KU-728-893

Also in the Never Mind the Botox series:

Rachel Altman is a corporate financier with a prestigious accounting firm who's desperately trying to keep on the straight and narrow. Hopelessly led astray by her bar diving boyfriend, she gets the chance to turn things round when her boss gives her the break she's been waiting for. But when the deal doesn't go as planned Rachel panics, sparking off a chain of betrayal and lies that threatens to ruin both her love life and her career.

Stella Webb is a successful but bored cosmetic surgeon whose career is going in a very different direction to that of the A&E doctor she's dating. With credit card bills larger than the latest implants, this deal should be the answer to her prayers, but it seems that not everyone has been playing by the rules. Desperate to leave her working-class roots behind, will she be forced to choose between money and love?

Meredith Romaine is an ice cool senior banker whose competitive world revolves around men and money. This deal will cement her reputation as the office rainmaker and put her in line for a huge bonus. But only if no one finds out about her relationship with a doctor at the American buyers and the completely unethical way she set the deal up. Can she pull it off without her past coming back to haunt her?

The series can be read in any order.

MIXING BUSINESS WITH PLEASURE

Never Mind The Botox

Alex

PENNY AVIS AND JOANNA BERRY

Matador
5 Weir Road
Kibworth Beauchamp
Leicester LE8 0LQ, UK
Tel: (+44) 116 279 2299
Fax: (+44) 116 279 2277
Email: books@troubador.co.uk
Web: www.troubador.co.uk/matador

ISBN 978-1848766-617

British Library Cataloguing in Publication Data.
A catalogue record for this book is available from the British Library.

All characters in this publication are fictitious and any resemblance to real persons,
living or dead, is purely coincidental

Typeset in 11pt Aldine 401 by Troubador Publishing Ltd, Leicester, UK
Printed and bound in the UK by TJ International Ltd, Padstow, Cornwall

Matador is an imprint of Troubador Publishing Ltd

MIX
Paper from
responsible sources
FSC® C013056

For Peter and Grant, without whom this would have been possible but not as much fun.

CHAPTER 1

Alex hitched up her strapless dress and frowned at the designer sink in front of her. It was a seemingly perfect slab of marble. Okay, so where's the tap? she thought. Clearly she wasn't alone in her inability to work it out, as she tried not to stare at the surprisingly supple girl in the hot pink number limboing under the hand dryer attempting to dry out her skirt. The last thing Alex needed tonight was also to look as though she'd wet herself; Emma would kill her. She decided to opt for e-coli instead and, leaving pink dress girl tutting to herself, she wrestled with the handleless door and escaped the bathroom with no knobs.

Alex was almost thirty years old and had attended enough industry award dinners to know the form. The PR Industry Awards had all the usual ingredients: egos, alcohol and cleavage – in that order. It was the regulation cavernous ballroom from a bygone era lit with blue up-lighters and with a local radio host doing his best to add some showbiz to an industry back-slapping exercise.

She nodded to the waiter to refill her glass as she sat back down to resume pretending to be on the edge of her seat over who would win Best Internal Communication Leaflet of the Year.

'Congratulations!' she said to the man sitting next to her, pointing to his Perspex runner-up trophy for Best Communicator of the Year.

'Thanks,' he grunted while shovelling down his passion fruit cheesecake.

Alex rolled her eyes at Emma, who was on fine form this evening. With immaculate blow-dried hair and carrying off a beautiful champagne satin dress, she was the perfect hostess. When Emma had been let down at the last minute by the global head of communications at Clinton Wahlberg, an investment bank, Alex had agreed to fill the empty seat at her table. The only downside was that Alex, a lawyer, knew nothing about PR, and it showed.

As the final award was announced to the strains of 'Simply the Best' everyone stood up, whooping and cheering, and Alex was able to escape the social imprisonment of the table plan.

She headed for the bar, leaving Emma to schmooze her clients. It was easy to shuffle to the front of the queue: everyone else knew everyone else and was deep in conversation. She surveyed the row of optics. Vodka? Bacardi? Wine? Or should she play it safe with a soft drink?

The bartender interrupted her deliberations. 'What can I get you, miss?'

'Erm, not sure.' How difficult could it be to decide

what to have? She smiled at him as he pretended he had all the time in the world. 'A vodka and tonic, please. Er, no, a gin and tonic. Thanks.'

'You're sure about that?' he asked, holding the glass up under the optic and looking back at her before he pressed the glass against it.

'Absolutely,' she said.

She was squeezing her way through the crowd with her glass aloft when she was almost taken out by an impressive pair of breasts artfully displayed on a shelf-like structure attached to an otherwise petite woman.

'Whoooaaah!'

'I'm so sorry!' said the pneumatic-breasted woman as she grabbed on to Alex to avoid crashing to the floor. 'These heels are just ridiculous.'

Alex smiled. Fortunately her G&T had survived the collision. Then she saw him: tall, attractive in a slightly worn way, and with that familiar asymmetric smile and eyebrow combination… it was Rob, an early encounter from university.

Rob had been a permanent feature at the student union. A medic, he'd taken even longer than Alex to qualify (vets took the longest, followed by dentists, then doctors, then lawyers). Alex had always thought it strange that it took more study to care for animals than humans. Anyway, Rob certainly knew how to care for humans, especially the female variety. She'd spent three years almost getting off with him, but somehow it had never happened. Looking at his well-endowed companion she could see he'd certainly settled for the cliché. Perhaps her instincts had been right all along: there were no hidden depths to his shallowness.

'Rob! Hi!' she said.

'Hello, stranger. You look fantastic!' He kissed her on each cheek and appraised her slender frame. 'So you've met my wife?' he said, gesturing to the top-heavy girl. 'Annabelle, this is Alex. Alex, Annabelle. We were great friends at uni, weren't we, Alex?'

'Of course we were.' She raised her eyebrows. 'So how are you? How's the world of medicine?'

'It's great. I'm a surgeon now at a cosmetic surgery business.'

'Oh.' Alex was surprised but realised that she probably shouldn't be. 'So the African AIDS work? Did that happen…'

'Well, I did the whole qualification thing in London and realised while working in a burns unit that my true vocation was in plastic surgery. Then I met Annabelle and the rest, as they say…'

'… is history!' Annabelle giggled.

'What about you? What are you up to?' Rob asked.

'I'm at MacArthur Warren in the City specialising in corporate law, for my sins.'

'Well done you! Knew you had it in you. So are you on track for partnership?' Rob knew from many a night of career planning that Alex had always aimed for fast-track partnership.

'Ever hopeful. Could really do with another deal in the bag before the end of the financial year. They need to know I can win work as well as do it, so I've got my ear to the ground for opportunities. Apparently I need to be more commercial and decisive. Anyway, it's why I keep turning up to events like these,' she said.

'Well, you certainly don't come for the food and the entertainment value, do you?' said Rob, scanning the room.

Annabelle, who Alex suspected had more impressive boobs than intellect, had already disappeared, and Rob and Alex sat down in a corner of the bar. He was carrying a bottle of red wine and kept topping up his glass. He nodded to Alex. 'Want some?'

'Don't mind if I do,' she said and drained her G&T so he could fill her tumbler with wine. It was that time of the evening.

'You really do look bloody fantastic. Did we ever?' He left the question hanging.

'No! We didn't! What are you like? I can't believe you can't remember,' she laughed.

'All a bit of a blur, those uni years. So many women, so little time. Actually in my case about six years. Anyway, I'm a changed man now I'm with my ideal woman. I met Annabelle two years ago. Never been happier. She was a patient of mine actually,' he whispered conspiratorially.

No shit, Sherlock, she thought.

'So, looking for a deal, are you?' he asked.

'Always, Rob. Why? Got one for me?' Alex asked.

'You know I might just have. Ever heard of the Beau Street Group? Specialists in BA and BR?'

'I'm not that up on the transport sector,' she said, racking her brain.

'It's not transport, you idiot! Breast augmentation

and breast reduction. My line of work. Between you and me, the finance director is a contact of mine. I bumped into Tom at a conference last week and apparently a major US player is showing them some interest. Looks like they want to expand into the UK market now us Brits aren't as squeamish as we used to be about the odd nip and tuck. He said something about getting advisers in place. Give him a call. I've got his business card somewhere.' Rob put his glass down, pulled out his wallet and extricated a card.

Alex looked at it and smiled. 'Thanks, Rob. I'll call him.'

'You owe me one.' He raised his glass.

'Still catching up on old times?' It was Annabelle again. She was carrying a sparkly jacket that looked a bit like the tin foil wraps they put round marathon runners. 'Come on, Rob, some of us have got jobs to go to in the morning. I need my beauty sleep. Sorry to drag him away, Alex.'

'Not at all. Be my guest. So what is it you do?' Alex couldn't imagine glamour models had to be up at too ungodly an hour of the morning.

'I'm an analyst on the Japanese desk at Bergelman Sykes. I have to be in before the Nikkei closes. Anyway, it was lovely to meet you, Alex. Good luck with the partnership.'

'Yeah, uh, thanks. You too,' Alex stammered.

'Bye, Alex. Give my best to Tom when you speak to him,' Rob said. He turned back as Annabelle walked on ahead of him. 'Told you she was the full package,' he mouthed.

Alex looked at the business card in her hand. Rob had always had the capacity to surprise and she felt rather ashamed about the judgement she'd automatically passed on Annabelle. She looked up again and smiled as she saw Emma striding towards her with a bottle of champagne and two glasses.

'Let's celebrate!'

'What are we celebrating?' asked Alex.

'All my guests have gone home, they're all happy and my dress has stayed up all night.'

'That's good enough for me.' Alex took a glass. 'I'm celebrating too. I bumped into Rob Sweeney. Remember him?'

'Of course. I invited him tonight. He was on my boss's table. We do the PR at his practice.'

'Well, thanks to Rob it looks like cosmetic surgery could be my route to partnership, power and money. He's tipped me off about a deal that might be going down at a cosmetic surgery business.' Alex raised her glass and giggled. 'What shall I get done first? Boobs, nose, lips?'

'Let's finish this bottle of champers and consider your options. We've got all night,' said Emma.

Alex scrabbled about in the bottom of her black hole of a handbag. Somewhere amongst the lip glosses, Oyster card, mobile, perfume, keys, Blackberry, chewing gum and assorted receipts was her purse. She smiled at the cabbie, who was staring at her in his rear-view mirror.

'It's okay. It's in here somewhere.'

'Been here before, love. I've got to earn a living, you

know. What'm I supposed to do? Dump you on your own in your state at the mercy of whatever nutter's out there?'

'It's fine, really, my purse is definitely in here somewhere. Definitely. Shit!' She lurched off her seat onto the floor as the cab braked suddenly.

'I'm not a bleedin' charity, you know. If it's not the missing wallet it's puking City boys,' he continued.

'Please, it's in here. I promise,' she said from the floor of the taxi. 'Anyway, there's always the Chinese jar.'

'The what?'

'Don't worry, I've got a jar at home with stacks of cash in. All my loose change.'

He groaned.

She emptied her bag onto her lap and there it was. She waved it at the cab driver and he shook his head.

As she stuffed the detritus of her bag back she saw the card Rob had given her. 'Aha! My ticket to fame and fortune!' she remembered. Now was as good a time as any, wasn't it? She was supposed to be more commercial, more decisive. She grabbed her phone.

'Hello, this is Tom Duffy from the Beau Street Group; please leave a message after the tone,' the voicemail message monotoned.

Had she not had the last two glasses of champagne, she might have hung up then. Had she not had the first seven, she wouldn't have made the call in the first place.

Alex sat at her desk warming her hands on her

polystyrene coffee cup. She was feeling lousy but was doing a great job of hiding the fact. As always she was dressed immaculately; today in a navy pencil skirt and neat tailored jacket. She and Emma had had a blast last night, but she was good at hiding her hangovers under smart suits.

Alex had experienced an epiphany nine years ago when she and Emma had been backpacking in Indonesia. After seven months of living on five pounds a day, wearing the same old washed-out t-shirts and generally delaying life, she'd been sitting at a roadside cafe when the most amazing woman had walked past. She may in fact have been an unremarkable woman, but at that time to Alex she was the biggest wake up call of her life. The woman was wearing a Chanel suit, had a sharp bobbed haircut and was carrying a briefcase so shiny you could see Alex's gob-smacked face in it. But that wasn't what threw Alex. It was the woman's stride, her sense of purpose, her apparent efficiency and her ability to make Alex suddenly look at herself and see a washed-up hippy thirty years too late for the hippy trail. That afternoon she'd booked her return trip to London. She'd started her training as a solicitor six weeks later.

Alex's mobile rang. It was Elliott, her fiancé.

'Hi, babe, how are you?' he said.

'Hi. I'm feeling dire.'

'What time did you get in? I stayed up watching some documentary about the Stones but crashed about two.'

'No idea. It was a monster night. What are you up to today?'

'Got a meeting at the record company this afternoon. Hoping they might let us record our own stuff instead of the sixties covers. We might make some cash then. Oh and then we've got a gig tonight in Acton at The Duck. You going to come and see us?'

Alex frowned. She'd hoped to have a few drinks after work with the guys from the office but it looked like she was going to be a groupie instead.

'Of course. You know I'll be there. Good luck at the record company.'

'Thanks. See you later.'

Alex had met Elliott on an island in Indonesia. Alex, Emma and Elliott had been part of a gang of Brits and American students who'd all landed on the island at the same time. They had a chilled week sleeping and snorkelling by day and drinking, singing and playing dominoes by night. Alex loved the whole vibe. For the first time in her life she actually started to like Bob Marley.

Elliott had been just one of the guys. He spent most of the time strumming a battered guitar and listening to the others. But he had a wit that took her by surprise and Alex found him engaging. They spent hours playing Scrabble and despite the fact that she had a frightening competitive instinct and he had an ambivalence that both fascinated and frustrated her, he beat her every time.

When she and Emma left the island on the glorified canoe that the locals called the ferry, he was one of the few who came to wave them off. Three days later in the crash pad in Singapore she was sorting through her rucksack when she found a note. It was short and to the point. He was intrigued by her and thought she was amazing. He'd scribbled his address and mobile number and said he'd leave it up to her if she wanted to contact him.

They came back to England as Alex and Elliott the couple, and rented a flat together while Alex did her training contract and he scraped a living as a musician. They would probably still have been renting that place if Alex hadn't bought the house where they now lived in Chiswick.

Alex jumped as the office phone rang this time.

'Alex Fisher, corporate department,' she recited.

'Ah Alex, good morning. This is Tom Duffy from the Beau Street Group.'

Oh my God, thought Alex. She tried to remember the contents of the message she'd left last night.

'Hello. Thanks so much for returning my call,' she said, composing herself.

'I must say I was very impressed that you took the trouble to call me at two thirty in the morning and from what you said your experience in the healthcare and beauty industries sounds very impressive,' he said.

What the hell had she said?

'Not at all. Obviously I was very keen to make contact with you when Rob Sweeny mentioned you to me,' Alex said.

'Well, you called me at opportune moment. We've been approached by the Equinox Practise in the US and they seem very serious about buying us. I need advisers in place as soon as possible and the one area I don't have tied up is the legal side. I need to hire a law firm in the next week or so. I've heard of MacArthur Warren, of course, but would be interested in meeting some of your lawyers. I need people who are commercial and sensible. I can't be doing with ivory tower types who look like Harry Potter – I want real people to work with.'

'Tom, I'd love to put together a team to meet you. Look, I can promise you we're not boffins here. We're commercial lawyers who want to facilitate your deal, not put obstacles in your way. When can we come and see you?'

'Would next Tuesday at eleven suit?' Tom said.

'Of course,' said Alex without even glancing at her diary.

'Well, that's great. I look forward to seeing you then. I think everything you need to know about us is on our website, but if you need anything further just give me a call. Preferably during daylight hours!'

'Of course. Thanks.'

'Oh and Alex, I'm not sure that having your colours done qualifies you to work for us. Just focus on your legal skills,' said Tom.

'Er, yes, of course. See you Tuesday,' she replied.

What on earth was he talking about?

CHAPTER 2

Alex grabbed her coffee and headed for the corporate department's weekly team meeting, where they discussed current deals and what they were doing to win new work for the department. As a senior associate Alex had to demonstrate that she was not just a clever technician who could do the work but someone who understood the business of being a lawyer in a big commercial firm. This meant she had to be able to negotiate fees, manage the lawyers on a deal and most importantly keep the deal flow coming so the department was busy and making money.

She walked into the room on a high. It was a large corner meeting room on the top floor of the firm's offices with panoramic views across the City. It was uber modern with glass tables and electric everything. There was even a button on the table you pressed to call for refreshments. Alex loved it up here. She always felt more glamorous somehow in the meeting rooms. This was more like the lawyers' offices in a movie. It was the lawyer's equivalent of a stage, where they showed off in front of their clients while all the real work was done downstairs in airless rooms with views of the next door office block.

Truman Barry, the revered head of the department, was already there, presiding over his team.

'Good morning, Alex.' He nodded at her as she sat down.

'Morning, Truman. Am I the last one?'

'Just Dan to come,' said Truman as a lithe thirty-something man jogged into the room. Dan was an American who'd joined the department on secondment from New York three years ago. He'd become an anglophile and had ended up staying with them at the end of his secondment. Technically Alex's junior, he was about her age and a good ally.

'Okay, morning all. Let's start with new business. Margaret, what have you got for us?' said Truman, turning to the woman next to him.

Margaret Kemp was the first ever female partner in the team. Phenomenally bright, she'd thrown everything into her career. Alex respected her but was also petrified of her. She was one of those career women who'd broken through the glass ceiling and pulled the ladder up after her.

Alex surveyed the room as Margaret spoke about the upcoming department away day when the team would get together for 'bonding' and training. Theirs was one of the strongest teams in the firm. Ross, Alex's trainee, was next to Dan. He was twenty-two, fresh from law school and would spend the next two years training as a solicitor. He shared an office with Alex and it was her job to supervise his work and educate him in the philosophy and politics of the corporate department. Ross already had the makings of a star. He was a quick learner, not afraid of hard work and tenacious. Alex liked him and already considered him an asset. She'd want him on the Beau Street deal if she won it. Who else? she thought as she scanned the room? Dan maybe?

'Alex?' said Truman, interrupting her thoughts. 'What have you been up to this week?'

She sat upright and instinctively smoothed her already poker straight hair.

'Well. I attended the PR Industry Awards last night and met a contact who's put me in touch with a cosmetic surgery business.'

'What are you getting done then?' asked Lisa, a fellow associate, to sniggers from the trainees and a frown from Margaret.

Alex smiled. 'Actually it's a major UK practice, the Beau Street Group. You may have heard of it, Lisa? They've been approached by a US business, the Equinox Practise, who are considering buying them. I'm meeting them next Tuesday to try to secure the deal for us.'

'That's excellent work, Alex. Exactly what we need. Well done. Who are you taking with you?' said Truman.

'Initially I thought I would take Dan with me, if that's okay with you, Dan?'

Margaret raised an eyebrow at this.

'That's cool. I'm just finishing up on the magazine

deal.' Dan had been working on the acquisition of a popular gossip magazine by a European newspaper group.

'And Ross of course,' Alex continued.

'Hmm. I think I should be there too, Alex. I think we need a partner there as this is a potential new client. Though obviously you'll lead it,' Truman said.

Alex nodded. She'd expected Truman would want to come and she was happy for him to lend his gravitas to their pitch.

'Well, if you pull this one off the department could hit our year-end target, which is good news for all of us,' Truman continued.

His comments resonated with everyone. Times were tougher but if they hit their target then they would all get bonuses.

As the meeting ended Alex caught up with Dan. 'I'll brief you on Monday about the deal. In the meantime check out the website and do some internal research. We need to know if anyone else in the firm has any experience in the cosmetic surgery field. We need to sound like we understand their sector. Speak to anyone you know who's had work done. Wendy in Accounts had a boob job; find out where. Anything. We need as much info as we can get.'

'Sure. And thanks, Alex, for putting me on the team,' he said while he jotted down notes in an awkward left-handed pose.

'No problem. Tom Duffy wants commercial people not stiffs, and your approach should suit him perfectly.' Alex knew that Dan's down-to-earth, businesslike attitude would be ideal. She also thought his US background would work well for them when they were dealing with the US lawyers who'd be working for Equinox.

'Er, and Alex? Maybe you could speak to Wendy?' he pleaded.

'Yeah sure,' she laughed.

'Okay then. See you Monday.'

He waved before getting into the lift, and held her gaze as the doors closed.

After work Alex made her way to Elliott's gig in West London. The Duck and Drake was an unsophisticated pub with green leather chairs, a stone floor and a vast selection of real ales. Alex was self-conscious in her work suit. She knew no one here apart from the band. The rest of the audience had a high beard count and seemed oblivious to any developments in fashion or music since early Status Quo. She cradled her half of lager and gazed in what she hoped was a supportive way towards Elliott as he sang Bob Dylan's 'Just Like a Woman' for what seemed to her like the millionth time. She adored Elliott but she couldn't help thinking that he'd been born in the wrong era. He would have been so at home in the sixties.

She felt her phone vibrate in her pocket. It was a text from Lisa at work: In Bar Q. All here. Wine? Alex sighed. She'd much rather be with the rest of the gang but she knew Elliott appreciated her support. Her thoughts drifted towards their wedding in three months' time. Everything was pretty much booked and organised, although her mother was still stressing about it. She phoned her at least once a day in a panic. The latest drama had been whether the colour of her outfit clashed with the wallpaper at the hotel.

Alex gazed at Elliott as he thanked the audience. She did wonder about their relationship sometimes. Elliott had been her boyfriend for such a long time and for years they'd complemented each other so well, but now she increasingly wondered if their differences were driving them apart. She'd gone from hippy chick to corporate chic. She wasn't sure Elliott was too keen on the transformation.

'Hiya, babe,' Elliott said as he joined her. His guitar was slung across his back and he was holding a pint of Guinness. 'What did you think?'

'Fabulous as always. Wembley arena doesn't know what it's missing!' She kissed him on the cheek and held his hand.

'I was talking to Barney before.' Barney was the drummer in Elliott's band. He was in his fifties, wiry and had a good line in leather waistcoats. 'He's off to Goa on a twelve-week tour in July. He's got some gigs booked. Andy and Rory are up for it too.' Elliott looked at her pleadingly.

Alex stared at him. She couldn't believe him. The wedding was booked for the end of July. Had he forgotten or was he hoping she could change the date? She dropped his hand.

'Elliott. We're getting married on the twenty-second of July.'

'I know, babe, of course I know.' He nervously

flicked his fringe from his eyes. 'But I thought maybe we could bring the wedding forward to the beginning of the month and then we could both go to Goa. Like a honeymoon?'

'What, for a romantic break with the rest of the band? Elliott, what planet are you on? Do you have any idea how long ago the church and the hotel were booked? Don't you understand that there's zero chance of either of them being free any other Saturday in the next twelve months? And you promised me you'd booked us a honeymoon. Don't tell me you haven't? Don't you understand how important this is to me?' She lowered her voice as she realised people were starting to look at them.

He stared back at her, confused and taken aback by her reaction. He raised his hands defensively, almost spilling his pint. 'Okay, okay. I just thought…'

'But that's just it, you didn't think. You haven't thought about the wedding since the day you proposed. Do you have any idea how much effort I've put into this?' Her voice softened as she registered his bewilderment. He really didn't get it. 'Look, you wrap up with the band and I'll see you at home. We can talk about this then.'

He nodded. 'Love you, babe,' he said, squeezing her hand.

She turned her back.

She walked out of the pub in tears. He was adorable and frustrating in equal measure but this time she was hurt and angry. She'd been planning her perfect wedding since she was a girl and to him it was like a dinner date that could be rearranged on a whim. He had no idea how long she'd agonised over the font type for the invitations, never mind the venue, the dresses, the menu. She drew her jacket around her and hailed a cab as she felt her phone vibrating again. It wasn't Lisa this time; it was Dan: Have great weekend. Looking 4wd 2 Beau St job with u.

Alex didn't know what to say to Elliott when he returned home. She was already in bed so she pretended to be asleep. She heard him stumbling around in the kitchen. He'd obviously had a few drinks after she left him. It could wait until the morning.

She was up first the next day. She sneaked out of the house in her pyjamas, ski jacket and trainers and bought croissants, bread and coffee at the local deli. She reran the previous evening in her head while she set everything out on a tray and then took it upstairs to Elliott.

'What's this?' he croaked, rubbing his eyes and brushing his unruly blonde hair from his face.

'Breakfast. We need to talk.' She got under the covers.

'Before you say anything, I'm sorry about last night. I got carried away after talking to Barney. The Goa trip is off,' Elliott said, reaching for her.

Alex looked at him. He seemed sorry. 'Look, let's start the weekend all over again. I hate it when there's an atmosphere. I've had a great week at work. The wedding's twelve weeks away. Let's be nice to each other.' She cuddled up to him.

'I know. I'm sorry. I've got no idea what you've

been working on with the wedding but I'm sure it's taken loads of effort.'

'Why don't I talk you through it?' Alex said excitedly, sitting up. She was thrilled to be able to share everything with Elliott. He was finally taking an interest.

'Some other time, babe,' he said, grabbing a croissant from the tray as he got out of bed. 'I need to be at Rory's for rehearsal by ten. We've got that wedding gig tonight and we need to brush up on a couple of slushy numbers.'

Her face fell.

'And don't worry, the honeymoon is under control.' He kissed her on the forehead.

She mustered a smile, then pulled the covers up to her neck and sighed. She stared out of the French window of their bedroom, past the miniscule Juliet balcony, at a supermarket carrier bag that was being blown across their postage stamp of a back garden. Another Saturday to herself. She decided to call her mum.

Two hours later and Alex was on the train to Hertfordshire going through her wedding to-do list. Okay, just the table plan and canapés to do. How difficult could it be?

She saw her dad's blue Jaguar as soon as she walked out of the station. He was always on time. She felt a pang of affection as she looked at him reading his *Daily Telegraph* in his chain store v-neck. She tapped on the window.

'Hello, darling. What a lovely surprise. Your mother was thrilled when you rang this morning.' He beamed at her.

After the usual performance where he insisted on putting her bag on the piece of old carpet laid out to protect the boot – 'Got to think of the resale value, Alex' – they set off for home.

'How's Mum?' she asked.

'She's good. She's really enjoying her aromatherapy course. Keeps her busy. But I'm bloody sick of those damn burner things she's got all over the house. It smells like a Moroccan souk.'

Her mum was waiting for her at the door in an unstructured floaty linen number.

'Alex, darling! You're as skinny as a bean pole. Are you eating? Is it stress?'

'Mum, I'm fine. Please, I've just got here.' Alex hugged her.

'Well, I'll feed you up. You work too hard. We can't have you wasting away. Come and have some tea and cake.'

'Ooh, I'd love a cup of tea. Normal tea, please, Mum. None of that fruity nonsense.'

'Are you sure? I've got some lovely rosehip and chamomile.'

'No thanks. Builder's tea is good.'

They sat in the conservatory, which hadn't changed a bit since Alex had left home. The same school photos were on the windowsill next to the same pot plants.

'So darling, the marquee. I thought it would be wonderful if we had some aromatherapy burners. A soothing bergamot and patchouli mix would be nice, don't you think? And Beryl says she can get them in bulk for me from the wholesaler.'

'Er, great idea, Mum, but what about Elliott's grandma? You know she has respiratory problems. I'm not sure she'll be able to cope with them.'

'Oh, no. I suppose not.' Her mum looked crestfallen.

'Maybe we could have a couple by the entrance where there's plenty of ventilation?' Alex conceded.

'Ooh yes. That would be nice. Something welcoming. Ylang ylang perhaps. I'll see what Beryl thinks.'

'Great. Now what about the table plan? I've done mine and Elliott's friends but I really need you to help with family and yours and Dad's friends.'

'Darling, it's a minefield. You're absolutely right, I must be in charge. Heaven knows what could happen. Imagine if Uncle Gerry ended up on Bridget-from-next-door's table! Aunt Janet would never forgive us.'

'Well, I was more concerned about Uncle Bill. Is there anyone left he hasn't offended?'

'Put him with the vicar and anyone who's a bit deaf.'

'And Victoria from the golf club?'

'With any single men who are coming. She'll hunt them out wherever they are so we might as well make it easy for her.'

'I think Elliott has got some single cousins.'

'Ah yes, Elliott. He's going to have to sort his family, darling. I only know his parents and obviously they'll be on the top table. Oh and you must find out what his mum is wearing. It's getting quite urgent. I don't know what I'll do if we clash. Though Beryl says I have priority as the mother of the bride so she'll just have to get something else.'

They spent ages writing and rewriting the table plan. Her mum was right: it was a minefield. It was like a complex family tree working out who'd fallen out with who, who'd shagged who, who'd been missed out of whose will, who had to be near the loo and who would take mortal offence if they were one metre further from the top table than their arch enemy. In the end it took them two bottles of elderflower wine and two packets of vegetable crisps to get it done.

'Darling, it's going to be worth all the effort. Who'd have thought it? My little girl marrying the man of her dreams.'

'That's not how it felt last night,' said Alex, and despite herself she told her mum all about Elliott and the trip to Goa and the unbooked honeymoon. Her mum looked more confused and upset than she had. She immediately wished she hadn't said anything.

'Oh darling, that's dreadful. You poor thing. You know what men are like, though. Take your father. He never remembers anyone's birthday, including mine. I had to buy my own present last year. But he is good in so many other ways.'

Alex tried to think of all the positive qualities that Elliott possessed.

'But you do love him, don't you?' her mother continued.

'Of course.'

'Well then, everything's going to be just fine. Come on, let's go and have some fish pie with organic carrots.

That will fatten you up. Yes, comfort food, that's what you need.'

For once her mum was right. Tucked up in her old bedroom feeling absolutely stuffed Alex felt sure everything would be fine. She stared at a poster of a muscle-bound man cradling a tiny baby and thought of Elliott. It was just the pressure of work and the wedding. Everything would work out; she was sure of it.

CHAPTER 3

Alex was excited to be back at work. She'd done her research with Dan and Ross and they'd discovered that the firm had done some litigation for a couple of other cosmetic surgery businesses defending claims of shoddy workmanship. They'd spent most of Monday morning picking the brains of the lawyers who'd worked for those clients. They had endless tales of boob jobs gone wrong, lumpy liposuction and botched nose jobs. Ross had ended up having the conversation with Wendy from Accounts, who'd regaled him with tales of the benefits of a teardrop implant and how her boyfriend loved her new look. They'd also put together a glossy document to leave with Tom Duffy that made them and MacArthur Warren sound like the best, cleverest, most experienced cosmetic surgery sector specialists and talented lawyers in the universe.

It was Tuesday morning now and they were ready.

'Good morning. Truman Barry, Alex Fisher, Ross Livingstone and Dan Furtado to see Tom Duffy,' barked Truman at the receptionist at the Beau Street Group.

'Please take a seat. I'll let Mr Duffy know you're here.'

The four of them sat down in the plush waiting area. It was more like a country house hotel than a medical practice. Copies of *Horse and Hound* and *Plastic Surgery News* lay juxtaposed on the large upholstered ottoman.

Alex tried not to look at Ross and Dan. They'd all noticed the receptionist's immobile waxen face and Dan and Ross were trying hard not to stare at the before and after pictures that hung in ornate frames on the walls. There was an undercurrent of hysteria. Only Truman seemed oblivious to the fascinating tableau before them. Alex's team were on the verge of giggles and all the other people in the waiting area were there to have something enhanced, removed, tightened or tucked. The well-groomed forty-something woman next to her looked coquettishly at Dan over her copy of *Country Life*, clearly unembarrassed by the large dressing on what was presumably her now-perfect nose. Another woman browsed a bizarre catalogue containing pictures of what appeared to be feet. Perhaps she was having the foot narrowing surgery that Alex had read about that enabled women with wide feet to wear Jimmy Choos? Ross's eyes were like saucers as he listened into the conversation another static-faced woman was having with her daughter about the boob job her father had bought her for her birthday. Alex noticed that the daughter had a rat-sized dog in her Louis Vuitton handbag that was glaring at Truman.

'Mr Duffy is ready to see you,' the receptionist said.

The four of them left the waiting area and followed her to a lift that took them to the management floor where Tom Duffy's office was situated at the end of a luxuriously carpeted corridor, decorated with more before and after pictures. It was a large wood-panelled room containing a traditional mahogany desk behind which he stood as they entered the room. Tom was in his fifties and had a stocky ex-rugby-player's physique and creased intelligent eyes.

'Good morning! You must be Alex, the night owl.' He smiled as he extended his hand towards Alex.

She introduced the rest of the team.

'Good to meet you. Call me Tom,' he said. He motioned towards a circular table in the corner of the room and then hurriedly removed the literature spread in a fanlike display on the table, advertising everything from Botox to penis enlargement.

'Mr Duffy, er, Tom, we're delighted to be given this opportunity to present to you today. Needless to say, we'd be delighted to represent the Beau Street Group,' Truman opened.

He proceeded to give his standard MacArthur Warren pitch. Alex had heard it so many times she could recite it in her sleep.

'... and most of all, what you get with us is a hundred and ten per cent commitment to you and your business,' Truman finished.

'Thank you, Truman,' Alex said. It was her turn now. 'Now Tom, what we thought might be useful would be for you to hear about our experience in your sector and what we think the issues might be for you on the acquisition of your business. Our firm has acted for a number of other cosmetic surgery providers and we understand that you'll need to demonstrate a breadth of offering, which as we see from your literature is already quite impressive. The businesses that can only do breast augmentation aren't enough for the US buyer. They want buttock lifts, penis enlargements, labioplasty, ear lobe reshaping, mouth lifts.' Alex didn't dare look at Truman. 'They want to know you can follow US trends into the UK market. So we need to help you present your experience and expertise in a way that demonstrates your safe track record but that also deals honestly and commercially with any negative issues such as litigation you may have faced. On the back of the strength of your business and brand we'll help negotiate you the best deal we can get, and one that won't come back and bite you two years down the line.'

Alex continued to discuss the firm's strengths in tax, medical negligence, employment law and everything else under the sun she could think of that might be relevant to Tom. She was desperate to win the deal and hoped it wasn't too obvious.

'You're right about the US market, Alex,' Tom said. 'It's different to the UK but the gap is closing. Equinox want us to recreate their US practice in the UK. As I understand it, we need to produce a set of reports that show them everything we can do, how much profit we make and what legal and regulatory issues there are, and produce a business plan going forward. You guys would be responsible for the legal report, and from what they're saying we'd need something fast. Maybe as quick as a month from now. Is that feasible?'

'If you let us into your offices with free access to what we need we'll work round the clock,' Alex replied. 'As you said, I'm a night owl.'

'I'm sure you want to know how we charge,' interjected Truman.

'Like a rhinoceros, no doubt, like all you lawyers,' Tom said to Alex.

She laughed politely.

'We'd be prepared to consider a fixed fee arrangement to secure the work on this transaction,' said Truman, taking Alex by surprise. Truman clearly needed this deal. Fixed fee deals were rarely offered, although many clients asked for them. Usually the firm charged an hourly rate. 'Although obviously if we got the deal away for you we'd be looking for completion uplift.' Ah, now she understood. Truman was gambling that the deal would be successful and MacArthur Warren would get an additional success fee.

Tom seemed to like Truman's proposal and they spent the next twenty minutes talking about the individuals on the MacArthur Warren team and the timetable of the transaction.

'Okay, guys. I think you've told me everything I need to know.' Tom stood up. 'I'll give you a call in the next twenty-four hours and let you know my decision. In the meantime, thank you for coming in.'

They said their goodbyes and the team of lawyers walked back through reception, leaving the building just as the rat-like dog spotted Truman, escaped from the handbag and headed after them into the revolving door. As they got into the waiting black cab Alex looked back at the creature jumping up to see through the glass panel of the door, snarling at them, while its owner pushed the door, forcing the dog round and round and in and out of vision. A security guard was berating the woman angrily for bringing a pet into the clinic. It was a far cry from Alex's local GP's surgery.

'Alex, I have absolutely no idea what you were talking about back there but you'd obviously done your research and he seemed to like it,' Truman said. 'I have to say that if you pull this one off your partnership prospects are looking very strong.'

Ross, who was bouncing about in the cab's jump seat, looked at Alex with a new respect. Partnership at Alex's age was a major achievement.

'Thanks, Truman. Let's just hope we've done enough,' she said, trying to conceal her excitement.

An hour later Emma and Alex were having a late lunch at Bar Q, a riverside wine bar in the City equidistant between their offices. They were sitting outside in the spring sunshine near a patio heater trying to convince themselves it was tropical.

'Alex, that's so great. God, I hope the deal comes off for you. If it does you must remember it's all down to me. If you hadn't come to my PR do you'd never have got the tip-off from Rob.' Emma took a large slug of wine. 'It's so great having a long lunch, isn't it?' she continued.

'I know, this is fab.' Alex put her face up to the sun.

'Don't forget, you're a potential client I'm wining and dining if anyone asks.'

'Who's going to ask? Chillax, as my baby brother always says.'

'Anyway, if the deal does come off I'm going to bring you here and buy you dinner, champagne, whatever the lady wants. You're right: I owe you. Which reminds me, that's exactly what Rob said. Maybe I should invite him and that bizarre wife of his,' said Alex.

'Excellent,' Emma said, scanning the menu. 'I'll make sure I order the lobster and the Krug then!'

'Ha ha. Actually if the deal does come off maybe I could get you some discounted surgery.'

'Thanks, Alex! Anyway, you know I'm perfect in every way!'

'Seriously. Would you ever consider getting any work done?' Alex asked.

'Ooh, I don't know. Still a bit young, I guess, but I know loads of girls back in the office who have Botox. Thin end of the wedge, I reckon. You start with a frozen brow and end up with tits like melons,' said Emma.

'Yeah, it's like Botox is the gateway drug,' Alex said.

'What do we know, anyway? I reckon I'd think about Botox when I'm closer to forty. Maybe a facelift in my fifties. Who knows? By the time we're that age it'll probably be available on the NHS. What about you?' asked Emma.

'I've already had Botox,' said Alex, watching Emma for a reaction.

'What! You never told me. How, where, why!'

'Not on my face; my armpits. And don't you dare tell anyone.'

'Why on earth?'

'Oh, it was a tip from one of those bloody wedding planners. She told an apocryphal story about some girl sweating all over some designer wedding dress she was trying on and then having to buy it. She said it was becoming standard practice and I should consider it. I was in "buy" mode and fell for it. Some dentist friend of hers did it for me.'

'Alex, you're bonkers. She was probably on a kick-back from her dentist mate.'

'I know. I can't believe I fell for it. It does work, though. I have the most fragrant unwrinkled armpits in the City!' Alex giggled. 'But it really hurt.'

'Would you do it again?'

'No way. I'll just buy deodorant. I'd probably get a lifetime supply for what it cost.'

'So if Botox is the gateway drug what's next for you, Ms Fisher?' Emma asked.

'No, that's it. Really. I don't want to look weird. You should've seen some of the people at the Beau Street Group. The receptionist was like a blow-up doll, for God's sake. No, I intend to grow old gracefully but with beautiful armpits.'

'While I'll have a top lip like a sausage, cheekbones you can eat off, the forehead of a waxwork dummy and sweaty pits.'

'They'll call us Fresh and Freaky!'

The wine had kicked in and they giggled hysterically.

'What did Elliott say about it? The Botox?' Emma asked when they'd calmed down.

'He doesn't know. Frankly I don't think he knows anything about the wedding. I'm not sure he even knows where the church is.'

'Hey, that's not good.' Emma wrinkled her unBotoxed brow.

'Tell me about it. Honestly, I'm not sure he even wants to get married. The only bit he's shown the slightest bit of interest in is the set he and the band are playing at the reception.'

'Well, you know Elliott. His strengths lie elsewhere. I'm sure it will be all right on the night,' said Emma.

'I really hope so. I've spent more time talking to the guys at work than I have speaking to him for the past few months.'

'Look, take him out for dinner. Get him on his own and talk to him,' said Emma.

'Yeah, I know. I will. It's just getting hold of him in the first place and then cutting the umbilical cord between him and the band. They're much worse than any in-laws could ever be.'

'Alex, you need to do this. Marriage is for life not just for Christmas. Well, unless you fancy a messy divorce where he gets half that house that you bought with your money.'

'He gave me some money towards the deposit,' Alex said.

'Yeah right, about fifty pence. How's his record deal progressing?'

'Hey, he's doing fine. He's really hopeful they're

going to put out an album of his own material and then he'll get some proper royalties.'

'Assuming anyone buys it.'

'Emma, stop it. I know you think he's a waster but this isn't helping,' Alex said.

'Okay, I'm sorry. But it's only because I'm worried about you. You know I think he's a sweetheart but he's not exactly Mr Reliable, is he? I just think you and he need to talk, pronto.'

'We will. I promise.'

An hour later Alex was back at her desk feeling drowsy. She rested her head on a thick file.

'You okay?' said Ross from his desk across the room.

'Yeah,' she mumbled. 'Lesson of the day: never have more than one drink at lunchtime if you intend on using your brain in the afternoon. It's a well-known fact that your brain turns to mush and work is two hundred per cent harder. Save it for days when you're internet shopping, not for when you're drafting complicated business sale contracts.'

'Right, of course. You are wise, Obi-Wan,' he said, pretending to write it down. 'Want me to have a stab at a first draft of it?'

'God, would you? You absolute star. Yes, yes, why not – it'll be good training. Okay, let me talk you through the deal.'

Alex was deep in conversation with Ross, explaining the clauses that had to go into the contract, when the office phone rang. It was Truman Barry. He wanted to speak to her in his office immediately.

'Of course, Truman. I'm on my way.' She hung up.

'Sorry, Ross. Got to go. Can you make a start on that for me?'

'Not a problem. Good luck.'

It wasn't often she was summoned to Truman's office. It wasn't often anyone was summoned to Truman's office, for that matter. Truman kept a low profile but his presence was somehow pervasive. It was very much his team and his department and although he wasn't one for fireside chats he was protective of his people. Being summoned to his office meant one of two things: either you were in big trouble or you'd done something very good.

Shit, shit, shit! Why did I have that third glass at lunchtime? Alex thought as she strode down the corridor, smoothing her skirt and her hair as she went. What could this be about? she wondered. Shit, had he heard about the completion party for the TV deal? She went cold at the thought of it.

She reached the door of his office, knocked and walked in.

'Ah Alex, great, come in. Well, I have some excellent news,' he said, beaming at her.

She immediately relaxed and smiled back at him.

'Tom Duffy has already called. We've got the job. And for a sensible fee too. He wants you there tomorrow.'

'Gosh, that's fantastic news.' Alex managed to stop herself punching the air and high-fiving her boss.

'Well done, Alex. Really. Excellent work.'

'Thank you, Truman.'

'He's expecting you and your team at nine a.m. sharp.'

'We'll be there.'

Truman's phone rang and he was already talking to someone else. He nodded at her as she reversed out of his office.

As soon as she'd run back to her office she reached for her phone and called Dan. 'Get here now! We've got the deal.'

'Wow, that's great,' said Ross, turning round on his swivel chair to face her. His enthusiasm was written all over his face. This would be the first deal he'd worked on from start to finish.

'I know, isn't it?'

She smiled as she heard Dan's heavy footsteps pounding down the corridor towards her door. He burst into the room, a pen behind his ear, his shirtsleeves unbuttoned and rolled up to his elbows.

'Hey, look at you, Miss Rainmaker. Good job.' He smiled at her and shook her hand enthusiastically with both of his.

Dan was tall and wiry with thick dark hair and beautiful American teeth. When he smiled it was like a toothpaste ad. Emma always said he had the 'ring of confidence'. But he wasn't in your face, which why Alex liked him. He was generally quiet and kept his own counsel at team meetings, letting others show off and, often, take the glory for his own work.

'Well, we've got the rest of today to clear our desks because we start in the morning,' Alex said. 'And guys, we need to suspend our judgement on cosmetic surgery. We don't want to lose this job because we all wet ourselves every time we see the Beau Street receptionist.

It's a serious business making serious money and there's clearly a market for what it does.'

'No big deal for me. I know plenty of girls who had nose jobs in high school. It's fairly normal in the States. It's just the more exotic stuff that freaks me out,' said Dan.

'Well, it all freaks me out really. I've got a needle phobia,' Ross said.

'No way!' said Alex.

'Seriously, I have. Embarrassing, I know. The thought of that Botox thing that celebrities have makes me feel physically sick.'

'Remind us to keep you away from the treatment rooms then,' Dan said.

CHAPTER 4

Alex took her time deciding what to wear the next morning. Tom didn't want them to be the lawyer cliché, he wanted sassy commercial people, and Alex wanted to look the part. So no black suit today, she thought. How about a dress? Maybe with boots?

Elliott watched her getting ready.

'You look sexy today.'

'Thanks,' she said, worrying whether that was a good thing. 'Big day for me.'

'Why?' he asked.

'I told you last night. We won that cosmetic surgery deal and it's my first day on the job.'

'Oh yeah.'

'Elliott,' she said suddenly, remembering her conversation with Emma from the day before, 'is there any chance we could have a night out in the next few days? It would be nice to spend a bit of time together and talk through the wedding.'

'Good idea. I'm meeting Rory and Barney for a curry tonight, why don't you join us after work?'

'That's not what I meant. You know, just the two of us. A date. Man, woman, bottle of wine. You remember how it goes.'

'Oh, okay, of course. Er, I'll check the band diary and text you later.'

'Great.'

She finished her make-up and studied herself in the mirror. It would have to do; she was meeting Dan and Ross in forty minutes and had to leave. She kissed Elliott and grabbed her bag and laptop.

She saw Ross and Dan chatting to the security guard at the Beau Street offices as she pushed her way through the revolving doors. Great, they were all on time.

'No cloud cover, you see, last night. That's why we had a bit of a frost first thing and why it's lovely and sunny now,' the security guard was saying. 'Ah good morning, miss. You must be Ms Fisher,' he said, handing her a personalised security pass. 'Lovely spring morning. Forecast is good for the next few days as well.'

'Yes. It's a beautiful day,' she replied, clipping the pass to her bag. Why did the manufacturers of those passes always assume you had a breast pocket you could pin them to?

'Good to meet you,' said Dan to the guard.

'And you too, sir. And don't forget: never cast a clout 'til May is out!' he shouted after them.

'Strange guy,' muttered Dan as they walked over to the reception desk. The same taut-faced woman was there answering the phone in a faux posh voice. When she'd finished her call she looked up at the three lawyers, her eyes lingering on Dan, and strained her mouth into a lipless smile.

'Ah yes, Ms Fisher and your team again. Good morning. Let me call Albert. He's going to be looking after you.'

Dan raised his eyebrows at Alex. A rare occurrence in this place, she thought, as she appraised her colleagues. Ross, who only had two work suits, had opted for his blue 'interview suit' and looked every inch the lawyer from his trendy thin designer glasses to his shiny brogues. Dan was sporting the preppy look with a button-down-collared shirt and loafers, his battered brown document holder under his arm. You could take the man out of America but you couldn't take America out of the man.

'Ah, Ms Fisher. I'm Albert.' A short dapper oriental man of indeterminate age bounded towards them. He had the smooth unblemished skin of a small child and that now familiar shiny forehead.

'Good morning. I'm Alex, and this is Dan Furtado and Ross Livingstone,' Alex replied.

'A real pleasure to meet you,' said Albert, practically bowing to them as he shook each of their hands. 'Now Mr Duffy has asked me to look after you all and get you whatever you need. This is my direct line, my pager and my mobile details. Call me whenever you want. I'm here to help.'

He passed Alex his business card, which read 'Albert Cheung, Clinic Patient Care Coordinator – Surgical'.

'Now if you'd like to follow me I'll take you to the room we have ready for you.'

They followed him as he almost moonwalked down one of the ubiquitous corridors, down a set of stairs and into a large conference room. There were no windows in the room and the only furniture was a large oval table upon which were rows and rows of lever-arch files stacked in piles of three. Here we go, thought Alex, our home for the next few weeks.

'I think everything is here. I went through your list of requirements personally. There's a photocopier in the corridor outside that's yours as long as you need it. I've checked it's set to A4 single sided and has plenty of paper. I'll show you the tea and coffee making facilities.' Albert led them to a small windowless kitchen down the corridor. 'As you can see we have a range of fruit teas, breakfast tea and Columbian and supermarket coffee. And you're all welcome to use our canteen, which is on the second floor − turn right at the top of the stairs. The special today is Cajun chicken wraps.'

'Great. That's perfect. Thank you,' Alex said.

'I'll leave you to it then.' Albert clapped his hands together like a clockwork monkey. 'Don't forget, whatever you need just call or page me.' He looked at his watch. 'Must dash − I'm off to counsel a man about a penis enlargement.' He whispered the last two words before retreating back to the stairs.

Alex turned to look at the uninspiring room. 'Okay, guys, let's get down to business. Ross, can you look at all the files and compare them to the list of stuff I sent to Tom Duffy. We need to check he's given us all the info we asked for. Dan, you and I can start ploughing through it all. You know the score. We're looking for anything unusual, uncommercial or potentially damaging to the business – particularly anything that could affect the price the purchasers will pay. We need to find the skeletons in the closet now while there's a chance we can bury them or at least tart them up a bit. So, any contracts where the business has paid over the odds, any employees who might have tribunal claims, any festering litigation against the practice that won't go away and anything that could cause reputational damage. If this outfit is doing dodgy boob jobs that keep exploding or something, we need to know now.'

'Yeah, rather than them exploding in our faces at a later date,' Ross chipped in.

'And everything going tits up,' added Dan, smiling.

'Precisely. If we can deal with any problems now and deliver a clean report on the legal exposure of the business then the sale is more likely to happen at the best possible price. Right, Dan, you look at the litigation files. I'll grab the employees' files.'

They sat in the windowless room for four hours taking it in turn to make coffees. None of them found out anything remarkable about the business. Dan researched a dispute with their electricity supplier and Alex looked at the employment tribunals they'd been involved in. Ross had the joy of looking at their photocopier leases.

'I don't know about you but I can't take any more of this excitement. Fancy a trip to the canteen?' asked Dan eventually.

'Definitely, I'm starving,' said Alex.

The canteen was like any other – a pocket of design

mediocrity deep inside the plush clinic where no clients ever set foot, resplendent with MDF tables, bright yellow walls and royal blue trade carpet. The three lawyers sat together as they ate, feeling very conspicuous.

Suddenly Albert materialised next to Dan. 'May I join you?' he asked.

'Of course, take a seat,' said Dan as Albert slid his tray onto the table and sidled up to him.

'So, folks, how's it going? Do you have everything you need?' he asked.

'Everything's fine, thanks, Albert,' said Dan.

'How long do you think you'll be here?' Albert asked.

Alex wasn't sure how much Albert knew about why they were there. She would need to speak to Tom. Usually clients didn't want their employees to know their business was being sold in case it caused mass panic. She decided to be vague.

'Maybe a couple of weeks. That's how long these sorts of review take,' she hedged.

'So what exactly do you do here, Albert?' Dan asked, changing the subject.

'Well, I'm the first person you see if you're considering a surgical procedure. If someone's come in for a consultation I advise them on the most appropriate surgery for them and what it involves, how long it will take, et cetera. I picture what they could look like and then tell them how to achieve it.'

'Wow, so you sell them a new face!' said Ross.

'Or body, darling,' said Albert.

Ross blushed.

'It depends what they're seeking to achieve really.'

As they spoke a striking older woman in a leather skirt and heels clicked passed. She nodded at Albert.

'That's Dr Cassidy's assistant nurse, Audrey. A fine example of what we can do here,' said Albert. 'Ms Fisher?'

'Call me Alex,' she said.

'Alex, perhaps I could use you as an example?' asked Albert.

'Er, okay,' said Alex, wondering what she was letting herself in for.

'Well…' He stared at her intently.

Alex immediately felt very uncomfortable.

'One or two things spring to mind,' he said.

'No!' said Dan. 'She looks great.'

'Well, certainly she's attractive, but we could do so much more.'

'Excuse me, I am in the room,' said Alex.

'Of course. Forgive me,' said Albert. 'What I should say is that if you were a patient I'd probably recommend some work on your nose. We could reduce the slight bump in the bridge and the width towards the end. You're a bit young for an eye lift but in five or so years you should think about that. Your chin is quite prominent so we could reduce that slightly. And let me look at your ears.' He pulled Alex's long hair behind her ears. 'No, they're fine. I just wondered if we'd need to consider pinning them. Obviously I don't work with non-surgical procedures but I'm sure my colleagues in that area would recommend a bit of Botox in the forehead area and some fillers for your nasolabial folds. Otherwise you look fine.'

Alex was stunned. She felt like the last chicken in the supermarket that had been mauled by a day's worth of customers and then left on the shelf to be reduced. Dan and Ross looked pretty shocked too. Dan recovered first.

'I can't believe what you just said. Alex looks fabulous. If she needs that amount of work, God help the average client who walks through your door.'

'Of course, I'm not saying she needs it, just that if she wants to enhance her looks those are the procedures I'd recommend. It's all about enhancing what we've got. The base point is different for every patient.'

'Would someone my age really have that amount of work done?' Alex asked.

'Absolutely. We get girls in their early twenties having preventative Botox and a large proportion of the breast augmentation clients are under twenty-five. Nose jobs are popular at every age. Apart from facelifts, eye lifts, that type of thing, which really are for the over thirty-fives, it doesn't seem to matter what age the client is.'

'It's more about confidence then,' said Dan.

'What do you mean?' Albert said.

'Well, I'd guess that someone confident with their appearance and with a healthy amount of self-esteem isn't going to be thinking about getting work done in their twenties,' Dan retorted.

'A matter of opinion. I'd argue that someone who's confident is keen to be the best they can be and that may mean surgery for them,' countered Albert.

'Well, it does seem that cosmetic surgery is much more common these days. It's on all the TV makeover shows,' said Alex, keen not to alienate Albert.

'Exactly.' Albert smiled. 'People can see for themselves the fabulous results and how safe it is.'

'Do you get many celebrity clients?' Ross asked.

'Well, we're not supposed to talk about individuals, of course. Client confidentiality,' Albert whispered excitedly. 'But yes, we have had a few. Most of them are obsessed with keeping everything top secret. The number of magazine interviews I've read where it's "all down to my genes" and I've had them in here having eye lifts, chemical peels, the full monty.'

'So the taboo about having the surgery in the first place has gone but somehow people can't bring themselves to be honest about it,' said Alex.

'No one wants to look shallow or self-obsessed, I guess,' said Dan.

'We'd love it if they were open about it. The free publicity would be fantastic. Instead we have to make veiled references to our celebrity client base. Not that we have any difficulties attracting new clients, I should add.' Albert stood up as he spoke. 'Can I get anyone a coffee?'

After a morning mainlining caffeine they all politely declined.

As they returned to the project room Dan walked next to Alex.

'You okay?' he asked.

'Yeah, sure. Just a bit stunned by what Albert said back there. I know I'm not the elephant man or anything but it does make you think.'

'Anything but. He's just a salesman desperate for his commission. Remember that.' He smiled at her and she felt his hand gently patting her back. 'At least your face moves,' he said.

She smiled.

'Okay folks, let's get back to the joys of being high-flying lawyers,' Dan said.

'Yep. It's back to the cave of doom for us,' said Alex as they returned to the entirely artificially lit room for an afternoon of due diligence. 'Let's liven things up a bit and look at the file of thank you letters.'

Alex had never enjoyed this stage of a transaction. Spending the best part of a month reviewing documents and looking for issues that might affect the price or structure of the deal was tedious. The fun bit was the nitty gritty of doing the deal. Negotiating the contract to buy the business in late night meeting rooms; that was where she got her kicks. However, as she watched Dan taking notes, his brow furrowed and his hair sticking up where his hand clutched his head, she had to concede there were some benefits of being shut up in a dark meeting room with two attractive men.

Alex's mobile rang. It was Emma. She decided to take the call.

'I'll just take this outside. Reception's dreadful in here,' she said, getting up from the table.

'Alex Fisher,' she said into the phone as she left the room.

'I know it's you, you idiot. I phoned you,' said Emma.

'I know,' Alex said. 'I was just maintaining a veneer of professionalism in front of my colleagues.'

'Ah, so you're on the job, are you. How's Dan?'

'Stop it. Though I have to admit I'm not sure it was a good idea having him on the team. I can't take my eyes off him.'

'Well, he is rather gorgeous. Why did you do it to yourself?'

'He's got the right skillset for this deal.'

'Yeah, right.'

'Oh and I need to prove to myself that that whole completion party episode was just a blip. I'm getting married in less than three months.'

'I know. That's why I rang. And stop beating yourself up about that night. It was a drunken snog. Happens to the best of us.'

'Not at MacArthur Warren it doesn't. Either Dan or I would be out on our arse if Truman ever found out. I'm sure Margaret Kemp suspects something. She keeps giving me funny looks,' said Alex.

'That old fossil? She probably fancies you. That firm of yours is in the dark ages. I thought you said the senior partner had married his PA?' said Emma.

'One rule for them and another one for the minions, I guess. Anyway, what did you want? Don't you know I'm a very busy person?'

'Okay, Miss Hotshot. Look, I need to sort this fitting out for my bridesmaid dress. Your mother's phoned me twice today.'

'Oh no. My mum's hassling you now? She's a nightmare. I've ignored four calls from her already

today. Okay, when shall we do it? Can you do a late night after work? The woman said you could do weekday evenings until nine. We could do tomorrow? I could come straight from here.'

'Yeah, that should work. Why don't I get a cab from work and pick you up on the way?' Emma suggested.

'That sounds good. I should be able to get away by seven thirty at a push.'

'Cool, see you then. Oh and what's all this about hand-reared butterflies?' said Emma.

'Oh don't get me started. Mum went to some blasted wedding fair and got it into her head that we'd release hand-reared butterflies after the meal. I did point out that with the number of candles and burners she's got planned for the marquee we'd have a butterfly massacre on our hands. I thought that had put that one to bed, but obviously not.'

'Do you want me to call her and tell her the RSPCA has banned butterflies at weddings?' laughed Emma. 'Go and get back to drooling at Dan and I'll see you tomorrow,' she said.

'Okay, Em. Oh and can you get Bex to call me about the make-up?'

Bex, Emma's sister, was a TV make-up artist. She'd promised to do make-up and hair for Alex and the bridesmaids.

'Sure. I might see if she can come along tomorrow and we could all go for a pizza afterwards.'

'Great. Thanks again. I must go. Bye.'

Alex could see Tom Duffy striding down the corridor. She put her phone down and walked towards him.

'Tom, good to see you,' she said as they shook hands.

'Hello, Alex. I'm sorry I wasn't here to welcome you this morning. I've been tied up in meetings on the deal. It's all kicking off, I can tell you.'

'Really? Nothing to be concerned about I hope?' Alex was well aware that a significant percentage of deals collapsed at the early stages.

'No, no quite the opposite. The Americans seem very keen to crack on with it. The pressure is on them to get it done before their year end so it's all hands on deck as far as we're concerned. There's going to be an all-party meeting here next week. The accountants and bankers are going to be here and obviously I want you at it too.'

'Well, I'll speak to Truman.'

'Look, Alex, no offence but it's you we want at the meeting, not Truman. He seems like a great bloke and all that but you seem to get our business better. His face when you mentioned buttock lifts at the pitch was hilarious. I want you there, not him. That's okay, isn't it?'

'Of course.' She was flattered but not sure how to convey the message to Truman that the client thought he was a dinosaur.

'Great. Now, do you have all the documents you need?'

'So far it looks like we do. At some point we might have some follow-up questions for you, but at the moment we're just working our way through everything.'

'I've got my secretary doing some copying at the moment so there'll be a few more files to come,' he said.

'Not too many I hope!'

'Actually she's rather snowed under. Do you think Ross could do some of the copying?'

'Of course. All part of the service. I'll send him up to your office,' said Alex.

'That's great, thanks. Anyway, I must go. I've got a conference call with the bank at three. So I'll see you at the all-party meeting. I'll email the details and the agenda.'

CHAPTER 5

'Good day?' Elliott asked.

It was nine o'clock. Alex had just walked in the door. Elliott was lying on the sofa, surrounded by sheet music, his guitar on his lap.

'Not bad. A bit dull, to be honest. How about yours? What happened to the curry with the guys?' She collapsed on the slouchy leather sofa next to him, causing several sheets of paper to float onto the floor.

He took the plectrum from between his teeth. 'The record company called us back. They want us to gig a bit more and practise the new material and see how it goes down before we record anything. Barney was a bit pissed off so the curry idea got binned.'

'But they haven't said no?'

'No.'

'Well, that's good then. What's for supper?' she asked.

'I hadn't got that far. Fancy a takeaway?'

'No thanks. I'm not that hungry. I might grab some soup.' She yawned.

'I'll do it. Tomato or chicken? Out of a tin, before you get too excited.' He got up and leaned his guitar carefully against the wall before kissing her on the top of her head.

'Ooh thanks. Chicken please.' She closed her eyes and rested her head back. She opened one eye and saw Elliott staring at her. 'What is it?'

'Nothing. Just thinking how lucky I am.'

'You better believe it,' she laughed.

'Oh and I checked the band diary. I can do dinner on Monday. Sorry, we've got gigs and rehearsals every night before then. Thought I'd book Elio's. Is that okay?'

'Lovely. Perfect. Though make it about half eight. Looks like I'm going to be putting in some long hours on this deal.' She closed her eyes again and felt herself drifting off.

The next evening Alex was running late. Emma had been waiting outside the Beau Street clinic for ten minutes and the meter on the cab was slowly ticking over.

'Good evening, Ms Fisher. Looks like you'll be needing that raincoat,' shouted the security guard as she raced through the revolving doors, almost tripping over the coat she was carrying, and flung open the taxi door.

'Bye.' She waved to him. 'Sooooo sorry I'm late.' She kissed Emma.

'I'll forgive you. Bride's prerogative, remember.' Emma smiled, unruffled.

'Okay, dress fitting first. Is Bex joining us for dinner?' Alex asked.

'Yup. She'll be there. So how's tricks?'

'Great, thanks. Work's going well and an okay evening with Elliott. We're going out on Monday to talk through the wedding.'

'Excellent. And Dan?'

'Emma, will you shut up about Dan! He's just a colleague, okay?'

'Okay. Sorry.' Emma put her hands up.

'Sorry, Em. Didn't mean to shout.'

Alex reclined on a Louis XV style chaise, watching Emma being pinned into her dress. Emma was statuesque with long, soft, strawberry-blonde curls. She had an intrinsic style of her own and always looked at ease in whatever she wore. The bridesmaid's dress was no exception.

'Can't you make her look fat?' Alex asked the dressmaker.

'Hey! I only agreed to do this if you let me have a decent dress,' said Emma. 'Can't you make me look like I have a waist?' she said to the dressmaker.

'She's not a miracle worker, you know,' said Alex.

'Watch it,' said Emma, pretending to throw her phone at Alex. 'Don't forget my black belt in taekwondo.'

'Okay, okay. Seriously, though, why do you have to look so great in it? It's my day. I wish I had ugly friends.' She pretended to be a spoilt princess. 'I'll have to hire some for the day.'

'You will be gorgeous. As the only one of us with dark hair you're really going to stand out. At least you aren't some freaky giant like me.'

'I hope so. And you aren't a giant. A bit freaky maybe…'

Emma threw her phone at Alex.

'So how was the fitting?' asked Bex a little later as they all sat down at the small corner table in Emma's local brasserie.

'Too good. Emma just looks fabulous. I knew I should have picked ugly bridesmaids,' smiled Alex.

'The dress is lovely but Alex will be the fairest of them all,' said Emma, smiling at her friend.

'Well, I'm going to make you eat lots of pizza so you get spotty!' said Alex.

'Don't worry, I'll stitch her up with my make-up skills. Some nice dark bags under the eyes should sort her out,' said Bex.

'Excellent! And can you give me a quick facelift?'

'I thought you could get one for free at work,' said Emma. 'Tell Bex about where you're working at the moment.'

Alex filled Bex in on the deal while they ordered dinner and wine.

'Today was a scream. We reviewed a file of all the testimonial letters. One woman said that having her boobs done was the most fulfilling thing she'd ever done. And this was a forty-two-year-old mother of three!'

'No way!' said Bex.

'Yeah and there were piles of letters from husbands thanking them for giving them a new wife. Lots of totally unnecessary references to how it had really improved their sex lives. And get this, we had one from a wife going on about her husband's penis enlargement and how he was a new man now and it had saved their marriage. Apparently he's now confident enough to wear Speedos on holiday! She enclosed a photo of him posing by a pool.'

'Ugh.' Emma choked on her bruschetta.

'Joking apart, though, I couldn't believe the difference it had made to these people. It's just bizarre to think how many people must be walking about really unhappy with their bodies,' said Alex.

'Yeah, but if they sort their bodies out do they then get unhappy about something else?' said Bex.

'Very profound! But I guess some of them then get addicted to surgery,' Emma said.

'Yeah, but that's great for Beau Street. Lots of repeat business.'

'So have you got many letters from dissatisfied customers?' asked Bex.

Alex put down her wine glass. Actually she couldn't recall any. 'Er, not really. Not sure we've got to those files yet,' she said. She made a mental note to ask Dan and Ross about the complaints files. Changing the subject, she asked, 'So how's the world of TV at the moment, Bex?'

'Same as ever. I've been having fun on a hospital drama doing all the blood and gore. I had to spend two hours yesterday making up a burns victim. He was gorgeous, though, so no great hardship there. He asked for my number actually.'

'No surprise there,' laughed Alex. Bex had the most beautiful face and was a total man magnet. The fact that she was quite aloof and non-committal seemed to make her even more irresistible to men.

'Not my type really. He loved himself. One of those who'll be stripping off for GQ before you know it.'

'Yeah, we know, Bex. Must be dreadful for you!' Emma said.

'Actually one of the production guys was talking about some cosmetic surgery type show he was doing a pilot for,' she said. 'A kind of makeover show, I think, but for celebs whose careers have nosedived. The idea is that they bring them on, spruce them up a bit and re-launch their careers.'

'Sounds cheesy,' said Emma.

'Cheesy is good apparently. Not sure it will take off, though. Might be hard to find the victims.'

'Well, if they need a surgeon I'm sure there are some good ones at Beau Street,' Alex added.

Bex looked at her thoughtfully. 'Yeah. I'll bear that in mind,' she said.

It was Friday morning and Alex was back at the office. She'd left Dan and Ross at Beau Street where they were continuing to trawl through all the files while she started to draft the report she would have to present to Tom and ultimately the buyers. One or two issues had cropped up relating to suppliers of medical equipment to the practice. The business was tied in to some long-term supply contracts that were very difficult to get out of. Alex knew these would have to be disclosed to the buyer. Equinox would need to know that if they were thinking of changing to a different supplier, or using their own supplier, they wouldn't be able to do so for at least eighteen months. Apart from this and a relatively high number of employment tribunal claims brought by disgruntled employees, they'd discovered nothing so far of any concern.

The other reason Alex was in the office was because it was her annual performance review. She was at her desk reading the feedback form she'd been given prior to her session with Truman and Wanda, the human resources director.

MacArthur Warren operated a three hundred and sixty degree appraisal system, which meant each employee was given feedback from a range of people in the firm, from the post boy to the senior partner. Alex's form was an eclectic mix of comments ranging from compliments about what a nice cuppa she made to an analysis of her technical understanding of corporate legislation.

Alex looked at her watch. It was time to get going.

She knocked and entered the meeting room to find Truman, Wanda and Margaret Kemp already there. She hadn't been expecting Margaret, and her presence made her unexpectedly nervous.

'Good morning,' she said.

The meeting proceeded much as she hoped it would. Truman was as effusive as he was able to be and was clearly delighted about the Beau Street deal. Margaret didn't say much, but spent the whole session listening to what was being said and making the occasional aside.

'We just need the deal to happen, Alex. If it doesn't

then our fee barely covers our costs,' Margaret chipped in.

'Well, we haven't found any issues yet. The business is as clean as a whistle,' she said.

'Don't count your chickens.' Margaret looked up from her paperwork. 'No business is perfect. You just need to know where to look.'

'Quite. I'm sure Alex is on the case, Margaret,' said Truman. 'All in all, Alex, I can see no reason at present why you can't be recommended to start the partnership process next year.'

'As long as the Beau Street deal happens and you follow all the other protocols,' Margaret added.

What's her problem? wondered Alex.

'Of course,' said Truman. 'Well, I think that wraps it up. A very good year for you, Alex. Well done.'

Alex got up to leave and Margaret followed her. As they walked back to the lifts, Margaret turned to her.

'Alex, you're fully aware of the firm's policy on personal relationships within the office?'

'Of course,' said Alex. What was she getting at? She followed Margaret into the lift. Margaret was so close Alex could see the blue eyeshadow settled in the creases on her eyelids.

'How is Dan Furtado?' Margaret said, looking directly at her.

'He's doing a good job, Margaret. He's an excellent lawyer,' Alex replied, angry now.

'Good.'

'Margaret, I'm getting married in less than three months.'

'Congratulations,' she said under her breath as she exited the lift on her floor.

Alex stopped the doors closing and ran after her. She headed Margaret off before she left the lobby area and faced her.

'Margaret, what are you insinuating?' she asked.

Margaret raised her eyebrows in mock surprise. 'Nothing at all, Alex. Why? Do you have something to tell me?'

Alex let the anger rise in her and then fall away. She took a deep breath and smiled. 'Of course not, Margaret. I just wanted to be sure there was nothing further you wanted to say to me.'

'No, nothing. Now I must get on.' Margaret turned and strutted down the corridor.

Back at her desk Alex reached for the phone to call Emma but it started ringing as she touched it. It was Elliott. As she spoke to him she started logging into her email account.

'Hi, babe. How's things?' she asked.

'Yeah, good thanks. You?'

'Just had my appraisal. It went well, I suppose,' she said.

'Great. Look, I'm just calling 'cause your mum phoned in a bit of a state. Said she'd tried to get hold of you.'

Alex looked at her mobile and sighed. Seven missed calls.

'What's she panicking about this time?'

'Something about a deadline for canopies?'

'Canapés.'

'Oh and some butterfly problem. She was fairly hysterical.'

'Okay, I'll call her. Look, if I ever show any signs of turning into my mother please tell me.'

'Yeah sure,' he laughed. 'See you later.'

She put the phone down and stared at the screen in front of her. As she started to work her way through the ninety-two emails in her inbox, Ross came into the office pushing a large metal trolley laden with familiar-looking lever-arch files.

'What are you doing here? Why aren't you at Beau Street?'

'Photocopier packed up. The engines could'na take the strain, Captain,' he said.

'Okay, Scotty,' she laughed. 'What are we going to do?'

'There are at least ten more files to copy so I thought I'd do them here then get back in a cab with them later.'

'Okay. Tell the print room to prioritise this. We can't afford to lose any time. Oh and Ross, have you and Dan come across any complaints files yet?' she asked.

'Well, I haven't. I've been too busy wrestling with the photocopier. Not sure about Dan.'

'Okay, I'll give him a call.'

Ross left with his trolley of files. Alex didn't know who to call first: Dan, her mum or Emma.

She called Emma. The conversation with Margaret was eating away at her.

'I have no idea how she knows about the completion

party. I can't even remember her being there.'

'Calm down,' said Emma. 'She probably doesn't know anything. She's just fishing for something. Anyway, I thought you snogged him in a cab? Unless she's taken up taxi driving in her spare time, you're home and dry.'

'I know but we were chatting and flirting at the bar for hours before that. What if he's told someone and it's got out?'

'Do you think he will have?' Emma asked.

'Well no, not really. He promised not to say a word. He values his career too. Anyway, I'm pretty sure he's got a girlfriend.'

'Exactly. Maybe she saw a bit of flirting and has put two and two together.'

'Yeah and made four,' said Alex.

'She has no proof. Anyway, would they really sack one of you just for a drunken snog? Aren't there laws against that?'

'It doesn't work like that. I'd just be discredited and marginalised 'til I left. You never sue a law firm for discrimination or unfair dismissal. It's career suicide.'

'God, the sexual tension at your place must be incredible. There's nothing like something being forbidden to make it more exciting.'

'It would be Margaret Kemp of all people,' said Alex.

'She needs to get a life. Anyway, why isn't she supporting you? Girl Power and all that?' Emma asked.

'She's an honorary man. She makes it quite clear that women need to work harder than men to prove themselves. As for any woman with kids, she makes their lives hell,' said Alex.

'I take it she's not married then?' asked Emma

'No and she definitely doesn't have kids. She once told me she'd had a hysterectomy as a career move and I don't think she was joking.'

'Bloody hell.'

'Until a couple of years ago she frowned on women in trouser suits. Said they were unprofessional. She's a weird mix. I think she gave up so much to get where she is that she finds it really galling to see "normal" women making it.'

'Calling yourself normal now?' said Emma.

'Far from it. I'm a total stress bunny. My mother thinks I'm some kind of wedding helpline, my fiancé will probably turn up at the wrong church and everyone keeps telling me this cosmetic surgery deal has got to happen. No pressure there then. Oh and on top of that I've got Margaret Kemp sticking pins in a voodoo doll of me. Apart from that I'm just tickety-boo.'

'You're just busy like the rest of us. Calm down. It's just this thing with Dan that's stressing you and there's no need. Even if this Margaret woman does know about it, where's her proof? Just bluff your way through it. You're getting married. No one would believe her.'

Emma was right, she knew it. Alex just wanted her career progression to be seamless and she didn't want there to be any doubts about her promotion to partnership when the time came. Her ambition took her by surprise sometimes, but she loved her job. Elliott didn't get it at all. He thought you could only be passionate about a creative pursuit, but she was as devoted to her job as he was to his music.

She phoned her mother and calmed her down. They agreed on the canapés and Alex finally persuaded her that butterflies were very passé, that there were all sorts of cruelty issues and they didn't want to be raided by the RSPCA on her special day, did they?

'You're right, Alex. Of course. What about doves then?'

Alex silently screamed into the speakerphone. 'Mum, what is this with flora and fauna? Can't we just have fireworks or something?'

'Mmm, I suppose so. We could play Tchaikovsky's Eighteen-Twelve Overture and set off the fireworks in time to the music, I suppose,' she pondered.

'Good idea,' said Alex. 'How's your outfit coming on?'

'Ooh, I went to the shopping outlet yesterday and got the perfect thing: a lavender shift dress with bolero style jacket. Beryl says it's just my colour.'

'Another outfit! How many is that now?'

'Only three, darling, and I'll probably take the suit with the pink piping back. I'll save the blue skirt suit for the alternative therapies conference I'm going to in September.'

'Won't that be a bit over the top? With all the others in gypsy skirts and broderie anglaise?'

'Don't be so prejudiced. The alternative therapies are getting proper recognition from the NHS now. People take it very seriously. I keep telling your father this is the future of a holistic approach to medicine. Don't mock it.'

At least she was off the subject of butterflies now she was on her soapbox, thought Alex as her mum gave her the lowdown on the latest academic paper on the benefits of crystal healing.

'Anyway, darling, enough about that. How are things with Elliott? Sort out your little problem, did you?' her mum asked.

'It's all fine, Mum, really.'

'Good. I'm sure it's just pre-wedding jitters, that's all. I was the same before I married your father. Got myself in a right tizzy and threw a jar of Brylcreem at him. You can see the bruise on his forehead on the wedding pictures.'

CHAPTER 6

It was the morning of the all-party meeting and Alex was on edge. All the senior people working on the deal would be together in one meeting room and she would be representing MacArthur Warren. There would be people from Beau Street, the accountants and the investment bankers who were advising the buyer on the transaction. This was the first time she'd done one of these meetings without a partner there to hide behind.

Persuading Truman that he didn't need to come hadn't been too difficult since he'd been invited by a client to an all-expenses-paid day out at an England cricket match on the same day. He'd suggested that Margaret might be able to stand in for him but thankfully Alex had convinced him that this was exactly the sort of thing she needed to be doing on her own in the run up to partnership. At the last minute she'd decided to bring Dan. There was safety in numbers and she had no idea how many bag carriers and hangers-on the other professionals would be dragging along with them.

She was conservatively dressed in her best black trouser suit with a pink tailored shirt and silver cufflinks. She had her dark hair up in what she hoped was a neat and professional looking pleat and her make-up was subtle. The meeting was being held at the Beau Street offices and Alex took the now familiar route to their dingy project room to catch up with Ross and Dan before she and Dan moved upstairs to the boardroom.

'Hi, guys. How's it going?' she asked as she scanned the neat piles of work. Ross had been meticulous in his organisation. The files that had been reviewed but that hadn't thrown up anything of interest were in one pile. The files yet to be reviewed, and there were still plenty of them, were at the other end of the long table. The files in which they'd discovered something that needed to be investigated were laid out and numbered in the middle section of the table. It was with these files that the three of them had spent most of their time, writing detailed analyses of the risks to the business; reports that would end up in the document that Alex would have to present to the business and the buyers.

'Not too bad,' said Dan. 'We've found the complaints files. Nothing too scary in them. Pretty much what you'd expect.'

'Such as?' she asked.

'Lots of minor stuff about fees. In a few cases people seemed to have gone for a few extras on the day of the procedure and not thought about cost and ended up with another bill they hadn't budgeted for. But the clinic has tightened that up now and gets patients to sign up for every little thing they choose, even if it is another syringe of Botox, so they can't argue about the bill at the end.

'The other problem area is where patients aren't happy with their results, but nine times out of ten that's because their expectations were too high in the first place. The clinic covers itself very well by explaining exactly what the results are likely to be. If a patient has signed up for a tummy tuck, Botox and fillers, they aren't going to come up looking like Cameron Diaz, unless they are Cameron Diaz, of course.'

'Yeah, I read one from a woman who wanted to be a glamour model who asked to go up from an A cup to a C cup and complained because they weren't dramatically big enough,' Ross chipped in.

It was funny how soon the guys had become comfortable with talking about patients' boobs and bits, she thought.

'Okay, but what about actual mistakes? Are there many complaints about surgery that's actually gone wrong or that needs putting right?' Alex asked.

'Nothing to speak of. Ross, you found one, didn't you?' said Dan.

'Oh yes. It was gross. A woman who'd had liposuction and the wound kept getting infected. The medical reports made me feel sick. She ended up getting one of those superbugs and was ill for months.'

'She didn't get the bug at the clinic, did she? God,

we don't want some MRSA scare story. That would really put the buyers off.'

'No. The wound was infected after she left the clinic. She went to her local NHS hospital to get it sorted and caught the bug there. It didn't look good for Beau Street, though. The NHS doctor was less than impressed that the woman had been allowed to go home so quickly after the procedure. But I've done some research into industry practice and Beau Street's recovery times look to be pretty standard.'

'Did Beau Street end up paying compensation?' Alex asked.

'Nope. She hired lawyers but at the end of the day Beau Street weren't legally responsible. When she left their care she was fine,' Ross said.

'Yes, but didn't they make some kind of ex gratia payment?' Dan asked.

'That's right. They didn't admit liability but paid her about a thousand pounds, I think it was, as a gesture of good will and then got her to sign a confidentiality agreement.'

'Very clever — so they wouldn't end up with any dodgy publicity,' said Alex.

'Exactly,' said Ross.

'Okay. Is that it? Any other cases I need to know about before this meeting?'

'Not at the moment. We've still got one more file on complaints. After that we just have the property stuff to look at — you know, their leases, upkeep costs, that type of thing,' said Dan.

'Great. It looks like we're in pretty good shape then.

Come on, Dan, we'd better get to the boardroom. We don't want to be the last people there and end up playing musical chairs.'

Alex and Dan waited for the lift to take them to the boardroom, which was on the top floor.

'What's the form then, Alex?' Dan asked.

'Well, usually the investment bank runs the meeting. Some guy called King Alfred, must be a code name, has circulated the agenda,' she replied.

'Code name?'

'You know. It's probably highly confidential that Equinox is looking to buy in the UK so the investment bank has gone all paranoid and given everyone and everything a code name. They've named the transaction "Project Pout".'

'Those guys sound like a laugh a minute,' Dan smiled.

They left the lift and strode towards the boardroom carrying their document wallets. Dan knocked politely on the door and then pushed it open with his right arm, signalling with his left to Alex to go in before him. She straightened her hair, moved forwards and promptly tripped over the silver carpet rod and plunged into the back of someone already sitting at the boardroom table.

'Ah, this is Alex Fisher who's leading the team from MacArthur Warren,' said Tom Duffy. 'Are you alright, Alex?' he asked.

'Yes, of course.' She smoothed her hair and straightened her jacket. 'I'm so sorry,' she said to the man she'd fallen on.

He stood up and held out his hand. 'Not a problem. Pleased to meet you, Alex. I'm Alfred King from Clinton Wahlberg.'

'Ah, you're King Alfred,' she said, tapping her nose and winking.

'Er, no. I'm Alfred King.'

'The emails? The codename?' she said.

'I think you'll find that our email account is set up so the surname reads first,' he said. 'Although I think I'm going to speak to IT and get them to change it,' he muttered.

Bugger, she thought. She laughed exaggeratedly as if she'd known all along and had just made some incredibly witty aside. Several heads in the room turned to look at her.

She sat down and pretended to study the agenda. Dan sat to her right and Alfred was to her left.

Tom formally started the meeting by introducing everyone. Tom's chief executive, Charles Sutton, and a lady doctor from Beau Street sat either side of Tom opposite Alex and Dan. Alex noticed that the lady doctor looked as nervous as she felt. A statuesque and extremely serious looking woman called Meredith was the senior banker on the deal and she was sitting on the other side of Alfred. On the right-hand side of the table were the accountants, a partner called Carl Stephens and a younger woman called Rachel. She was glad she'd brought Dan. It was true: professionals came in twos. Shame there wasn't a buy-one-get-one-free offer, she thought. The Beau Street clinic's professional fees on the deal would be huge. With the exception of the

Beau Street people, every person in the room was on an hourly charge out rate.

The introductions over, Meredith from Clinton Wahlberg took over the proceedings.

'Okay. You all have your agendas, I take it?' She looked over the top of her glasses at the rest of the table. 'I'll talk you through the Project Pout timetable first.'

Alex couldn't place Meredith's accent. She was pretty sure she was British but there was a twang of something else there too. French maybe? Meredith was certainly striking and had that whole Euro-chic thing going on. Extremely tall and with a haughty and well-bred posture, she was also intimidating. As far as Alex could pick up from what she was saying, the priority seemed to be to get everything done as quickly as possible but without cutting any corners. This didn't seem to concern Tom and the Beau Street people.

'A quick deal suits us as long as the advisers can facilitate that for us,' said Charles Sutton, Tom Duffy's distinguished looking boss.

'Good. But let's be clear: Equinox don't want a quick and dirty deal. They want a full due diligence exercise. If they're happy the business is clean then I'm pretty confident you'll get the agreed price, or thereabouts.' Meredith continued, 'Right, I'm going to patch in Ryan now, if that's okay with you all.' She perfunctorily scanned the room while pulling the speakerphone in the middle of the table towards her. It seemed that Ryan Miller was a big cheese at Equinox and he was going to be on the speakerphone for the rest of the meeting.

Dan took notes while Ryan, Meredith and Tom did most of the talking.

'You guys are a neat fit for us. Our priorities are reputation, quality and diversity. The synergy works because, like us, you have a good reputation in the marketplace, you're professional and use senior medically trained personnel, and you seem to be able to branch out into new areas. I can guarantee that the Brits are going to be looking for weirder and weirder stuff just like our US clients,' Ryan was barking down the line. 'Jeez, we need this to happen quick, though. I'm sure Meredith has explained we need to be announcing this deal before we release our year-end result. The timetable is tight and there's no margin for slippage.'

Alex exchanged a wry smile with Dan. They both knew they were going to have their work cut out delivering what was required on time.

'Thanks, Ryan,' said Meredith. 'Perhaps the advisers can give us an update now. Alex, how is your review progressing?'

'We're on track. We've reviewed the bulk of the documentation that Beau Street has provided and are working on the first draft of our report. We'll deliver our first draft followed by the final version to our client as per the timetable,' Alex said.

'Thank you for that update, Alex,' Meredith said, nodding at the lawyers. 'Rachel Altman from Payne Stanley is now going to give us an update from their side.'

Alex looked at Dan. They both knew what she'd promised was a tall order.

Thirty minutes later they were back in the dungeon with Ross.

'Look, guys, we really have to put in some long hours, I'm afraid. We're going to be spending a lot of time here and eating a lot of takeaway pizzas. It's probably a good idea to cancel our weekend plans now.' As Alex said this she remembered her date with Elliott that evening.

'Not a problem,' said Dan. 'It comes with the territory.'

As Ross spoke they heard a polite knock at the door and Albert Cheung came in. 'Good morning all. I've brought you some more documents,' he beamed.

'Great,' mumbled Ross.

'One of the doctors has a temp working for him at the moment and she found a file of papers that seemed to have been missed when we put the first set of documentation together,' Albert continued.

'Thanks, Albert. Do you think there will be any more?' Alex said. If they kept getting new files to review at this stage they'd never be ready on time.

'No. She seemed pretty sure this was the last one. I've asked everyone to have a final check.' Albert handed Alex another lever-arch file. 'Is there anything else I can get you?' He tipped his head to one side and smiled.

'The number for a good local takeaway would be helpful,' Dan said.

'Don't you like the canteen food then? It's Mexican chilli tacos today. They're excellent.'

'The canteen is great. No, it's just that I think we're going to be putting in some late nights, that's all,' said Alex.

'Ah, of course. I'll get right on it and text you the number.'

'Another one. Bloody marvellous,' said Ross after Albert had left. 'What's in it, Dan?'

Dan was leafing through the file's contents. 'Doesn't look too bad. Mainly thank you letters from happy patients. Won't take long at all. Don't stress. We'll be fine. This is nowhere near as bad as that magazine deal I was on. That business was full of holes. At least this one doesn't look as though it has anything to hide. On the magazine deal the finance director was sleeping with the head of legal and kept using her to keep some dodgy expenses scam away from us.'

'They could do with an in-house lawyer here really. They might end up spending less money on employment tribunals for a start,' said Alex. 'Mmm, I think I'll make that one of our recommendations.'

'Yeah and everything might be a bit more organised. Albert is really helpful but the files aren't in any kind of system. I found a letter about labioplasty in the middle of a photocopier lease yesterday,' said Dan.

'Yeah, what is labioplasty?' asked Ross. 'I keep seeing references to it.'

'I suggest you Google it!' laughed Dan.

Alex and Dan were still giggling as they saw Ross hide behind his laptop while he looked it up.

'Whatever you do, don't select Google Images,' said Alex.

'Ugh, this is grim,' said Ross.

'I tell you, our IT department are going to have a field day looking at our search history over the past couple of weeks,' said Alex.

The three lawyers continued their work all day, only breaking to sample the Mexican chilli tacos. By six Alex was wrestling with her conscience over whether to cancel Elliott or work on through and jump in a cab and meet him at the restaurant later. Her mobile phone vibrated. It was a text from Elliott. She sighed loudly as she read it. He'd cancelled her. Something had come up with the band and he was really sorry and could he move the table reservation to the same time next week? She'd been here so many times before.

'You okay?' Dan looked up.

'Yeah. My fiancé's just cancelled our dinner date. It's probably just as well. We've got plenty to do here.'

'Anyone for another caffeine hit?' asked Ross, gathering up all the dirty cups.

They toiled away late into the evening reading property leases. Beau Street rented two adjacent properties and it was important that the buyers understood the obligations and liabilities they'd be taking on. They made notes about the amount of the rent, when the landlord could increase the rent and by how much, the length of the leases and the obligations on Beau Street to maintain the premises. It was tedious but necessary work. Five lever-arch files and two large pizzas later they'd had enough.

'Okay, guys, shall we call it a day?' said Alex. 'Don't know about you but I'm losing the will to live.'

'Good plan. Anyone fancy a quick drink?' Dan suggested. 'I need to wind down.'

'Go on then, just a quick one,' Alex said. Elliott wouldn't be back until after midnight.

'I think I'll pass,' said Ross. 'I haven't seen my girlfriend much this week.' Ross's girlfriend was a trainee solicitor at another City firm.

This is fine, Alex told herself as she and Dan walked to the nearest bar. It's perfectly normal behaviour to go for a drink with a colleague after work.

They went down some steps into the basement of a Tudor-beamed building that housed a bar-come-steak-house. The walls were panelled in dark wood and the floor was stone flags. Dan went up to the bar and ordered a beer and a white wine spritzer and they took a table in a corner dimly lit by a mock candle wall-light.

'That was a productive day. I thought the meeting went well this morning. Though that banker woman was a bit over the top,' Dan said.

'Yeah. We could have done without me flinging myself at that King Alfred chap on the way in. I was mortified. I can't imagine that ice queen Meredith ever does anything like that.'

'Hey, it wasn't such a big deal,' he laughed. 'You did great in that meeting. Oh and how did your appraisal go? I've been meaning to ask all day.'

'It was good, thanks. Truman seems to think I could start jumping through the hoops for partnership next year. It will really help if this deal happens, though,' she said.

'Good for you, Alex, that's amazing. There doesn't

seem to be any reason why it won't happen at the moment. They all seemed desperate to get it done as soon as possible at the meeting.'

'Fingers crossed. So what about you? What are your career plans now you're staying in the UK? By the way, how did you wangle that?' she asked.

'My mom's a Brit. I've got dual nationality. And, well, I'm not sure. I think MacArthur Warren is a great firm but I've toyed with the idea of going into business and working on the other side of the fence,' said Dan. Many lawyers considered leaving the familiarity of their law firm to go and work 'in-house' as the lawyer working in a business.

'You'd be great at that. You're very commercial.'

She wondered whether to tell him about Margaret. The spritzer had started to kick in.

'Dan, you probably should know that Margaret Kemp is onto us.'

'What do you mean?' He frowned.

'You know, the completion party? She made some pointed reference to you. I think she has her suspicions,' Alex said.

Dan put both hands to his temples and stared at her. 'What is wrong with that woman? She was asking me how I found working with you the other day.'

'Well then, she's definitely on to us,' said Alex, panicking.

'Hey, hey, Alex. Let's get this into perspective. We kissed. In a taxi. It isn't a crime. It was actually very nice.' He smiled.

Alex couldn't look at him as he spoke.

'This ridiculous firm rule is wrong and probably contrary to any number of employment laws. You're getting married, for God's sake.' He was angry now.

'I know. I told her. Look, it's her word against ours whatever happens.'

'Yes, of course.' He sighed. 'I'm sorry I put you in this predicament.'

'It takes two to tango,' she replied.

They finished their drinks, making awkward small talk.

Outside, as Alex hailed a taxi she turned to Dan. 'Want to share with me? No funny business this time.'

He laughed. 'No thanks. I've moved. I'm up in Islington now.'

'Oh.' Alex was surprised.

'Yeah. Melissa and I split up. She's gone back to the States so I had to get out. It was her flat.'

'Ah. Right, well, I'll see you in the morning. Thanks for the drink.'

What is the matter with me? she thought to herself on the way home. She couldn't stop thinking about Dan. Why did he have to be so good looking and newly single and why oh why had she put him on the team? Who was she kidding?

CHAPTER 7

The next morning Alex decided to work from home. She had to work on the draft report and didn't really want to see Dan again until she'd got her head straight. Was it right to have a crush on someone when you were getting married to someone else? She'd assumed that being engaged somehow made you immune to it.

She left Elliott still asleep. Just looking at him next to her made her feel guilty. She made a coffee and sat at the kitchen table with her laptop. She sent an email to Ross and Dan explaining what she was doing and telling them to email their work to her so she could review it for inclusion in the main report.

A couple of hours later Elliott staggered into the kitchen.

'Hey, babe. What are you doing here? Where's the sharp suit and the briefcase?'

'Working from home. I've got loads to do and need to concentrate.'

'You might not be in the best place then. The guys

are coming round later to do some writing. Cup of tea?' he said as he flicked the switch on the kettle.

'No thanks. When are they coming?' She made a mental note to relocate to the local coffee house before they arrived.

'About four. Hey, I'm sorry about last night. I'll call Elios and try to book next week instead.'

'No worries. I'm snowed under at work. But please book us in next week. I really need to go through this wedding stuff. I'd do it now if I wasn't so busy.' She watched him move around the kitchen in a languid fashion, taking his time to make his toast and dunk his teabag. 'I suppose I could do it now actually.' She leaned back in her chair. At least he was a captive audience; maybe she should seize the chance.

'No, you do your work. I need to go out and get some new strings for my acoustic and a cable for the keyboard. I won't be in your way. We'll talk weddings next week.'

'Yeah, okay. I suppose I should get on with this.'

'Oh and Alex?' he shouted from halfway down the corridor. 'Your mum phoned last night. Something about doves this time.'

Alex rested her head on her keyboard and groaned.

By mid afternoon Alex was dressed and feeling positive. She'd phoned her dad and he'd agreed to put her mum back on track. 'Tell her doves have got fleas,' she'd suggested. She'd written at least half the report and was heading for the local coffee shop to do some more work while Elliott, Barney, Andy and Rory were transforming her sitting room into some kind of creative brainstorming den.

'See you later, guys,' she said, poking her head round the door. They were sitting on the floor, instrument cases strewn all over the sofa and deep in conversation.

'Bye, city slicker,' said Barney, looking up at her. He had an unlit roll-up in his mouth.

'Don't forget, no smoking in here,' she said.

'Don't worry, I'll keep them in check,' said Elliott.

As she walked down the street past the combination of gentrified and run-down terraced houses she wondered about the lives going on behind those closed doors. Who lived in the neglected ones? she wondered. Students? Elderly people, as neglected as their houses? She hoped it was the former. She'd tried to discuss with Elliott where they might move to when they had children. They would soon outgrow their small house. She was sure she wanted children at some point but it might be a good idea to get partnership first. She had no illusions; she would be the main breadwinner. Elliott had looked at her as though she'd asked him to do a Britney Spears cover when she'd raised the subject of children. He lived one day at a time but she had no doubt he would be an amazing father. He just wouldn't engage in the process until he had a baby in his arms.

As Alex queued in the coffee shop, Bex called her. She was working on location in West London.

'I just wondered if you'd be home early. I'm in your neck of the woods and thought I'd pop round for a quick drink,' she suggested.

'I'm in the coffee shop on Eldon Street. I'm going to be here for a couple of hours. Why don't you join me?' said Alex, balancing her mobile under her chin as she picked up her latte.

Two hours and five more pages of the report later, and after stringing out her coffee for as long as she could, Alex was back at the counter ordering another one as Bex came in.

'Perfect timing. What can I get you?' Alex asked.

'A G&T's what I really want, but go on, I'll have a skinny latte, please.' Bex pulled her messenger bag over her head and took off her jacket. 'God, I'm boiling. Just been sardined on the tube for ten minutes.'

They sat down at the corner table where Alex had been working. Alex closed her laptop and put it back in its bag.

'Why are you working here?' asked Bex.

'It's a long story involving a man I want to avoid at work and a man at home who wants to avoid me.'

'Ah, clear as mud. Think I might have an inkling who the man at home is. Who's the guy at work?' Bex asked.

'A guy on my team. Dan. The American?'

'Ooh yes, I remember him from that Christmas drinks thing at Bar Q. Lovely teeth. Nice guy too I seem to remember. Why would you want to avoid him?' As Bex said this Alex could see the penny drop. 'Oh Alex, you haven't!'

'No I have not! It's complicated. I've just got a bit of a crush, that's all. I don't need that sort of complication at the moment.'

'Enjoy it while you can. No more crushes in twelve weeks' time.'

'Eleven actually, and counting,' Alex said.

'I'm sure it's perfectly normal. You don't stop fancying other men just 'cause you've got a partner. Anyway, it's great to see you.' She raised her mug of coffee.

Alex chinked her mug against it. 'Yeah, you too. How's the world of make-up?'

'Thrilling as always. It was a road accident scene today. Prosthetics, broken limbs, bloody faces — the lot. Not really what I had in mind for my career but it pays the bills, I suppose.'

Alex was surprised. She'd always assumed that Bex loved her job. 'What would you rather be doing then?'

'Ooh, I don't know. Changing people's lives, I suppose.'

'Retraining as a heart surgeon, are you?'

'I just mean doing something where you get some appreciation. Making people look nice rather than injured or dead would be a start!'

'Well, you need to make me and Emma look fab at the wedding. How is Em, by the way? Whenever I see her at the moment all we seem to talk about is me and my traumas.'

'She's good. Working her tits off on some celeb perfume launch. You know that actress Olivia Meddoes?' said Bex.

'Yeah. The rom-com specialist?'

'That's the one. Well, she's putting her name to an upmarket perfume and Em is handling the UK launch.'

'What's she like?' asked Alex.

'Olivia? Bloody nightmare apparently. Total diva.

She's getting on a bit now too so is obsessed about the right lighting, her dietary requirements – you know, the whole nine yards.'

'Em should get you on the make-up,' said Alex.

'Yeah, not a bad idea. I'll mention it but I'm pretty sure that woman has a team of thousands doing all her personal grooming.'

There was a brief silence while they both took a sip of their drinks. Then Bex looked around her as if she was about to share some highly secret piece of gossip. She leant forward. 'Look, Alex, you know this deal you're working on at the moment? The cosmetic surgery one?'

'Yes,' she said, intrigued.

'Well, the thing is, I've been thinking about having a boob job for years now but I've never plucked up the courage or had the money. But now Granddad has left me five grand in his will. Do you think I should? Have you come across any scare stories? Anything I should worry about? Beau Street is one of the clinics I was thinking of going to.'

'Gosh. I can't believe it. Why would you want to do that? You're gorgeous,' Alex said.

'Not from the neck down. I'm so self-conscious. People expect me to have boobs 'cause I'm quite curvy, but I'm flat as a flatbread.'

'I'd never realised you were so bothered by it. Do you really want to go through surgery, though?'

'I'd go through a week at your mum's to have a decent pair.'

Alex laughed. 'Okay. Well, to be honest the whole

safety side of it is pretty good. It does seem that a lot of clients end up going back at some point and get new implants or get them lifted after they've had kids. Think long and hard about it. You could do a lot with five k.'

As Alex finished speaking her phone rang. It was Dan. 'Sorry, I need to take this.' She smiled apologetically at Bex. 'Hi, Dan. What's up?'

Bex raised her eyebrows and made kissing noises at her. Alex turned her head away from her.

'Alex, I'm at the office. The shit's hit the fan.'

'Oh God, has someone found out about us?'

'What are you talking about? It's the deal, Alex. I've found a very worrying letter. I think you need to see it.'

'What's it about?' Alex asked, kicking herself for revealing to him how obsessed she was about the ramifications of their drunken moment.

'Blackmail, botched surgery, threats. It's not good.'

'I'm on my way.'

'What on earth's the matter, Alex?' Bex said as she saw her ashen face.

'So sorry, I've got to go.' She grabbed her laptop bag and pecked Bex on the cheek. 'Major work crisis. Oh and I've also just made a total idiot of myself.'

'Bye. Hope it works out,' Bex called after her.

Alex hailed a taxi to the City. Half an hour later she hurried through the front entrance of MacArthur Warren to the glass atrium where the lifts were located. She was acutely aware that even though it was now after seven p.m. she wasn't suitably dressed for the office in her jeans, sandals and floaty top. The lift door opened. There was no one in it. She breathed a sigh of relief and headed up to the fourth floor to the corporate department.

As she ran down the corridor towards Dan's office she saw Margaret Kemp come out of the coffee station. She knew what was coming.

'Interesting choice of clothing for the office, Alex,' she said.

'Yes, sorry, Margaret. I was working from home and something urgent has cropped up. I needed to get back to Dan as soon as possible.' She regretted it the moment she said it.

'Quite,' said Margaret with a disapproving smile. 'Nothing that's going to hold up the deal I hope?' She was clearly not expecting an answer.

Alex carried on to Dan's office. As she entered he was just getting off the phone. He hung up as he saw her and turned his chair towards her. He ran both sets of fingers through his hair and then cradled the back of his head in his hands.

'Take a seat and I'll talk you through it.'

She pulled a chair round to face him and sat down, feeling her cheeks flush.

'This is the letter. You'd better read it. It was in the file Albert gave us yesterday; the one the temp found.' He passed her the letter.

Alex read it. It was from a C list actress called Felicia Monroe. She'd had a breast augmentation operation that, from the sound of things, had gone disastrously wrong. She had the opinion of an independent doctor, which said that Beau Street's work had undoubtedly been negligent. She'd ended up in her local NHS hospital and, according to her, had nearly died. Felicia had clearly complained on a number of occasions previously. She was now threatening to go to the General Medical Council, clinical negligence lawyers and the newspapers. It was the kind of publicity that could scupper the deal. And there was a cryptic comment at the end that sounded like blackmail.

'What's this at the end about her telling "the agency" and Beau Street losing all its clients?' Alex asked.

'I've no idea, but it looks like she's going to do a lot of mudslinging if they don't deal with her. The weirdest bit is where she says it's her fourth complaint letter and that they haven't even bothered to reply to the previous three,' Dan said.

'It doesn't sound like Beau Street. They seemed quite together on handling complaints. I take it you and Ross haven't seen any of these other letters?' Alex asked.

'Nope. The other thing is she mentions the doctor who did the surgery. Some guy called Lloyd Cassidy. Have you come across him yet?'

Alex shook her head.

'Well, I checked his client list and couldn't find her on it, so I just phoned Dr Cassidy. His assistant nurse answered. It's that Audrey Fox; remember the glam older woman Albert pointed out in the canteen that day? I told her about the letter. She seemed very surprised and said that Felicia Monroe had never been a client of Cassidy's.'

'Well, someone's lying then. What do we do now?' said Alex.

'I don't know. I was hoping you might have a bright idea,' Dan said. 'The obvious thing would be to get hold of Felicia's number and get her full version of events. If she's some total fantasist we might be able to work that out from a phone call. Her address is on the letter but there's no number. I don't suppose she'll be in the phone book, though.'

'Hmm. You Google her and I'll phone a friend.'

'Yeah and I'll ask the audience,' he said.

She smiled as she dialled Bex's number.

'Hello again. Crisis over?'

'Not exactly. Bex, is there any chance you could help me get hold of a number for an actress — Felicia Monroe? It's obviously totally confidential.'

'Ooh, how exciting. It's like Charlie's Angels.'

'Not exactly.'

'Felicia Monroe. She was in that daytime soap set in Derbyshire. Yeah, I could speak to Mark in the Talent Department. He might be able to help. He fancies me, I think.'

'Well, that should help. Use your charms. If there's any way you could get it tonight I'll be eternally grateful.'

'I'm on the case. I'll do my best.'

'Thanks so much. Oh and Bex, please don't tell anyone why you need it.'

'Shouldn't be difficult seeing as I don't know. Byeee.' She rang off.

Dan was speed-reading celebrity gossip sites. Alex looked over his shoulder and read some of the highlights. Felicia's name had generated numerous hits.

'She sounds like a classy lady. She was an actress in a soap until four years ago. Since then she hasn't done much apart from turn up at premieres and parties. She's dated two footballers and a game show host and married her hairdresser. That lasted six months. She's done two reality TV shows and managed to appear naked in one of them. She's forty-three. Oh and her favourite colour is purple,' Dan said.

'It doesn't tell us much. Any pictures of her new boobs?' asked Alex.

'No. The trail goes dead about nine months ago. It seems she's been keeping a low profile.'

'Well, that would make sense if what she says in that letter is true. She'd hardly be hanging out at Stringfellows if she's wrapped up in bandages. Okay. Now what?' said Alex, looking at Dan. He looked exhausted. 'What's Ross up to?'

'Not sure. I've been here all day. I spoke to him this afternoon and he was finishing off the property stuff.'

'How come you didn't go to Beau Street?' she asked as her phone started ringing.

'You'd better get that. It could be your friend,' said Dan.

She answered the call. It wasn't Bex.

'Hi, Em. How's things?' she asked.

'Good. Look, I've had Bex on the phone. She can't get you that number – her flirting didn't work for once. But I can get it for you.'

'How can you do that?' asked Alex.

'Felicia is on our rent-a-celeb list. Bear with me while I look her up.'

'She's on your what?'

'Our list of B- to Z-listers who we invite to some of our PR dos. You know, whenever we need to get some headlines the next day. Felicia was one of our regulars. She would turn up to the opening of a bag of crisps. Looking at her file, though, it seems she's gone a bit quiet recently. She's turned down our last three requests to go to events. Maybe she's trying to reinvent herself as a serious actress or something. Anyway, here's her mobile number but you mustn't tell her how you got it. I could get fired for this.'

'Thanks so much, Em, you're a total star.'

'Why do you want it, anyway?'

'Long story. She claims to have been a client of Beau Street. She says they messed up on some work they did for her. Don't tell anyone, though. It's confidential.'

'I won't if you won't.'

Alex hung up and stared at the number. Then she looked at Dan, who'd been watching her intently while she was speaking to Emma. Even when he was stressed and exhausted he generated an aura of easy capability. Could she ask him to call Felicia?

'Would you like me to call her?' He read her mind.

'Would you? Do you know, I somehow think it might come better from you. I don't know why. Something tells me she might be more of a man's woman than a woman's woman, if you know what I mean,' she said.

'Of course. Not a problem.'

Alex passed Dan the number and together they

drew up a list of the questions they needed to ask. They decided to call her on the speakerphone so Alex could listen in.

'Okay. Here goes.' Dan dialled the number.

'Hi, Felicia here,' said a clear, well-spoken voice.

'Good evening. My name is Dan Furtado. I'm a lawyer and I'm calling you about a letter of complaint you recently sent to the Beau Street Group,' he said.

'About time. I've been waiting for a response for weeks now. I've been calling Lloyd Cassidy and leaving messages with his PA and no one has had the decency to get back to me.'

Alex looked at Dan. Felicia clearly thought Dan was calling on behalf of Beau Street to sort out her case. They should have anticipated this.

'Ms Monroe, I should make it clear that I'm not representing Beau Street on your case. I came across your complaint in the context of another matter I'm working on and am keen to know more about it.'

Alex gave him a thumbs up.

'I'm sorry, I'm not sure I understand. Do you want to help me or not?' Felicia asked.

'I'd love to know more about the allegations in your letter and then I can bring them to the attention of the right people for you,' Dan said.

'Okay. But look, I'm not talking through all this on the phone. I've got photos and everything you need to see. Can I meet you?'

Dan looked enquiringly at Alex. She nodded vigorously.

'Absolutely. When would suit you?' he said.

'I'm away at the moment but I'm back in town on Monday. How about Tuesday evening?'

'Can you do any sooner? It is rather urgent.'

'You're telling me. I've been through hell and back and still look like a freak. Tuesday is the earliest I can do. I'll have my agent with me.'

'Okay, I'll see you then.'

Dan and Felicia agreed a meeting place.

'And can you just confirm it was Lloyd Cassidy who did your surgery?' Dan asked.

'Yes it was. He came highly recommended but I wouldn't recommend him to my worst enemy after what I've been through. And you can tell him that from me.' Felicia hung up.

Dan clicked the speaker button and turned back to face Alex. She was perched on the edge of her chair swinging her legs like a child, lost in thought. If Dan wasn't meeting Felicia until Tuesday she had the dilemma of whether to include anything in the report she was preparing for Tom Duffy for Monday.

'It just doesn't stack up. She doesn't sound like a fantasist but either she or this Cassidy chap is lying,' she said.

'Or his assistant is lying. We haven't actually spoken to Cassidy,' said Dan.

'You're right. Perhaps we should track him down tomorrow. Are you okay to do this meeting with Felicia?' Alex was conscious that next Tuesday was when Elliott was supposed to be taking her out again.

'Yeah, fine. Her agent is going to be there as well so it isn't going to be one on one. Look, I'm sure this is nothing to worry about. Beau Street will probably have to make her a payout, maybe offer a bit of corrective surgery, and it will blow over.'

'Yeah, you're probably right. Nothing more than a storm in a D cup,' said Alex.

She returned home late that evening, exhausted. The tube journey had taken for ever and she hadn't eaten since lunch. All she wanted to do was grab a sandwich, sink into her slouchy sofa and watch trashy TV for an hour before going to bed.

As she clicked the front door closed behind her she could hear Barney's voice. 'Yeah, but that riff is so wrong at the bridge. We need something less showy there.'

'That's bollocks,' said a voice she recognised as Rory's.

She opened the door to the living room and the smell of marijuana hit her. The room was trashed. The guys were sprawled on the sofas, cereal bowels overflowing with cigarette butts and spliffs were balanced on the arms of the sofa, and half empty fish and chip wrappers were mixed up with the sheet music that was strewn everywhere. Alex surveyed the scene with mounting anger. She looked at Elliott.

He smiled back, clearly oblivious to her reaction. 'Hi, babe,' he slurred.

Alex didn't know what to say. If she bawled him out now the other guys would laugh at her and she would feel like an idiot. That was the worst thing about Elliott and the band. They always made her feel like she was uptight and some kind of obsessive compulsive.

'Hi. I thought we agreed no smoking in the house?'

'Oh yeah. Sorry, it's only the band,' said Elliott.

Yeah and that's an excuse, she thought.

'Just because you're "musicians" doesn't mean you can trash the place. Look, I'm knackered. I'm off to bed. Can you keep the noise down.'

She closed the door and resisted the temptation to listen to what they were probably saying about her.

CHAPTER 8

For the next two days Dan, Ross and Alex kept their heads down. The first draft report had to be with Tom Duffy on Monday. Dan and Ross churned through the final dozen files of documents while Alex continued drafting the report. They were in a rhythm now and worked together silently and effectively, breaking the monotony with their daily trip to the canteen and occasional visits from Albert.

On Friday Alex had arranged with Tom for them to have access to various members of the management team at Beau Street, to ask them follow up questions on areas where they needed clarification. Dan was spending an hour with the businesses property manager and Ross was meeting with the lady doctor Alex had seen at the all-party meeting. Her name was Stella Webb and it seemed she was a rising star on the management team.

Alex had an appointment with Lloyd Cassidy. She approached his assistant Audrey's desk armed with her legal notepad and a smile.

'Hello. I'm Alex Fisher from MacArthur Warren. I'm here to see Dr Cassidy.'

'Dr Cassidy is just with a patient, but he's nearly finished. Take a seat,' said Audrey.

Alex sat and leafed through a copy of *Country Life* while watching Audrey at work. The nurse was probably in her late forties. She was glamorous in an obvious way in leather trousers and heels and had a weird lip-liner-outside-her-lips thing going on.

The door opened and an attractive middle-aged woman left the office. Alex found herself assessing her face for any evidence of what she'd had done but found none. She looked naturally pretty.

As the woman left, a dashing grey-haired gentleman appeared behind her. He strode towards Alex, thrusting out his tanned, well-manicured hand. 'Ah, so you're the legal eagle who's come to see me. Charming to meet you, Ms Fisher,' he said, keeping hold of her hand slightly too long.

'Er, yes. Good to meet you too, Dr Cassidy.'

'Lloyd! Call me Lloyd. Come in. Audrey, please can we have some tea?' he asked as he ushered Alex into his office.

Alex looked around the room at the various certificates, commendations and awards the doctor had accumulated over the years. There were also several large photographs of him at industry events looking very pleased with himself.

'Now, young lady, what can I do for you?' He beamed at her from behind his desk, revealing a full set of white veneers.

Alex felt uneasy under his gaze. She was sure he must be assessing all the work she could have done.

'Just a few routine questions about insurance and complaints procedures.'

Alex asked him the questions on her list and he was polite, helpful and professional in his answers. He even got Audrey to provide her with an up-to-date copy of his medical negligence insurance policy.

'That's great. You've been extremely helpful,' she said. 'There's just one more thing and then I think I can leave you in peace.'

'Of course. What is it?' He leant back in his chair and rested his expensive looking shoes on the desk.

'Well, we came across a letter of complaint from a lady called Felicia Monroe who says she underwent a breast augmentation procedure here. Apparently she had numerous post-surgery complications and she now has lopsided breasts and horrific scarring. She says you were her surgeon.' Alex had been watching his reaction as she spoke. He was impassive.

'I'm so sorry I haven't a clue. But that name is familiar to me. An actress I think?' he asked.

'Yes, that's right.'

'But a patient, no. I've never treated her. She must be mistaken. She has the wrong surgeon. It sounds like she's had some poor quality surgery somewhere else. I don't know. But she's definitely not one of my patients,' he said. 'Where did you say this letter came from?'

'It was in one of the files we were given by Albert.'

'How peculiar. Well, I'm sorry I can't help you.'

'Dr Cassidy, is there any way she could have been

referred to you initially but then treated by a colleague of yours?'

'Absolutely not. All my patients are my patients. They come to me, usually by recommendation. I didn't receive all these commendations for nothing, you know.' He waved his arm towards his wall of certificates and awards. 'I don't refer my patients to any other doctor unless it's for a procedure I don't do, and there aren't many of those I can assure you.'

'As you say, this lady is clearly mistaken.'

'Or a little mad,' he said, tapping the side of his head.

As Alex left his office he called loudly, 'Audrey? Does the name Felicia Monroe ring a bell? Not one of mine, is she?'

'No, not at all. I've never heard of her. I can run a quick check of your patient lists if you like,' she said.

You've heard of her, thought Alex. Dan only called you last night.

'No, please don't go to any trouble. We've already had copies of your patient lists and she's not on there. That's why it's so odd,' said Alex. 'Anyway, thank you for your time,' she said to the doctor. 'It was a pleasure to meet you.'

'The pleasure was all mine,' Lloyd replied.

Alex returned to the project room. On balance she thought Felicia was in the wrong. Perhaps she wanted publicity or free remedial work or was crazy? Dr Cassidy was a bit smarmy but he'd seemed pretty convincing and Audrey had backed him up. Alex felt much happier now about keeping silent about the complaint in her report.

Even so, she spent a couple of hours checking out the potential cost to the business, just in case Felicia was telling the truth. It seemed that it would be Dr Cassidy who'd probably be legally liable, unless one of his assistants in theatre could be shown to have been at fault. It was likely that any claim would be made against his insurance rather than Beau Street's policy. He could also be subject to proceedings before the General Medical Council if his work had been seriously negligent. Despite all this Alex knew that, whether or not the allegations were true, if Felicia wanted to make a big fuss then the impact on the business could be huge. It was the bad publicity and the damage to Beau Street's reputation that would scare off Equinox. She had no doubt that Felicia had to be managed very carefully.

That evening the Beau Street team found themselves inexorably drawn back to the City and Bar Q. Alex always missed the office when she was working away from it. Somehow she felt out of the loop on the politics and, more importantly, the gossip. They arrived at the waterfront bar later than most of the City professionals and it was already packed. The bar was three people deep and on every table, windowsill and decorative niche there were assorted briefcases that had been dumped while their owners let off steam after a week of keeping the image together.

Dan got the drinks while Alex and Ross tried to locate the MacArthur Warren posse. They tracked them down at the front of the bar, near the huge bi-folding doors that opened onto the outside paved area that looked onto the

Thames. Alex spotted Lisa's red hair straight away. Lisa had started at MacArthur Warren six months after her. She was sassy and scarily clever, but knew it. Some of the junior lawyers couldn't stand her but Alex didn't mind her. She'd never tried to boss her around.

'Hi, Alex. How's it going?' said Lisa.

'Hi, Lisa. Yeah, not too bad. We're putting in the hours but we're getting there. How are you? What's the gossip in the office?' she asked.

'It's a bit quiet, to be honest. Truman was giving us all grief to get out there and bring in more work. He was singing your praises for pulling in the cosmetic surgery deal,' Lisa replied. 'And old Maggie Kemp is going round with a face like a bag of spanners. When she's not working on a deal she's a nightmare. She walked in on me reading a gossip magazine and gave me hell. More or less implied I'd single-handedly set back the women's movement by twenty years.'

Alex laughed. 'Yeah, she's clearly got too much time on her hands at the moment. She sat in on my appraisal for some reason.'

'Really? That's a bit odd. She wasn't at mine,' said Lisa.

Dan appeared with the drinks. He'd bought one for Lisa too.

'Thanks, Dan. You read my mind. I was just ready for another one,' said Lisa.

'My pleasure,' he said, passing around bottled beer to the men and glasses of Pinot Grigio to Alex and Lisa.

'So how's the deal, Dan? Alex working you hard?' Lisa asked.

Just then Alex spied Emma and Bex weaving their way through the crowd. She excused herself from Dan and Lisa and went to meet them.

'Hi, guys! Didn't know you were coming down tonight,' she said, pleased to see them.

'Where else would we be on a Friday night?' said Emma, trying to hug Alex without spilling either of their drinks.

'Did you sort out your problem with Felicia Monroe?' Bex asked, too loudly for Alex's liking.

'Shh! That's confidential.'

'Oops, sorry,' said Bex, putting her hand over her mouth.

'No, we didn't really,' Alex said. 'Dan is going to meet her next week.'

'Which one is he again?' asked Bex, looking over at the crowd of lawyers by the window.

'The tall one with the dark hair with his sleeves rolled up. He's waving his arms around at the moment,' said Alex.

Dan was still talking to Lisa and had been joined by a group of guys from the post room. They were having a heated discussion about whether American football was more physically demanding than rugby. The girls looked over at Dan. His head was thrust back and he was laughing, revealing his perfect teeth. Lisa was laughing with him.

'God, he's gorgeous, isn't he?' said Bex reverentially. 'I didn't get a good look at him at the Christmas do. No wonder you've got a crush on him. Is he single?'

'Apparently so,' said Alex.

Emma looked at her quizzically.

'Yeah, he split from his girlfriend recently,' Alex said.

'She must be blind,' said Bex. 'I suddenly feel the need to mingle.'

Alex and Emma watched as Bex went over to the group and inserted herself between Lisa and Dan, much to Lisa's annoyance. She immediately began her well-practised flirting routine.

'What is she like? How long before all those men are eating out of her hand?' said Emma.

'Yeah, and how long before Lisa wants to kill her?' said Alex, still staring over at Bex and Dan.

'It bothers you, doesn't it?' Emma said.

'What do you mean?'

'Don't get defensive, Alex. You can't fool me — I've known you too long. You've got it bad, haven't you?' It was a statement rather than a question.

'Oh Emma, what am I going to do? You're so right. I just fancy him like mad and I can't help it. Every time he looks at me through those long eyelashes I just want to kiss him. The pheromones just ooze out of him. Then I have to keep reminding myself I'm getting married to Elliott. And I do love him. Really I do.'

'The problem with you and Elliott is you've been together too long. You're so past the lovey dovey stage. You should have got married years ago and then you'd be in a different phase.'

'I know what you mean. I feel like one of those planes that has to keep circling over Heathrow. I should have landed by now. I've missed my slot.'

Emma laughed. 'So what's Dan then? Your emergency parachute?'

'I wish,' she sighed.

'You know what it is — it's last chance saloon. You know you'll officially be off the market soon, so this is your last look round to make sure there isn't a better offer out there. It's perfectly natural. I'm sure everyone does it.'

'I hope you're right.'

At nine o'clock the next morning Alex, Dan and Ross met at Beau Street to spend the weekend finalising the first draft of the report that Alex would be presenting to Tom Duffy on Monday morning. There was something surreal about working the weekend, thought Alex. Wearing casual, though not too casual, clothes was part of it, but also the different pace of the rest of life. The bus journey to the clinic had been slower somehow, even though there were fewer cars on the road. The queue at the coffee shop had a completely different make-up. Instead of suited and booted executives, it comprised couples holding hands and giggly girls on shopping trips. The pounding headache didn't help either. Although Saturday was a working day for the team, it hadn't stopped any of them putting in the usual Friday night at Bar Q.

Dan got up from the conference table to replace a file and Alex watched as he moved round the room. He was wearing jeans and a polo shirt that skimmed his chest. She thought about her conversation with Emma the previous evening and decided that once the deal was finished she would keep away from Dan for a while.

Her thoughts were interrupted by a knock at the door. Stella Webb, the doctor who'd been at the all-party meeting, poked her head around the door.

'Please excuse me. I just wanted to check on Ross after yesterday,' she said.

'I'm absolutely fine,' stammered Ross, going bright red.

'That's great. You gave us all a bit of a shock there.' She looked at Alex. 'I expect you heard about Ross's dramatic collapse in my office. My patient was most concerned about him.'

Alex looked at Dan. He clearly had no idea what she was talking about either.

Ross spoke first. 'Well, everything's fine now. I'm so sorry if I upset anyone.'

'Not at all. Now you take care and I suggest you stick to the law. I'm not sure medicine is for you.' She smiled at Alex and Dan and closed the door gently behind her.

'What was all that about?' Dan asked Ross.

'It's a bit embarrassing really,' he replied.

'Come on, spill the beans,' said Alex.

Ross took a deep breath. 'Well, I went for my meeting with Dr Webb to go through the questions on the medical negligence insurance, like we discussed.'

'Yes. And?' said Alex.

'Well, when I got there her assistant made a mistake and showed me into her office just before Dr Webb came in with a patient. An enormous German woman. Very jolly. Massive boobs. Anyway, it was all a bit awkward but this German lady told me to stay. I think she thought I was a medical student and she kept banging on about her son training to be a doctor. She was really insistent. Dr Webb said it was okay and I didn't know what to do. She was only having a non-invasive procedure, she said.'

'Oh no. I think I know what's coming,' said Alex.

'Well, it was some sort of filler in her face and Botox, I think. It's all a bit of a blur after that.'

'No! You didn't faint.'

'Yup. Spark out. I came round to the sight of the German woman's cleavage. She was kneeling over me. I nearly passed out again when I saw her. I was petrified she was going to try CPR on me.'

Dan and Alex couldn't suppress their laughter any more.

'More likely to try the Heimlich manoeuvre,' said Dan.

'Dr Webb was trying to get to my arm to check my pulse or something but I think she fell over the German woman who was on all fours over me and then Tom Duffy came in and found all three of us on the floor. God knows what he must think.'

Alex and Dan were in hysterics at the thought of what Tom must have walked in on.

'You must have looked like some bizarre game of Twister,' said Alex, trying to compose herself.

'I know. It was mortifying,' said Ross.

'What did Tom Duffy say?' Dan asked.

'Something about coming back when the orgy was over, I think.'

For the rest of the weekend the three of them

spent their waking hours at Beau Street, stopping only at lunchtime to pop out to the local sandwich bars as the canteen was closed. They were a good team and worked well together with the right amount of banter and chat to make the experience bearable. By Sunday evening they were in good shape. The first draft of the report was finished and Alex had read it enough times to be confident that she could deal with any questions Tom might throw at her in the morning. They all knew that there would still be many revisions to the document and probably several more drafts before it was ready to be presented to the buyers. Alex just hoped that they wouldn't need to add a section to deal with the Felicia Monroe complaint. That would depend on the outcome of Dan's meeting with her on Tuesday.

'Thanks, guys, for all your hard work this weekend. Let's call it a day now and I'll see you back at the office tomorrow after my meeting with Tom,' said Alex after emailing the document to Tom Duffy.

'Not a problem, Alex. You guys have a great evening,' said Dan, leaving first.

'Oh and Alex, I'm so sorry about the incident in Dr Webb's office. I hope Tom doesn't mention it tomorrow,' said Ross.

'Hey, don't worry about it, Ross. You get back to that girlfriend of yours or she'll be forgetting who you are.'

Alex packed up her briefcase. She wasn't looking forward to going home. She hadn't spoken to Elliott since Tuesday and didn't think she had the energy to be mad at him any more. It wasn't easy always being the bad guy. She felt like a nagging wife and she wasn't even married yet.

CHAPTER 9

It was the evening of Alex's night out with Elliott. It was also the evening of Dan's rendezvous with Felicia. As Alex was getting ready she sent Dan a text asking him to text her back after the meeting. She'd told him she was out and wouldn't be able to take a call. If Elliott could make a space in his schedule for her then she should do the same for him, she'd decided.

She looked in the mirror and held up two necklaces against her pale skin. Dangly pearls or silver ethnic pendent? She chose the silver one. It was less safe and more Elliott, she thought. She massaged some of her ridiculously expensive wrinkle-reducing moisturiser onto her cheeks before applying her make-up and straightening her already straight hair.

Elliott was watching TV, a beer in his hand. Wearing his best jeans and a clean Nirvana t- shirt, he'd made an effort. He looked up as she entered the lounge.

'You look great,' he said. 'Shall we get going?'

They walked to the restaurant hand in hand. Elliott

was telling her all about the band's mini tour of the university freshers' weeks. The band had done the same tour for seven years now but each year he was convinced it would be their big break.

'Well, things are looking good for me at the moment too,' said Alex. 'This cosmetic surgery deal is in good shape. I presented the first draft of our report to the finance director yesterday and unless anything scary comes out of the woodwork in the next couple of weeks then I think the deal should happen. That will mean my bonus is safe, which is great news for us. We'll need every penny when we get back from our honeymoon. I know Mum and Dad are paying for most of the wedding but all the extras are really adding up,' Alex said.

'That's great, but didn't your dad say he wanted to pay for everything?' Elliott said.

'I know he did, but I don't want to take advantage. I've gone totally over the top with the flowers and I don't want him to get stung for that. And I don't think he should pay for the honeymoon. How's that going, by the way? Look, I know you want it to be a secret but are we on budget?'

Elliott looked uncomfortable. 'Look, I've done loads of research and I've been on the internet for ages,' he said. 'I've got the perfect place. Honestly, you're going to love it. Pretty sure it will be on budget.'

'Haven't you booked it?' she asked.

'Kind of. The accommodation is all sorted. I just need to fix the flights.'

Well, that's some progress, she thought.

They arrived at the restaurant. It was a fairly typical Italian from the outside with its red-checked curtains and Italian flags, but the food was something else. The proprietor, Elio, was from Naples. His brother Mario was the chef and they only employed fellow Italians. Alex didn't have the heart to explain equal opportunities law to them. Elliott and Alex were regulars.

'Signor Elliott and the beautiful signorina! Benvenuto!' Elio greeted them as long-lost family, planting a kiss on each of Alex's cheeks and pumping Elliott's arm up and down.

They were seated at a dimly lit corner table. Alex faced the wall, every inch of which was adorned with photographs of a younger Elio celebrating with long gone diners, and paraphernalia from Italian football teams. They ordered wine and Alex relaxed into her chair.

'To us,' she toasted, determined to have a lovely evening and forget about Dan and work.

When they'd ordered the food Alex delved into her handbag and pulled out the small notebook where she'd been keeping all her wedding notes.

'Okay, mister. You can't get away now.' She smiled. 'Let's talk weddings.'

Elliott looked into his glass and then slowly raised his eyes to her. 'Look, babe, before we do that there's something I need to say. Been trying to do it for a few days actually, but can't ever seem to find the right time.'

'Oh, Elliott. I thought you said the honeymoon was pretty much sorted?' she said.

'It's not that.' He looked down again.

'Elliott, what is it? You're starting to scare me.'

He took a large slug of wine and then, stumbling over his words, he said, 'We need to get checked out at an STD clinic before the wedding.' He stared at her almost defiantly.

'Okay. But why now? We've been together for years …'

'Do I really need to spell it out, Alex?' he pleaded.

The truth washed over her with a dreadful coldness. She couldn't say anything. She looked through him as the implications of what he'd said sank in.

'I got an email to the band website. A girl in York. Look, she wasn't specific about anything; she just said she was contacting all previous partners. I'm booked in at the clinic next week but I don't have any symptoms. I'm really sorry, Alex.' He couldn't stop talking now.

For a moment she was numb.

'It was only the once. Honest. It doesn't affect us,' said Elliott.

As he said this the anger, resentment and disappointment of the past months welled up inside her and Alex felt herself going red with fury.

'You total bastard! You are unbelievable. You sit there as if you're at confession and I'm going to absolve you. As if you seriously think I'll say it's okay and go back to my garlic bread. But it's not okay; for so many reasons. Elliott, we're getting married. The fact that you were so totally selfish to have unprotected sex with some tart is bad enough, but that you can just drop it on me and expect to carry on and get married at a wedding that I've organised, that you've shown no

interest in and that me and my family have paid for…
You're unreal!' She shook her head in disbelief.

'Look, babe, I know you're angry. I'm sorry. I really
am.'

'No, Elliott, you're not. You'll do it again. Another
groupie, another gig. I'm not stupid.'

'Alex, I won't, I swear,' he pleaded.

'How do I know that? You just don't get it. It's not
just the whole shagging the groupie thing. It's
everything. What do you do for me? Ever? It's just you
and the bloody band; that's all you care about. You
don't care about me or what I do. When do you ever
support me? You didn't even come to my work
Christmas party 'cause it was Barney's birthday. And
the wedding! Do you even know where we're getting
married?'

'You've changed, Alex. That's all I know,' he said.

'Don't throw that one at me. Yeah, you know what?
I have changed. It's called growing up, Elliott. You
should try it sometime.'

'It's since you started that job,' he said.

'You know what? I love my job. You just don't get
that either. It may not be making music or writing
lyrics but it's real. I work with great people, using my
brain and out in the real world. You don't have a
monopoly on loving your work, you know.'

'You've sold out. You're not the girl who trekked
through the jungles in Thailand,' he said.

'That's where you're wrong. I'm exactly the same
girl, but one who's faced up to reality. I have just as
much fun with the guys from work as I did back then.

It's just different. Anyway, why is this all about me? You're the one who's played away.'

Elio appeared with their starters, oblivious to their conversation.

'The gamberoni for Signorina and calamari for Signor Elliott,' he said with a flourish. 'Enjoy your starters.'

There was silence for a moment.

Alex felt suddenly calm. 'Elliott, I can't do this now. I'm going.'

'Alex, please. We need to talk,' he said.

'I know we do. But not now. I'm too angry, Elliott.' She scraped back her chair and picked up her bag.

He called after her as she left. 'Alex, don't go.'

She looked back at him. She was crying now. She needed him to say the right thing now, to hold her and convince her everything would be alright.

'I haven't got any cash. Can I borrow some?' he asked sheepishly.

'You are fucking unbelievable!' she said, throwing some notes onto the table.

Outside the restaurant she stood on the pavement, unsure what to do. She watched other couples walking past, enjoying the balmy summer evening, and felt bereft and liberated at the same time. She was shaking as she searched for her mobile in her bag. She decided to call Emma. She needed to be with someone.

She noticed the two missed calls and the three texts immediately. They were all from Dan. Why had he called, she wondered, when she'd asked him not to? Instinctively she called him, forgetting that she was still crying.

He picked up immediately. 'Alex. I'm so sorry for calling you. I just thought you should know what happened with Felicia. It's not good, I'm afraid,' he said.

'That's okay,' she said, sniffing.

'Are you okay? You sound a bit odd.'

'Yeah, I'm fine,' she lied. 'Go on, fire away. What did she have to say?'

'It's quite complex, but Alex, I believe her. I'm sure she had surgery at Beau Street and they're covering it up,' he said. 'But look, I can tell you about it tomorrow. You go back to your meal. Sorry for disturbing you; I was just so shocked when she left I had to call you.'

'Honestly, Dan, it's fine. Look, if you give me ten minutes I can join you if you want. My dinner got cancelled at the last minute.' She thought she might as well find out now. She didn't want to go home and at least she could drown her sorrows with Dan.

Dan gave her the address of the wine bar where he and Felicia had met and Alex hailed a cab. On the way she tried to fix her make-up. She fished out her small handbag mirror and almost laughed at her own reflection. She looked like Alice Cooper on a bad day. Ten minutes and lashings of concealer later she arrived at the scene of Dan's assignation with Felicia.

The wine bar was glamorous and contemporary, with a black glass bar and funky paper chandeliers. She found Dan at a table by the window, sitting on an uncomfortable looking chrome stool and drinking champagne. As she saw him she wondered why she'd come. Was it work or his company? If it was the latter it was one hell of a rebound.

'Hi, Alex,' he said, getting up. 'Are you sure you're okay to be here? I didn't mean to interrupt anything.'

'It's fine. Elliott had a band crisis and had to leave early. Come on then, tell me what happened.'

'Do you want some of this?' He pointed at the champagne bucket on the table. 'Felicia ordered it.'

'Why not,' she said. She'd barely had a chance to sip at her wine before she'd left the restaurant. Alex almost started to cry again when she saw the label on the champagne bottle. It was the same brand she'd selected for the wedding. She bit her lip and blinked ferociously.

'Okay. Let's start at the beginning,' he said. 'Felicia says she had the boob job in February. She's had a number of procedures with Lloyd Cassidy in the past. A nose job, some Botox and some vein removal thing.'

'And yet he claims he's never heard of her!' interrupted Alex.

'I know. But this is why. She was referred to him by her agent, who didn't come tonight by the way. I'll fill you in on that bit of the saga later. Cassidy operates some sort of secret surgery for famous people who want to keep the fact they've had work done confidential. It's just him, Audrey and some theatre staff who are in on it. They're all sworn to secrecy and get backhanders to buy their silence.'

'But what about their patient records? Surely other staff would have access to them. And anyway, wouldn't they get seen at the clinic?'

'That's the clever part. Cassidy only sees them out of hours when the clinic is officially closed and he gives them all pseudonyms so none of their names will feature in the client lists. Felicia doesn't think he keeps proper patient records for them.'

'Oh God. It's a legal minefield,' said Alex.

'And a reputational one. If the newspapers found out it would be a disaster for Beau Street. Especially as it seems Felicia really has a claim for negligence. My God, Alex, she showed me the photos. She's a mess. I felt really sorry for her.'

'What's the problem exactly?' Alex asked.

'You really want to know?' he asked.

She nodded.

'Well, for a start her boobs are totally lopsided. One is pointing one way and one another, if you know what I mean. And she has this horrendous hole, really, like an open wound where the scar has split or not healed properly. She's been really ill with infection. The NHS medical notes she showed me were damning. She's desperate to get it sorted but the NHS will only sort out the medical issues not the aesthetic problems. She's not rich by any means and her career is in freefall because she can't work at the moment.'

'The poor woman. What's she going to do next?' Alex asked.

'She was going to go to the papers, and her agent was right behind her, but apparently in the last few days the agent has changed her position. Felicia thinks Cassidy has leant on the agency.'

'Probably because we've alerted him,' said Alex.

'Exactly. The agency is now saying that if she goes to the papers she'll be blackballed and will never work again. The agency has referred loads of other clients to

Cassidy. I guess they don't want any of their other clients exposed and I'd have a wild guess that Cassidy has threatened to do just that.'

'Gosh. So for the moment at least we don't think she's going to go public?'

'No. But Alex, what should we do? We can't keep this quiet. If the buyers find out about Cassidy's dodgy practice — and, worse still, find out we knew and didn't tell them — they'll go ballistic.'

'Yeah and worse still, we'd be negligent and in breach of all sorts of professional rules of conduct,' said Alex.

'But if we do tell them? Will the deal happen?' he asked.

'I don't know. I wonder if Tom Duffy knows about this. It's probably best if Cassidy is just a maverick operating on his own. If the whole clinic is implicated then it will be a nightmare.'

'Oh and the other thing,' Dan continued, 'is that it seems Cassidy was charging celebs well over the odds, so he was probably making quite a lot of money. What we don't know is whether he was putting it through the Beau Street books or keeping it for himself.'

'I'll need to speak to one of the accountants, I suppose,' said Alex. 'What a mess.'

They sat in silence sipping the champagne. Alex was reeling from the effect of two glasses of champagne on an empty stomach and the shock of her conversation with Elliott. It had been a surreal evening.

'Look, I think I should go,' she said, standing up. 'I'll see you at work tomorrow. Don't mention this to anyone; not even Ross. We need to think carefully about how we play it.'

'Are you sure you're okay?' he asked as she swayed towards him. She steadied herself and then slowly got back on the stool. She might as well tell him.

'No, not really.' She took another sip of champagne. 'I just had a huge row with my fiancé. At the rate we're going at the moment we'll be lucky to make it to the altar.'

'Oh Alex, I'm sorry,' he said, filling up her glass. 'I've been there too, if it's any consolation. Melissa and I had talked about getting engaged but we just couldn't make it stick. We didn't spend enough time together, I guess. But you have to want to.'

'Exactly,' she said, staring at him. 'Yes, exactly. All Elliott wants to do is spend time with his band mates. I practically have to schedule an appointment to see him.'

Dan moved closer to her and put his mouth close to her ear. 'He must be mad. If you were my girlfriend I'd want to spend every minute with you.'

She stared back at him. He was so close to her. She could smell the scent of his aftershave. She noticed a single blonde eyelash amongst his thick dark lashes.
He reached his hand to draw her face even closer to his. Instinctively she closed her eyes, and then she felt his lips on hers.

They sat on their precarious barstools kissing like teenagers until eventually they pulled apart.

'God, you are so gorgeous, Alex Fisher. You're a dangerous lady.'

'Me? You're the dangerous one, Mr Furtado,' she smiled. 'What would Maggie Kemp say?'

'I don't give a damn about her. It's you I'm interested in. You do know how much I want to take you home right now, don't you?'

She nodded, embarrassed. 'Me too,' she said in a small voice.

'God, I shouldn't have kissed you again. I'm sorry,' he said.

'Please, I wanted it too.' Alex moved to him and kissed him again, more slowly this time.

'We shouldn't take this any further,' he said.

'I know,' said Alex. Just because Elliott had played away didn't mean she could. 'But…' She didn't finish.

'Let's go,' said Dan, jumping down from the barstool.

The next thing she knew was she was in a cab on the way to Dan's flat. They held each other's hand in silence. Her mind raced. She felt such a physical yearning to be held by him, to be loved by him. She glanced at him. He looked grim, determined. He caught her gaze and within seconds their hands were all over each other and he kept telling her how beautiful she was.

He held her face and looked at her intently. 'Alex, are you sure about this? I can't tell you how much I want you but I don't want to make your life difficult. If you're going to regret this in the morning, tell me now.'

She stared back at him while he scanned her face frantically for a response. She was overwhelmed by desire, confusion, guilt and excitement. It wouldn't matter, she thought. Elliott would never know.

'Oh God, this is so hard.' She dropped his hand.

He looked gutted.

'I can't. I can't do this to Elliott, or myself. The problem is it wouldn't just be a one night stand, would it? It would be more than that. Please understand, Dan. I'm sorry.'

She turned to the window so he couldn't see the tears come to her eyes. Dan took her hand again, more gently this time, and turned her face back to his. 'Alex, it's okay. I knew this would happen, but for a second back there I thought maybe we could, you know…' He left the sentence hanging and she nodded.

'Alex, you need to know that I find you impossibly attractive. I know you're getting married and I'm sorry I got carried away. But you're right; it wouldn't be a one night stand. It would be more than that.' He paused. 'Look, I really think we should try not to work together for a while.'

She smiled back at him. 'You're right.'

'You're not good for my concentration levels, you know,' he said.

CHAPTER 10

Alex woke to blinding sunlight flooding through the large gap in the curtains. Memories of last night immediately filled her head and she groaned and turned her back to the window. Thankfully there had been no sign of Elliott when she got in. She looked at the digital alarm. If she was going to put in an appearance at the office she would have to move now. She dragged herself out of bed and went to the bathroom. As she passed the mirror on the landing she saw the damage inflicted on her face by the events of the night before. She looked dreadful. She didn't think she could face anyone today. She decided to give the office a miss.

She stayed in bed with her laptop and mug of tea, trying to work but mostly replaying the events of the night before. She was feeling panicked now about the wedding. How could she get married when Elliott had shagged a groupie and she was lusting after a colleague at work? It wasn't exactly the dream start to married life. There was a more serious worry nagging at her too. She knew she felt more than lust for Dan and that was worse than any quickie with a groupie. Did that mean there was something seriously wrong with her and Elliott or had she just got too close to Dan?

She rubbed her eyes and closed her laptop as her mobile rang. She fumbled around under the duvet trying to locate it and answered it without looking at the caller name.

'Hi, it's me. Are you okay?' said Elliott.

'Fine. Um, what do you want?' she stammered.

'Look, about last night. You have to know I'm really sorry, babe. I totally get why you're so angry,' he said.

'Well, the reason is pretty obvious.'

'Look, I know I can be a prick and I haven't really been around much for you recently. The band's really starting to take off and I've been so focused on that I've had no time for you. For us. And I know I've been crap about the wedding, but to be honest, I thought you wanted to do it all. You seemed so organised and into it, I just left you to it, but if it's not too late then let me know what I can do to help. That's assuming it's still on.'

'Really? You really want to help?'

'Yeah, if I can. Alex, I do love you,' he said.

'And what about the groupie?'

'She wasn't a groupie actually. She hated our music,' he said.

'I don't really care about her musical tastes.'

'No, of course not. Look, I was totally out of it, if that's any consolation at all.'

'Not really. But Elliott, I do need to know one thing.'

'Anything, babe. Fire away.'

'Was she the only one?'

'I swear, yes. It's never happened before and it won't happen again, I promise,' he said.

Was she being easy on him because of her own guilt? she wondered. Should she still be screaming and shouting at him? She was so confused and desperate for some normality to return that she asked him to come home tonight so they could talk properly. They hung up and she sighed and threw the phone down onto the bed. It immediately began ringing again.

'Hi, Mum.'

'Hi, darling. Ooh, I'm so glad I got hold of you. You're like Lord Lucan. Well, obviously not, but you know what I mean. Look, I think I've found the perfect thing to bring you and Elliott from the church to the reception.'

'Mum, I booked the cars months ago. It's all sorted.'

'Mmm, I know, but I've found something so wonderful. Anyway, your dad and I could have your car as it's too late to cancel now. You'll never guess what it is.'

'No, Mum, I don't suppose I will. Go on, put me out of my misery.'

'Well, it's the most amazing open top carriage, like the one the Queen goes in at royal weddings, but it's pulled along by two unicorns,' she said.

'Mother, have you been at the vodka? You are aware that there's no such thing as a unicorn?' Alex lay back on the bed, staring at the ceiling. Could this day get any worse?

'They're not real, you silly thing! Just the most beautiful white ponies with gold horns made from fibre glass. Honestly, they're spectacular.'

'And I suppose you'll need footmen, dry ice and a couple of centaurs to greet us when we arrive?' said Alex.

'Well, I think that might be a bit over the top,' her mother said.

Alex opened her laptop and checked her emails while her mum continued.

'And they're relatively inexpensive too. The only problem would be if it rained.'

There was an email from Dan. Alex's face flushed at the sight of his name. He needed to talk to her about the Felicia Monroe problem. He didn't say anything about what had happened the previous night. She should really be at work.

'Though the long range forecast is looking very good,' her mother continued.

'Look, Mum, something's just come up. I have to go. Why you don't get a quote and check availability? I'm not saying I definitely want them.'

'Of course, darling. Lovely. I'll pop their brochure in the post for you.'

That might keep her quiet for a couple of days, thought Alex.

An hour later, wearing her wrap dress and heels, she was at her desk. Ross was working on revisions to their report and Alex knew she had to find out more about Lloyd Cassidy and his practice. She decided to call Rob Sweeney. He was in the same business and might have some inside info on him.

'Hi, Rob. It's Alex, Alex Fisher,' she said as he picked up.

'Alex! Great to hear from you. Did anything come of that lead I gave you?' he asked.

'Couldn't possibly say. Early days still,' she hedged.

'Well, don't forget me if it does.'

'How could I, Rob? Look, I was wondering if I could have a bit of a chat with you, off the record of course, about a doctor I've come across. He's in your line of work and a friend of mine is thinking of going to him but I just need to know he's okay?' she bluffed.

'Yeah, sure. Though you are talking to the best guy in town,' he said.

'Yeah, yeah, I know,' she laughed.

'Okay, who is it then?'

'A Lloyd Cassidy.'

'Ah. He's at Beau Street, you know. You sure this is nothing to do with that tip-off I gave you?' he asked.

'Just a coincidence, honestly.'

'Hmm. Well, he's a lot older than me and generally has a reasonable reputation. Loves himself a bit. He's South American. Qualified in Brazil, I believe. Quite a low profile but claims to do loads of work on celebrities, though I don't know any stars who've admitted to using him.'

'Would you recommend him?'

'I don't really know enough about him, to be honest. He popped up on the London scene about ten years ago.'

'Okay. Thanks anyway.'

'Oh and one other tip: if your friend is going to use

him, tell her to go through his assistant nurse. He's as thick as thieves with her. It drives Tom Duffy mad. No one else can deal with his patients at Beau Street. She's been with him since he got to the UK. If you ask me, they're having an affair. She goes to all the conferences with him.'

'Is that unusual then? To take your assistant?' she asked.

'Yeah, pretty much. Some people do occasionally but she's a permanent fixture. Wherever he goes, she goes.'

'Okay, thanks.'

'Not a problem. Anytime I can be of any assistance you know where I am.'

Well, that would explain why Audrey was prepared to lie for Lloyd, thought Alex. She was obviously in on whatever scam he was operating. There must be others too, though. What about theatre staff and anaesthetists? She needed to speak to Dan.

Alex picked up the office phone and called him.

'Hi, Dan. We need to decide what to do about Felicia's allegations. I've spoken to the guy who referred the deal to me in the first place and he seems pretty sure that Cassidy is having an affair with Audrey, the assistant. That would explain why she was less than helpful. There must be others involved. The two of them can't do boob jobs on their Jack Jones.'

'Of course not,' he said.

'The issue is, do we dig around more and find out exactly what's going on, or do we ignore what we've found and get Cassidy to sort Felicia's problem out?

Then she keeps quiet, no one is any the wiser and the deal isn't threatened.'

There was a short silence.

'You're not serious, Alex? That would be a cover-up.'

'I know. I'm not really sure why I suggested it.'

'To safeguard the deal and guarantee your partnership?' he said.

'No! Absolutely not.'

'Is that also why you can't contemplate a relationship with me? You don't want to upset the guys upstairs? Or is it really because you're getting married?' he said.

Alex couldn't believe what he was saying. 'Dan, no. You've got me all wrong. God, what do you think I am?' she whispered. Ross had walked in the room.

'I'm sorry. I shouldn't have said that. Let's stick to business.' He sighed, and then said in a calmer tone, 'For what it's worth, I think you should talk to the accountants and see if they've come across anything in their due diligence.'

'Okay. I'll talk to Rachel from Payne Stanley. I'll see if we can support Felicia's claim that his patients pay over the odds,' she said.

She hung up.

She was upset by what Dan had said. Did he really think she was so obsessed with her career that she would do something unethical? Or sacrifice her personal life? Why had he sounded a bit like Elliott back there?

It was after two when she met Emma at Bar Q. Alex was already impatiently sipping her mineral water as Emma burst in, her titian hair looking slightly wild.

'Sorry. I had that Olivia Meddoes on the phone again. That bitch is making my life hell. She's as high maintenance as they come. She wants to move hotels for the second time. This time the view is "too urban". She's the one who wants to be in central London, for crissakes! Sod it, I'm having a gin.' Emma gestured to the waitress for a gin and tonic. 'So, Bridezilla, how's things with you? Sorted the butterflies and the doves yet?'

'They're the least of my problems. Anyway, Mum has moved onto mythical creatures. She wants unicorns now.'

'Bloody hell. She's going to want the real Elvis next.'

'Believe me, she's probably got some clairvoyant working on it.'

The waitress arrived with Emma's gin and two menus, which they didn't need to look at; they always ordered exactly the same thing.

'Two chicken Caesar wraps, please,' said Emma.

'Oh and a glass of house white wine, please,' said Alex. She needed it today.

'So, how are things really? You look a bit stressed,' Emma said.

'Well, it's been an interesting twenty-four hours,' Alex replied.

She proceeded to fill Emma in on the argument with Elliott, the groupie, the passionate interlude with Dan and the work crisis.

'So apart from the fact your engagement is hanging by a thread, you had an almost fling in a cab and your deal is on the rocks, how are you doing?' said Emma when Alex had finished.

'Totally confused,' she replied.

'Look, this thing with Dan. Is it something I should be worrying about? I was planning to buy your wedding present on Saturday but I'm more than happy to spend the money on some cool wedges I've seen.'

Alex half smiled. 'If the wedding doesn't happen it will be because of Elliott not Dan, but the whole Dan thing's really not helping. I don't know, Emma. I felt like I was at the top of a rollercoaster with him and if I'd gone a few feet further that would have been it — I couldn't have gone back.'

'Yeah, but that doesn't mean he's the love of your life and worth risking your relationship with Elliott for,' said Emma.

'I know. But I'm also pretty sure that it wouldn't just be a fling. He and I have always connected. He said I was a dangerous lady.'

'Gosh. And what about Elliott? Can you forgive him?'

'I don't know. I feel like I'm almost as bad as him. I may not have slept with Dan but I so wanted to.'

'Yeah, but you stopped yourself. Unlike him.'

'I suppose so,' said Alex. 'Emma, can I ask you something?'

'Of course, as long as it isn't to do a solo at your wedding or ride a unicorn or something.'

'No, nothing like that. Both Elliott and Dan have implied I'm obsessed with my career. Do you think I am?'

'No, babe. No more than anyone else. It's obvious you're ambitious and you take it seriously but you're not obsessed.'

'Dan thinks I won't take things further with him because of the rule about no relationships at work.'

'Is he right?'

'Well, I'd hate to give Margaret Kemp the satisfaction. But it's so much more complex than that – the small matter of a resident fiancé being the main obstacle. Not to mention the thought of telling my mum that the wedding's off.'

'So are you and Elliott still together?'

'It's a mess but I think I want to forgive him. He sounded so sorry on the phone this morning and I really think he's going to make a big effort. He admitted he'd been neglecting me. I guess we've got to the seven-year itch phase.'

'So do I still need to organise your hen do?'

'I guess so.' Alex took a large sip of wine.

'And you're sure you want to have it in London?'

'Yeah. I can't expect everyone to pay for a weekend in Amsterdam or wherever and then pay to come to the wedding and buy me a big expensive gift. A day in a spa and a night on the tiles is what's called for.'

'Okay. I'm on the case as soon as Olivia Meddoes gives me a break. Which reminds me, I must call Bex. Olivia fired the make-up artist this morning.'

'How is Bex?' asked Alex.

'Oh, full of the usual body insecurities. She's on some crazy diet where she drinks shakes and eats bars of rabbit food. Will she ever get used to the fact she's a curvy girl and will never be stick thin? It's not like she has any trouble with men.'

'Mmm, I know.' Alex wondered if Emma knew her sister was about to blow her inheritance on more messing with her body.

'So come on then. When's it going to be?' said Emma, opening up her diary. 'We need a date if I'm going to organise this hen do.'

They compared diaries and agreed on a date in a few weeks' time. Alex hoped the deal would be all but done by then and she and Elliott would be back on track. She felt more positive about the wedding again, now that the hen do was in the diary.

'So do we invite your mum?' Emma asked.

Alex cringed. 'Do I have to?' she asked pleadingly.

'It's increasingly the form. My wedding etiquette book says so. Obviously you'd have to invite Elliott's mum too.'

'Leave that one with me. But you can definitely invite Bex, the uni crowd, Lisa from work.'

'Anyone else from work?' Emma asked.

'Nope, don't think so. I don't want anyone reporting back to Truman on my drunken behaviour.'

'And you're not obsessed about work?' Emma asked, raising an eyebrow.

'Hey!'

'Only kidding! Okay, who else?'

They sat in Bar Q for the rest of lunch finalising the guest list, the shortlist of spas to try and the watering-hole's location. Alex got Emma to agree not to hire a stripper but Emma refused to give any guarantees about what clothing and accessories Alex might have to wear. As she walked back to the office Alex felt a lot better. She wasn't sure if it was the effect of the wine or the fact that planning the hen do made her feel back in control of her destiny. Either way, it was better than the confusion of the previous evening.

CHAPTER **11**

It was Friday morning and Alex was on her way to Beau Street to see Rachel from Payne Stanley. She'd decided to take Dan's advice and speak to her. As she arrived in the reception area she had the usual exchange with the security guard about the weather.

'Exceptional temperatures this month compared to the five-year average,' he told her.

'You're quite the meteorologist,' she said.

He puffed out his chest. 'Well, I've been on a few courses. Got me NVQ, you know.'

'Really? How fascinating. You'll be on the local news next,' she smiled. 'Do you think you could possibly direct me to wherever the accountants from Payne Stanley are basing themselves?' she asked.

Armed with directions, Alex headed for the lifts. As she waited she was joined by Tom Duffy and, to her horror, the inimitable Lloyd Cassidy who, dapper as ever, was wearing one of those stripy shirts with the plain white collars that politicians favour and a pair of red braces. She inwardly cringed, wondering what to say, and then quickly decided now was not the time to be discussing her concerns about Felicia with Tom.

'Ah Alex,' said Tom. 'You know Lloyd, don't you? We were just reliving a momentous victory on the golf course,' he continued. 'Lloyd and I were in a four ball yesterday against a rival clinic and we stuffed them.'

'I was the Tiger Woods of the medical world,' said Cassidy, smiling at Alex.

Yeah, in more ways than one, she thought, recalling what Rob had said about Cassidy and his assistant, Audrey.

'Great,' said Alex. 'Good for you.'

'Anyway, how are you?' Tom asked. 'How's the report coming on? Have there been many changes since the first draft?'

'Oh, fine thanks. Not much to report.'

'I'm going to take you up on the recommendation in your report to hire an in-house lawyer, by the way,' said Tom. 'I've got my HR people starting the recruitment process. You were absolutely right, Alex, we do need some extra legal help. I ran it past Equinox and they agreed. I think they're going to get involved in the interviewing.'

'That's good to hear, Tom.'

The lift arrived and they got in.

'We're just waiting to start negotiating the sale and purchase agreement. Have you had anything through from the US lawyers yet?' asked Alex.

'Yes, I got a list of all the people working on the deal this morning.' Tom rummaged in his briefcase for a moment and then produced a document. 'Look, there's the chap at the US lawyers acting for Equinox. Give him a call and chivvy him along. If we're going to stick to that Meredith's timetable we need to get negotiations underway.' Tom handed the list to Alex.

'Thanks, Tom.'

The lift doors opened and the three stepped out.

'If you'll excuse me,' said Tom, 'I have a meeting shortly.'

He headed for his office and Alex turned to Lloyd. 'Good to see you again, Dr Cassidy,' she said.

'A pleasure to see you too,' said Lloyd, looking directly at her. 'Did you sort out that little problem?' His smile wasn't quite as friendly as before.

'Er, yes. Just a misunderstanding,' she said.

'I knew it would be,' said Lloyd, and sauntered off towards his office.

Alex found her way to the Payne Stanley team's room. She saw the temporary sign on the door and knocked politely. The accountants seemed to have got themselves a better working space at Beau Street than the lawyers. They weren't in the basement for a start.

'Come in,' a female voice called.

Alex opened the door and found a familiar scene to the room she'd just left. Piles of lever-arch files, laptops and coffee cups were scattered across a large desk. A petite brunette in a navy suit jumped up to greet her.

'Hi, I'm Rachel,' she said.

'Hi, Rachel. Good to meet you. I'm Alex. Do have time for a quick chat?'

'Sure. I thought our paths would cross at some

point. How's your stuff going?' asked Rachel.

'Not bad, thanks,' said Alex. 'Our first draft report is with the Beau Street guys. We're just working through all our revisions and latest findings. I'm expecting the first draft of the sale and purchase agreement from the US lawyers any day now. It's an interesting business. How about you?'

'Oh, we're getting there, I think. It's certainly interesting reading about all the procedures they do,' Rachel replied.

'Well, we could recite the menu of their procedures in our sleep. My trainee, Ross, has certainly had his eyes opened,' said Alex, smiling.

'Isn't he the one who passed out the other day?'

'Oh no, have you heard about that too? Yeah, he has a needle phobia,' said Alex.

'Sounded hilarious. Tom Duffy said he walked in on a woman with an arse the size of Belgium on top of Ross and one of his doctors on top of her. He said he almost jumped on himself. I think he used to be a rugby player or something. Anyway, what is it we can do for you?'

'Well, it's a tricky one, and obviously confidential,' Alex began. She told Rachel about Felicia Monroe and Lloyd Cassidy and their conflicting accounts, and the lack of any records to back up Felicia's version of events.

'The other thing Felicia told my colleague was that all the celebs paid inflated rates for their procedures, and I was wondering if you'd come across any evidence of that.'

Rachel didn't seem surprised by what Alex was saying and reached for a black file in her laptop bag.

'Here, take a look at this,' she said. 'At the moment this is all we have, but look, here are the names of some celebrities.'

Rachel laid out a photocopied document on the table in front of them and pointed to a list of names. It was a handwritten ledger with various columns and headings. 'Look, these are the real names and these are the pseudonyms Cassidy used. This column shows what procedures they had. And these final columns here show how much cash they paid him for it.'

'So you guys knew about this,' said Alex, staring at the document in front of her. She couldn't see Felicia's name but she did see one very familiar name.

'Well, we came across it by accident.'

'And these fees? How do they compare to what they charge your average client?' Alex asked.

'There's a significant mark up on all of them,' said Rachel.

'So Felicia is right. Do you have proof anywhere that she was a client?'

'Sorry, this is all we have. But I'm sure there are loads more in the ledger I copied from, and probably other ledgers too. Believe me, it was hard enough getting this.'

'Wow,' said Alex, the implications sinking in. 'So it's highly likely that Felicia is telling the truth, which means if she does go public a lot of other celebrities will be worried their little secret might come out.'

'Yeah, and Cassidy will be livid and Beau Street's

reputation will be in tatters. Oh and they'll lose a vital income stream,' added Rachel.

'What do we do?' Alex asked to no one in particular.

'We have to do what we think is right, but I'm not a hundred per cent sure there's anything fishy yet, although it doesn't look good. It could just be a case of poor record keeping and willing celebrities happy to pay a bit more for a degree of privacy,' Rachel said.

'Hmm, maybe. But if Felicia goes public it's not as simple as that, even if it is above board. It'll be all over the tabloids,' said Alex.

'Yeah well, I suggest you need to come up with a way to keep her quiet while the rest of us dig into Dr Cassidy's activities a bit more,' Rachel said, carefully folding up the document and putting it back in her bag.

'Well, she's keeping her mouth shut at the moment but I'm going to have to discuss it with Tom Duffy.' Alex stood up.

'Good luck with that. And Alex, keep me posted,' said Rachel.

'I will do, and thanks for your help, Rachel.'

They shook hands awkwardly.

'Not a problem. See you around,' said Rachel.

Alex walked slowly back to their room in the basement, considering her options. As Rachel had said, there was still no evidence of any wrongdoing. They couldn't prove Cassidy was pocketing the cash or that the celebs weren't getting proper treatment. However, if Tom didn't know about it then that was a different matter. It would mean the clinic was being used out of hours without senior managers' knowledge and possibly without proper insurance. But the main issue was still publicity. If Felicia decided to speak out then the clinic's reputation would be damaged and all the other celebrities would be furious if she somehow blew their cover. Equinox would run a mile.

Back in their dingy conference room, she rewrote her report. She wasn't sure if she was doing the right thing but she put in everything Felicia had told them. She would email it to Tom and then deal with the fallout.

'Fancy a coffee in the canteen?' she asked Ross, who was still pouring over employee records.

He looked up and smiled. 'Yes, please. I need to get out of this room.'

'It's a bit grim down here without any natural light, isn't it?' said Alex.

'Yeah. My girlfriend says it's like a veal crate. I look paler every day.'

Alex laughed. 'Yeah, it's not all glamour in the beauty clinic.'

They sat in the corner in the canteen cradling their cappuccinos. Ross had insisted they keep away from the Beau Street staff. Apart from Albert and Audrey, who were having a tête à tête, there were no other staff in view. Ross seemed relieved by the lack of people; he was still mortified by his fainting incident. Alex smiled at Audrey as she sat down. Audrey gave her a nod in acknowledgement.

'So what's next on the deal? The report's pretty much done now,' he asked.

'Well, it's time to start negotiating the sale contract with Equinox's lawyers,' she said.

'Presumably that should be straightforward. We've not discovered any nasties about the business,' said Ross.

'Yeah,' said Alex. Assuming Felicia kept her mouth shut and there was an above board explanation for Lloyd's 'out of hours' activities, she thought.

'Are you going to Chris and Gemma's barbeque tomorrow?' Ross asked. Chris was a libel lawyer at the firm. He'd recently got engaged to Gemma Kirk, a TV actress and former client of his. He'd helped her win a high profile libel case against one of the tabloids and they'd become inseparable afterwards. Most of the young lawyers had been invited to a celebration barbecue at their house.

'Yeah, I was planning to.' Alex had been looking forward to Saturday night all week. She and Elliott had had several long conversations and he'd agreed to spend more time with her. He had even moved the band's set on Saturday night so he would be able to come along to the barbecue with her. He'd been incredibly attentive to her all week. He'd bought her flowers and even made her dinner last night, though he'd used every pan in the house in the process. She had to admit he was really trying.

'It should be a good one. They've got caterers and everything,' said Ross.

'For a barbeque?' Alex asked.

Just then her phone rang. It was her mum.

'Sorry, Ross. I'd better take this.' Alex walked briskly out of the canteen, talking as she went.

'Hi, Mum. Everything okay? I'm at work, you know,' she half whispered.

'Hi, darling. Yes, I'm fine. Just a couple of things. Invitations really need to go out this week — have they come yet?'

'Mum, it's still two months away.'

'They need to go out this week. Your dad says so.'

'Dad? Since when has dad been worrying about the wedding? Anyway, everyone got save the date cards months ago.'

'Well, you need to chase up the printers, darling. We do need to get them out pronto. Next thing, I've booked a barbershop quartet to sing during the meal. Don't worry, Alex – it's a little treat from me.'

'Mum! Elliott's sister is playing the flute. We'd agreed that.'

'But when will she get to eat? The poor thing. I just thought it would be nice to hire professionals.'

'Christ, Mum. She's studying music at one of the best colleges in the UK. She's not exactly a busker.' Alex knew Elliott detested a cappella groups.

'Oh and I've booked the unicorns. They were very reasonable. That way your dad and I can use your car,' her mum finished.

'Mum! You promised me you were just getting a quote. Whose wedding is this?' Alex barked into her phone.

'Now, now, darling. I'm just trying to save you some of the wedding stress. You know, I've read all about it — how many brides don't enjoy their big day because they have so much to worry about. That reminds me, I've booked you in for a nice massage.'

Alex was crouched on her haunches in the corridor,

her back to the wall, her hair in her hand, pleading with her mother as Dan walked past with Albert Cheung. He mouthed to her 'You okay?'

She nodded and looked down.

'Mum, promise me you won't book anything else without checking with me first. I've got to go now. I'm coming home next weekend. Don't do anything else. We'll do the invitations then,' she said through gritted teeth.

Alex walked back to the basement still fuming. She'd be glad when the whole wedding thing was over and her relationship with her mother could return to normal. She was the one who'd turned into Bridezilla, not Alex. She decided to ask Bex to go shopping at the weekend for bridesmaids' presents, her bridal underwear, her tiara and anything else she could think of before her mum could do it for her.

She slammed the door behind her as she entered the project room and sighed as she surveyed the now too familiar room. She decided to call the US lawyer and get that out of the way. She checked his details on the list Tom had given her and dialled the number in New York.

'Beckmann, Grossberg, Fitzpatrick and Hale, how may I direct your call?' said the receptionist.

How many names did a law firm need?

'Good morning. Please could I speak to Warren Wickens?' she asked. Great name too, she thought. She hoped he didn't have a speech impediment.

'This is Warren Wickens.'

'Good afternoon, this is Alex Fisher from

MacArthur Warren in London calling regarding Project Pout,' she said.

'Huh,' he grunted.

'I was given your name by my client, Tom Duffy of Beau Street. I was wondering when we could expect a first draft of the sale and purchase contract?'

'When I've had my client's instructions,' he said. It was like pulling teeth.

'Okay. And when might that be?' she said as though speaking to a small child.

'It'll be with you by next Monday,' he said.

'Thanks. And good afternoon to you too,' she replied.

'It's morning here,' he said and hung up.

Alex stared at her phone in amazement. This was going to be fun.

CHAPTER 12

It was Saturday morning and Alex was on the bus heading for the King's Road. She stared out of the window and made a mental note of what she needed to buy. Bridesmaids' presents would be easy. Bex would help her with those. Something shiny for Emma and something sparkly and pink for her twin nine-year-old cousins should do the trick. Then she needed to track down some underwear to avoid any VPL on the day and then go to a specialist wedding shop she knew for a tiara. She also needed to buy twenty disposable cameras for the tables and organza bags for the wedding favours, and phone the printers. How hard could it be?

She saw Bex straight away when she jumped off the bus.

'Hi, Alex. You okay?' Bex gave her a hug.

'Yeah. Though I've just spoken to the bloody printers and they've got some boring technical problem going on, which means the invitations won't be ready for another fortnight.'

'That's not a big deal, is it?' asked Bex.

'Not really, but it's something else for Mum to freak about.'

'So what's first then today? Let me be your personal shopper and steer you seamlessly through the retail wonders of West London,' said Bex.

'Knickers,' said Alex.

They spent the next hour in a department store where Alex tried on every pair of body-enhancing seam-free knickers and a selection of figure-enhancing basques and corsets. She negotiated a range of nail-defying clasps and fasteners and shimmied in and out of millions of tummy-flattening horrors. Nothing was quite right.

'None of the basques fit my boobs and my bum at the same time, and the knickers are about as sexy as my Gran's big pants and give me a muffin top,' she moaned.

'I think you need to try them with your dress. And anyway, no one's going to see them,' said Bex.

'But I will,' said Alex.

'Okay, let's park underwear. I'm losing the will to live. What else do you need to get?' Bex asked, yawning.

'My tiara. That should be easy. I know exactly where to go. Yeah, I'm done with pants for one day.'

The tiara hunt was more successful. Alex found a beautiful pearl and crystal one that was exactly what she'd wanted and would go beautifully with the pearl detail on her dress. As she modelled it she felt nervous. She really was getting married. It was only when she tried on her dress and now her tiara that it felt even vaguely real. The tiara was obscenely expensive but

Bex and the shop assistant oohed and aahed so much she just had to have it. She linked arms with Bex as they sashayed out of the shop with the beautiful beribboned bag bearing the prestigious logo of the boutique. This was more like it.

They made a pit stop for lunch at a cafe and Alex filled Bex in on things at home with Elliott.

'So he's really making an effort. The last few days have been more like when we first met. He's been focused on me, not the band, and I really think he's sorry about what happened.'

'Well, that's great, if you're sure.' Bex didn't sound convinced. 'It's just such a big thing, Alex. Marriage, I mean. Have you thought about postponing the wedding for a bit? Just so you're sure.'

'God, no way. The thought of organising the wedding all over again is a nightmare. No, we either do it as planned or not at all,' she said.

'Okay. Whatever you say,' Bex replied.

There was a short silence while neither of them dared say what they were really thinking.

'How's work?' asked Bex.

'Okay. The deal is in the balance at the moment.'

'That cosmetic surgery one?'

'Yeah. Have you had any more thoughts on that subject?' Alex asked as she tucked into her sandwich.

'Not really. I've been speaking to some guys at work about it. That reality show I mentioned looks like it might be happening — you know, the one where the celeb whose career is on the slide gets the makeover?'

'Yeah. You did mention it.'

'Well, the pilot was a big success so the team have been researching clinics and have got hold of all the price lists for me. Beau Street isn't the cheapest, you know,' said Bex.

'I'm sure it isn't, but I'm not sure you should be looking for the no-frills option when you're getting your boobs done. You want to be sure they're not skimping on the anaesthetic, you know.'

'Take your point.'

'It's not double-glazing you're buying. It's your body.'

'I know. Hey, Alex, do you think that Rob guy, that surgeon you and Emma know, would be interested in working on the show? The guys need a camera-friendly surgeon.'

'Well, he totally loves himself so he's worth a try. I'll call him if you like.'

After lunch they started the hunt for bridesmaids' presents. They traipsed from one shop to another and on the way ruled out picture frames, scented candles, earrings (the little bridesmaids didn't have pierced ears), keyrings and trinket boxes. Finally it was getting late and Bex had to get back to North London.

'It's okay. I'll keep looking on my own, although I think we've exhausted the meaningless crap section of every shop on the King's Road,' said Alex.

'Sorry, Alex, if you're sure. I did say I'd meet Em and the guys for an early supper before the film. Good luck!'

'Not a problem, Bex. I need to get going myself soon. Thanks for putting up with me.' Alex hugged her and watched her bright red T-shirt disappear into the crowd, heading for the tube.

She decided to go to a jewellery shop she knew that specialised in unusual silver pieces. She had to get back to get changed for the barbeque so this would be the last chance to find something today. An old-fashioned bell above the door rang as she entered the shop. It was small, with panelled walls and a bright turquoise carpet and a handful of glass-topped display cabinets. She circled the shop, leaning over each table, examining every item on show.

She'd edged her way around the shop to the cabinet closest to the door when she saw the perfect thing. It was a charm bracelet that came in different sizes and with a huge selection of cute charms, ranging from teddy bears to mini diamond rings. It would fit both the little bridesmaids and Emma, and she could select a couple of individual charms for each. It was perfect.

The shop assistant looked up from her desk as she sensed an imminent sale.

'Can I help you?'

'Yes, please. I'd like three of these bracelets. Two small ones for children, and one that would fit me. Oh and six charms as well, please.'

'Of course. I'll just check availability,' said the girl, tapping away on her computer with her manicured nails.

'I'm terribly sorry but we only have one child's bracelet left. I could order one for you?'

'Oh no. I was hoping to take them with me today. How long will it take to come?'

'About a fortnight,' replied the assistant.

'Okay,' said Alex. She then pointed out the charms she wanted. The assistant took the two bracelets and the six charms carefully from their boxes for Alex to approve and then replaced them and painstakingly wrapped each box in turquoise paper. After tying a perfect bow in white ribbon around each box she placed each one in a small bag and sealed it with a white sticker. It seemed to take for ever. Finally Alex handed over her credit card. She was wondering what to wear that evening when the assistant coughed politely.

'I'm sorry, madam, but your card has been declined. Perhaps you have another card I could try?' she said with a forced smile.

Alex felt her face go red. 'Well, that's not right. I've just been paid and the balance is cleared automatically. I'm sorry, it must be a mistake. Could you try again?' She started to panic. She'd left her debit card at home and she didn't have nearly enough cash. The assistant plugged the card back in the machine and Alex tapped in her PIN again.

'I'm sorry but it's been declined again,' the assistant said defiantly.

She might as well have added 'Told you so', thought Alex.

'Well, that's weird. I don't understand it. Can you hold these until Monday?' she asked.

'Of course, madam, but you'll have to collect them no later than midday. Do you still want me to order the second child's bracelet?' She took the bags from Alex and put them under the counter.

'Yes, please. Thanks. I'll see you on Monday. Sorry.'

Alex closed the door behind her. She was mortified and confused. As she put her purse back in her handbag a group of kids with beer cans in their hands and a scruffy dog barged past her and caught her off balance. She fell back onto the step of the shop awkwardly, ripping the bag with her tiara in as she went down, and heard the boys laughing as they carried on. Humiliated and embarrassed again, she started to cry. This wedding preparation stuff was supposed to be fun and so far it had been one big anticlimax. For a split second she wished her mum was there. She caught the patronising gaze of the shop assistant, who was starting to lock up, and immediately shook her hair and stood up. 'Pull yourself together, Alex Fisher,' she said out loud, and set off to catch the bus home.

Elliott had already left for his gig when she got in. She was meeting him at the barbeque. She poured herself a glass of wine and ran a bath. As she lay there, face mask on, up to her neck in bubbles, she made a note to self that tonight was make or break night. If she had a good time tonight with Elliott then it would be a sign. Of what, she wasn't entirely sure.

After the usual negotiation of various tube lines to get south of the river, Alex approached the house in Clapham. They'd clearly gone to some trouble. The tiny front garden was lit with what looked like flaming torches but on closer inspection were pieces of cloth up-lit by floor-lights and blown by a fan. She arrived at the same time as some of the trainees from the office.

She recognised two girls, Naz and Jo, who'd worked with her earlier in the year.

'Hi, Alex. Is this it?' asked Naz.

'Yeah, I guess so. Unless there's a fire eaters' convention going on here or something,' she replied.

As they spoke the door opened and Chris greeted them, beaming from ear to ear and brandishing a bottle of beer.

'Come in, ladies. Welcome,' he said, kissing Alex on the cheek. 'Come on through. Everyone's in the back.'

He led them through the house, which Alex noted was designer neutral perfect, to some French doors in the kitchen that opened onto the small back garden. Though petite, the garden had also received the designer treatment. Chinese lanterns were hung from the branches of the trees, a huge gas barbecue was set up on a raised deck area, already attracting a crowd of men, and chrome storm lanterns were positioned around a patio that was clearly intended as a makeshift dance floor.

'Wow, Chris. This place is amazing,' said Alex.

'Yeah, it's a proper grown-up house,' laughed Naz to Jo. 'Nothing like our scummy student house.'

'It's all down to this lady,' he said as Gemma approached them. Her face, familiar from the TV, was expertly made up and she was wearing a diaphanous baby-pink shift.

Chris put his arm around Gemma proprietarily and introduced her to them.

'Hi. So glad you could come. It's lovely to meet Chris's colleagues. What do you do, Alex?' she asked.

'I'm on the corporate team. You know, doing deals, that kind of thing. You have a lovely house, Gemma,' said Alex.

'Thanks. It was Chris's place but I've given it a bit of a makeover. It was a bit of a bachelor pad, to be honest – lots of matt black furniture, an oven that had never been used, two years' worth of Sunday papers. You get the picture.'

Chris had disappeared to greet other guests and Jo and Naz had gone off in search of drinks. Alex was alone with the TV star.

'Congratulations on your engagement,' she said.

'Oh thanks. We're so excited. We've already planned most of the wedding. Ooh, you're engaged too.' Gemma had instinctively looked at her own dazzling solitaire and then glanced at Alex's left hand.

'Yes I am. The wedding's in a couple of months now.'

'Wow. You must be so excited now. Where's your other half?' Gemma asked, looking around Alex as though her fiancé was somehow permanently attached to her.

'He's coming along in a bit. He plays in a band and they have a gig tonight.'

'Well, you must introduce him when he gets here,' said Gemma. 'Isn't it great when you meet The One? I just knew with Chris. Almost from day one. I just can't wait to get married,' she said. 'Please excuse me, Alex. I can see some people from work who look a bit lost. Lovely to meet you.' Gemma squeezed her arm and planted a kiss on Alex's cheek before scuttling off.

Alex needed a drink. She headed back to the kitchen to forage for something as one of the caterers passed by with a tray of wine. She grabbed a glass at the same time as Ross.

'Hi. Not exactly your average barbeque, is it?' she said to him.

'No, it's unreal. Last one I went to we had economy burgers on one of those disposable tin foil things,' he replied.

'There's going to a lot of disappointed men tonight,' said Alex, nodding towards the circle of men watching the professional chef in charge of the barbecue.

'Yup. At least there won't be any cremated sausages or pink chicken,' laughed Ross.

'Just a lot of frustrated men talking each other through their marinade recipes,' she said. 'So are you here on your own?' she asked.

'No. Jenny's here somewhere. What about you?'

'Elliott's coming along later. Who else is here?' she asked, scanning the garden.

'Lisa's inside; most of the trainees should be here.'

'I saw Jo and Naz as I arrived.'

'Look, there's Dan, behind the barbecue crowd,' he said. 'Shall we go and join him?'

'You go. I'll go and mingle inside,' she said. She'd been half hoping Dan wouldn't be there tonight. She went inside.

Lisa was in the living room picking cushions off the sofa when she found her.

'Caught you,' said Alex.

Lisa jumped and just avoided spilling her red wine

on the cream carpet. 'You muppet! You scared the life out of me. I thought you were Miss Interior Design herself.'

'What were you doing?' Alex asked.

'I was trying to suss out whether these cushions were the real deal or high street fakes.'

'And?'

'Don't ask me. I haven't a clue. Could be from IKEA for all I know.'

Alex laughed. 'It's a cool place, isn't it?' she said.

'Yeah, Chris has done well for himself. I'm kicking myself. He asked me out when I first started at the firm,' said Lisa.

'Did he? I had no idea.'

'Stupid firm rule. We had one date and both got cold feet. We were worried we'd get chucked out before we qualified. I've never told a soul before. I should have gone to another firm and then I could be mistress of this place.'

'You're not serious?' Alex asked.

'Nah. We would never have worked out. I think Chris wanted a girly girl, not a gob on a stick like me.'

Alex laughed.

'Anyway, I've got my sights set on someone else now.'

'Anyone I know?' Alex asked.

'Yes, as a matter of fact.' She pushed the door closed so no one else could hear them. 'Dan.'

'Furtado?' asked Alex.

'The very same. And you know what; I don't give a stuff about the firm rule.'

'What about him?' asked Alex.

'No idea! He doesn't know about my cunning plan yet, but I'll keep you posted.'

Alex watched Lisa disappear on her mission to find Dan as the front door opened and Elliott came in. She rushed towards him and hugged him tight.

'Hi, darling,' she said.

'Hey, babe. That's a nice welcome,' he said, kissing her. 'You look gorgeous.'

'Hi! You must be Alex's fiancé. How lovely to meet you.' It was Gemma.

'Hi,' he said. He looked at her, bemused. 'Don't I know you?'

'Elliott, this is Gemma. She's an actress. You've probably seen her on TV,' said Alex.

'And you're in a band, Alex tells me,' Gemma said.

'Yeah. Lead guitar.'

'Well, perhaps you could play later? Chris has got a guitar upstairs.'

With that she floated off. Elliott took Alex's arm and they headed out to the garden.

It was a beautiful evening and Elliott and Alex spent most of it together. Alex finally got to tell Elliott all about the wedding she had planned and he seemed genuinely excited for the first time. Alex kept one eye on Dan, who was in the corner with a group from the office, and she noticed that Lisa never left his side. As it got later and darker the music changed and started to get mellower. The dancing changed from frenetic to romantic as more couples took to the floor.

Elliott grabbed Alex's hand and pulled her onto the

dance floor. His arms were around her waist and hers were around his neck as they performed the standard penguin shuffle that passed for a 'slow dance'. Alex inhaled his familiar smell and looked up at his face. He smiled back and they kissed and for a moment she felt safe.

Elliott suddenly broke away from her and she realised that someone was talking to him. It was Gemma, brandishing an acoustic guitar.

'Please. Would you play for us?' she begged.

Elliott looked at Alex and shrugged his shoulders.

'Go on,' said Alex.

He took the guitar and sat on a low wall that edged a neat row of box hedging. Alex looked round at everyone staring at him as Gemma turned the music off and he tuned up. She caught Lisa's eye. She was standing next to Dan and giving Alex a thumbs up.

Then Elliott began to play and everyone stopped talking. He started with a gentle James Taylor song. Alex could sense the audience's reaction. He flicked his hair out of his eyes and looked up at her as he moved onto 'Hey Jude'. He sang it to her, oblivious to anyone else. She looked down as she felt everyone's eyes on her.

Gemma whispered to her, 'He's really good.'

'I know,' said Alex. Sometimes she forgot how good he was. He was looking up now and nodding in time to the rhythm and working the audience.

'A real showman,' Gemma said.

CHAPTER 13

'Alex, I need to see you right away. I'm in my office.'
It was Tom Duffy and he sounded agitated.

'Okay, Tom, I'm on my way,' she replied.

She'd half expected a call over the weekend but he obviously hadn't read the revised report until this morning. Alex stood up, straightened her skirt and ran up the stairs to Tom's office. As she rounded a corner she almost collided with a trolley carrying a heavily bandaged patient with several drips being pushed along behind it. 'Sorry,' she called out.

Tom was standing by the large sash window in his office. The report was in his hand. As she entered he swung round to face her.

'Alex, you could have warned me about this. When did you find out?' He threw the report onto his desk and sat down, gesturing for her to do the same.

'I'm sorry. I wanted to last week but the only time I saw you, you were with Lloyd. We found out about Felicia a couple of weeks ago but it was only when I spoke to the accountants that I realised it could be more than an isolated case of one unhappy patient. Did you know about Lloyd?'

'No, I didn't. The accountants have been filling me in but it doesn't look good. It looks like he's been pocketing money on the side, so there's a whole fraud issue as well,' said Tom.

'So he was taking the difference between the advertised rates and the inflated rates he was charging? Rachel and I did wonder about that,' Alex said.

'Yup. It would explain his lifestyle,' Tom said, seemingly to himself. 'What I need to know is how much of this we need to tell Equinox about. I'm assuming I'm going to have to get rid of Cassidy and his practice. I also need to find out who else is involved.'

'Well, Audrey Fox for a start. But we don't know who he's been using as theatre staff,' Alex said.

'Probably just people from the bank.'

'The bank?' she asked

'Yes. We have a bank of freelance people we use for procedures when we're short-staffed – everyone from anaesthetists to orderlies. Look, Alex, I can handle Cassidy. What I'm worried about is whether there are any more smoking guns out there like this Monroe woman. The last thing we need is a stream of people who've had disastrous treatment selling their stories to the papers, especially if they're famous. The reputational damage would be huge. How did you find out about her?'

Alex explained how they'd found her details in a file that a temp had uncovered.

'So there could be more somewhere?' he asked.

'I've no idea, Tom. All I know is that Audrey Fox claimed we'd had all of Lloyd's files and then the temp found a file that had been overlooked.'

'Mmm, Lloyd is a good surgeon and generally gets excellent results. He's not had many complaints in the past. For now, I've suspended him while we investigate. Right, leave him to me. Get one of your employment lawyers to call me. I need to handle him carefully and I don't want to end up on the wrong end of a claim for unfair dismissal. And now he's gone get your guys to scour his office for any other files. In the meantime I need you to track down this Felicia woman and find out how we can get her off our backs.'

'Tom, we're going to have to disclose this to Equinox, you know, but you're doing the right thing. If we tell them and can then show we've done what we can to resolve it then it doesn't look so bad,' Alex said.

'I guess so, but those Americans are very risk averse. They aren't going to like it. The other big problem is the loss of revenue. Cassidy was one of our biggest earners, even with him creaming his own money off the top. Shit, Alex, I hope this doesn't stop the deal happening. Mrs Duffy is already spending our share money.' He tried to smile but Alex could see he was really concerned

'Tom, let's manage this problem and see where we get to. We've got a couple of weeks before the presentation meetings.'

'You're right. Okay, you track down the actress and keep me posted.'

'And what about Equinox? I've got their lawyer sending me the contract today,' she said.

'Can we keep it quiet a bit longer?' he asked.

'A bit longer, I suppose. But Tom, we'll have to disclose it sooner or later.'

'I know. Bloody Cassidy. I should never have trusted a man who cheats at golf like he does.'

'Don't worry, Tom. We'll sort this,' she tried to reassure him.

Alex returned to the project room where Dan and Ross had arrived and were now busy cataloguing all the documents that supported the findings in their report. She sighed as she sat down. Her phone rang. It was her mum. She let it go to answerphone.

'Everything okay?' asked Ross.

'Yeah. I've just been with Tom. Look, I may as well tell you that I put a new section in the report on Friday to deal with potential litigation. You should read it. Page sixty-one. Dan knows about it already.'

Dan looked up. 'Is it the Felicia thing?' he asked.

'Yeah.' She told them about her conversation with Tom. 'I really need to meet Felicia and assess how much of a risk she is.'

'Oh and Alex,' said Dan, 'someone called Warren Wickens called. The sale and purchase agreement is on its way.'

Alex called Felicia and arranged to meet her.

'Okay, but will anything happen this time?' Felicia asked.

'What do you mean?' said Alex.

'Well, I'm sick of talking about my boobs. I want

something doing about them. I need to get back to work.'

'Look, let's discuss this face to face. Can you meet this afternoon at the Kensington Royal Hotel reception, say three o'clock?' Alex asked.

'Okay. I'll be there,' Felicia replied.

At two thirty Alex jumped into a cab just as her phone started ringing.

'Hi, Em. How's things?'

'Okay. Work's a nightmare but otherwise okay. Look, I need to chat through the hen do stuff at some point. You free for a quick drink after work?'

'Yeah, sure. I'm on my way to a meeting but should be free by five-ish. I could meet you somewhere central then.'

'Cool. Covent Garden at five?' said Emma.

'It's a date.'

As she hung up she saw the missed calls from her mother. She reluctantly picked up her messages. There was one from the bank, one from her secretary reminding her about the department's away day and two from her mother stressing about the printers and bridesmaids' gifts.

'Shit!' Alex said out loud. She'd forgotten to pick up the charm bracelets from the jewellery shop.

She arrived at the hotel and strode into the reception area. She scanned the room, searching for Felicia. It was a huge impersonal area with small collections of armchairs and sofas dotted about amidst enormous potted palms. Felicia saw Alex first.

'Ms Fisher?' she heard someone call and then

noticed a tiny woman sitting on a red velvet sofa to the left of the reception desk. She walked over to her.

'Yes. Hello. You must be Ms Monroe?' Alex held out her hand.

'Yes. Pleased to meet you,' she said. She had a nest of blonde hair, huge green eyes and a petite frame that was dwarfed by her poorly disguised boobs. Despite the heat Felicia was wearing a beige leather jacket, which she was clutching together across her chest.

'Felicia, I'm Alex. It's a pleasure to meet you. How are you?'

'I'm good, thanks. I just need this whole ghastly business sorting out. I really need to get back to acting and promotional work as soon as possible. To be frank, I really need the money.'

'I understand.'

'With respect, Alex, I'm not sure you do. I've been out of work for the best part of six months now. I'm sure you think my money just goes on boob jobs and Caribbean holidays but that's not the case. I had the operation because I need to work. To work, to get in the papers and to keep getting paid by the promotional people I need to look good. I'm no spring chicken these days. I know my limitations. I can act but I'm never going to get serious stuff. Soaps are perfect for me because they give me a guaranteed income. No one's going to employ me at the moment. I'm a freak.'

'Okay.' Alex was taken aback. Felicia was more articulate and straightforward than she'd expected.

'Look, the bottom line is I'm thirty-nine,' said Felicia.

Not what the website said, thought Alex.

'I've got a big apartment and an even bigger mortgage, not to mention my handbag habit. I need to work. My savings are almost gone.'

'Right. Of course. I didn't realise. So that's why you do all the stuff for the PR companies?' Alex said.

'Of course. God, I don't turn up to those dos for the free champagne and the goody bags, although they're quite nice. I often get a fee, I usually get profile and often get work on the back of it. I have no illusions about where I am in the food chain, Alex. Unfortunately I don't have a law degree,' she said.

Alex cut to the chase. 'Right. Look, I'll be brutally honest. I've spoken with the managing director at Beau Street this morning. We need to know if you plan to go public. There's something important happening at the clinic and the last thing they need is bad publicity.'

'Well, since I spoke to your colleague I've had an offer for a story. It's really cloak and dagger stuff and my agent doesn't know about it but it would be a significant sum. I'm sure you must know that I'm not the only person in town who's been using Butcher Cassidy's out-of-hours services.'

'Do you know who the other people are?' Alex asked. If she and Rachel couldn't get the names, perhaps Felicia could.

'I know at least five names for certain. My agent told me. That was before she started threatening me. One of them is Hollywood A list,' Felicia replied.

'What if I could get everything sorted out for you by another surgeon from Beau Street?'

'Well, that would be a start, I suppose. But that's another couple of months out of work while I recover. What about compensation?' Felicia asked.

'I don't know but I'll look into it.'

'Okay, but Alex, I need action now, not words. The only bargaining chip I have is that you're petrified I'm going to go public. I need a response from you in the next forty-eight hours or the stories will start leaking out.'

'Okay, message received and understood,' said Alex.

'I don't like this at all, you know,' Felicia said, looking down. 'This isn't what I want to be like. I just want to work hard and have nice things, like anyone else. Please understand, I'm desperate,' she pleaded.

Alex believed her.

'Have you ever had any work done?' Felicia asked.

'Er, no.' She didn't think Botox on your armpits was what Felicia had in mind.

'No. Why would you? I sometimes wish I'd never started.'

Alex found herself patting her on the hand and saying, 'Don't worry, we'll get this sorted. Trust me.'

'Thanks. I really hope we do.' Felicia got up to leave.

'Here's my card. Please don't do anything without calling me first.' Alex gave her the business card and watched her leave.

She called Tom. 'Okay, Tom. I've just met Felicia. In a nutshell we've got forty-eight hours to put together a deal for her. She wants her breasts put back to normal and a compensation package otherwise she'll sell her story.'

'Charming. Sounds like a lovely lady,' he replied.

'To be honest, I feel a bit sorry for her. Dr Cassidy did the op months ago and she hasn't been able to work since. See it from her point of view. I'm surprised she'd even consider coming back to Beau Street.'

'Ouch. The truth hurts, Alex. Okay, fair play to her. I'll talk to the other doctors and get back to you. I've just had a call from your employment guy. I now know what to do to get rid of Cassidy. But unfortunately my initial plan of punching him and pinching his Porsche is apparently unfair dismissal.'

'Oh what a shame. Tell me, has he completely cleared his office?'

'Not quite. He still has to come back for a couple of boxes of certificates and awards and stuff he had on display. He'd brought so much to the office he couldn't carry it all the day we suspended him.'

'Hmm,' said Alex thoughtfully. 'Wouldn't it be a shame if some of his stuff got accidentally broken…'

'Well, if that's your advice as my lawyer then I might just carry the boxes down to reception myself, and oops, I might just trip up on the way,' he said.

'Well, let me know if you hurt yourself when you trip. I know a good personal injury lawyer.'

'Thanks. I'll bear that in mind,' he laughed.

Alex arrived at the bar in Covent Garden first. It was a one of a chain of themed bars pretending to be cowboy saloons. Stars and stripes, fake saddles and spurs and framed bourbon adverts adorned the wall behind the high mahogany bar. She pushed her way through the saloon style doors and ordered two beers from a nineteen-year-old Essex boy wearing a Stetson. Emma crashed her way through the doors moments later.

'Howdie, partner,' said Alex, handing her the beer.

'Hi. It's a bit OTT here, isn't it?' she replied, admiring the fake buffalo head mounted above their table.

'We're not having my hen do here, before you get any ideas,' said Alex.

'You sure? We could all dress up as Daisy Duke and go line dancing after.'

'No way. Not if you want to live.'

'Don't worry. I've organised something fun yet tasteful.'

'Good. So what do you need to talk about?'

'Okay, well, I've emailed everyone and they can all make it apart from Lucy,' said Emma.

'What's her excuse?' Alex asked.

'It's pretty watertight. She's getting married that day.'

'No way! Not to that geek with the cagoule fetish she was going out with at uni — Timothy or whatever he was called?'

'Jeremy, you mean. Yup, the very same. Pretty sure it's shotgun too.'

'Well, on the basis that I didn't even know that, and haven't been invited to her hen do or wedding, I can't say I'm bothered.'

'So, we've got twelve people. I've booked a hotel in town and got a restaurant and nightclub sorted. It's just the spa we need to sort. I've narrowed it down to three. Do you want final right of approval?'

'Who do you think I am? Olivia Meddoes? I'll leave it to you, Em. You choose.'

'Oh right, okay. Well, that was the easiest conversation I've had all week. That diva is still driving me insane. Latest request – get this: "Emma, darling, would you be so kind as to get the carpets cleaned in my suite between two thirty and four. I specifically requested odour-free carpets."'

'Christ. When will the launch be over?'

'Oh the perfume launch was last week but she likes us so much we're now working on her book.'

'She sounds like a spoilt cow.'

'She makes Veruca Salt look like a saint. Anyway, how are you? How's things?'

'Fine, thanks. I think we're back on track,' Alex said.

'Good, I'm glad. Look, Alex, I've got a bit of a confession. You know that actress I gave you the number for?'

'Felicia Monroe,' said Alex.

'Yes. Well, Bex has been banging on about some TV show that's in the pipeline, something about transforming fading D-listers into shiny new celebs.'

'Yeah, she's mentioned it to me. She asked for Rob Sweeny's details the other day.'

'Well, the thing is, I told her what you'd told me about Felicia and the dodgy surgery. I think she's going to ask her to be on the show. I promise I didn't tell her it was Beau Street or mention your deal. I'm really sorry. I know what you told me was confidential.'

'Okay,' said Alex, thinking through the implications.

'As long as you didn't mention the deal, Beau Street or me then we should be okay. But Felicia is bound to ask Bex how she knows about what happened. Do you know if she's spoken to her yet?'

'I only told her this morning.'

'Great. I'll call her before she speaks to Felicia. Don't worry, Em. I can sort it.'

'Sorry again. Me and my big mouth.'

Alex phoned Bex on the way home. Bex hadn't got round to calling Felicia yet and agreed to hold fire until Alex had spoken to her. Alex decided to wait and see what sort of proposal Tom came up with for Felicia before mentioning the reality show possibility. She needed to be absolutely sure she had Felicia signed up to a deal that would keep her mouth shut before dangling any other carrots under her nose.

She jumped onto the tube and found herself balanced precariously between a man hiding behind his *Financial Times* and a girl with more piercings and tattoos than virgin skin. She had nothing to hold on to so she positioned her feet as far apart as she could and tried to rock from side to side over the bumps. She started to plan what to pack for tomorrow. She was going on an overnight trip to a hotel in the home counties for the 'team-building' day with the rest of the department. This was the annual oxymoron that usually involved late night drinking competitions, bitching about each other's dress-down wardrobes and middle-aged partners regaling the junior lawyers either with stories of deals they'd worked on in the 'good old days' or about their latest boat/car/second home. She decided to take jeans for the day and a beautiful electric blue silk dress for the evening. The tube pulled into the station and she limboed under the tattooed girl's arm out onto the platform.

CHAPTER 14

It was before seven a.m. when Alex met Lisa under the clock at Waterloo. They had to get to the hotel near Ascot by nine and wanted to be on time. This was one of those days when everyone pretended to be relaxed and jolly, but Lisa and Alex had been at the firm long enough to know that, until the partners were safely tucked up in bed, every late arrival, inappropriate outfit and drunken monologue would be used in evidence and held against you.

'Glad you're in jeans too,' Lisa said. 'I was up 'til the early hours trying to decide what to wear.'

'I know what you mean. It's a fine line between the relaxed/in the spirit of the day look and the scruffy/can't be arsed look.'

'Yeah and the worst are the ones in the "tried too hard" category,' said Lisa.

'Remember that guy from the Property Department last year in the mustard cords and the checked shirt and waistcoat?' said Alex.

'That was the end of a promising career managing some millionaire's property portfolio.'

'I can't wait to see Margaret Kemp's dress-down look. Remember the cat jumper?'

'God, that was a fashion crime. Could be sheep this year, of course,' Lisa said.

'Let's play fashion bingo. If she's wearing sheep or farmyard animals you win. Any kind of pet and I win. Loser has to down a cocktail of the other's choice,' Alex said.

'Deal,' said Lisa and they shook on it as they walked to their train.

They arrived at the hotel to find Truman's PA, Pippa, in reception with a clipboard and pen ticking off all the arrivals. She looked like she was dressed for a nightclub in a bright pink dress with contrast zip up the back.

'Alex and Lisa, okay, you can dump your bags here.' She looked at her clipboard. 'You're both in the red team,' she said.

'Red team?' said Lisa.

'Yes, we've split you all up into three teams: red, white and blue.'

'How original,' muttered Lisa.

'After the welcome speech you'll have a series of breakout sessions. Legal updates in the morning and team-building activities in the afternoon. You'll all be scored and there'll be a presentation to the winning team at dinner,' Pippa said in a singsong voice.

'Sounds great,' said Alex with a forced smile. 'Where can we get a coffee?'

They were directed to a function room where rows of chairs were set out facing a flipchart. Lisa and Alex gravitated to the refreshments table where a number of other lawyers were already chatting.

'So does anyone know what the team-building activities are this afternoon?' Alex asked.

'Hopefully not the obstacle course and cargo net again,' said Jenny, one of the junior lawyers.

'Well, it would be interesting watching Pippa do that in her outfit,' said Lisa.

'I think her outfit is a clue that it won't be quite so physical this year. It'll probably be Suduko and brain training type stuff,' said Ross.

'As long as we get plenty of time in the bar afterwards I'm not fussed,' said Lisa.

They all settled into their seats to wait for Truman to start. Alex looked around for Margaret Kemp and couldn't see her, but she did notice Dan sitting behind her. She smiled at him, then whispered to Lisa, 'Have you seen Maggie K yet?'

'No. But I'm feeling pretty confident,' Lisa replied.

As they spoke Truman walked to the front of the room and a hush descended. He spoke for twenty minutes about the direction of the firm, the quality of the department and its people and the importance of them all working together as a team. It was the usual stuff but nice to hear anyway, Alex thought. He then focused on the performance of the team and Alex noticed when he jotted down the figures for the year to date he'd included the fee for the Beau Street deal. Alex was surprised. The deal hadn't even happened yet and it might not happen at all. Truman was clearly banking on it completing. Great, a bit more pressure; just what I need, she thought.

The rest of the morning involved them all being lectured on various updates in the law by specialists. By lunchtime everyone was ready for a break. Alex grabbed her mobile and headed outside. She needed to speak to Tom and Felicia. There were the predictable missed calls from her mum and a text from Elliott telling her he missed her.

'Hi, Tom. It's Alex. I just wanted to check on how you were getting on with Felicia's offer?'

'Oh hello, Alex. It's been an interesting morning. Cassidy popped in first thing. He didn't take his dismissal very well, I'm afraid. Lots of screaming and shouting and empty threats. I had to get the security guards to escort him off the premises again,' Tom said.

'Oh dear. Well, these things are never easy. So what about Felicia?' she asked.

'Well, I was thinking of a free rectification op and three thousand pounds compensation,' he said.

'Okay. That might just be enough,' said Alex.

'What do you mean? I thought that was pretty generous.'

'I agree, but I think she's sitting on a pretty big offer from someone,' said Alex.

'I'm not a big fan of blackmail, Alex,' said Tom.

'Me neither, but let's face it, she's got us over a barrel. Do you want the deal to happen or not?' Alex said.

'Of course I do. Leave it with me, but I'll need

approval from another director for anything over five thousand.'

'Okay, Tom, but don't forget we've only got 'til tomorrow.'

'I know, Alex. Oh and by the way, I managed to smash Lloyd's Golden Scalpel award this morning.'

'Fantastic! Well done,' she laughed.

'I think that was why he lost it with me!'

As Alex hung up she noticed at least a dozen other colleagues pacing the lawns on their mobiles. As she walked back inside to join the others she heard Margaret Kemp's distinctive voice from behind a laurel bush. She was on her phone barking orders to someone. Alex stopped and tried to crane her neck around the bush to see what she was wearing. Margaret had her back to her. It was definitely a jumper, v-neck, no sleeves, but Alex couldn't discern any pattern.

After a mediocre buffet lunch comprising sad quiches and unimaginative salads they split into their groups. The red team was made up of ten people including Pippa, Jenny, Dan, Lisa and Alex. They had a series of three tasks to undertake.

'It's like the trials of Hercules,' said James, a senior partner in his fifties. 'Come on, chaps, let's win this.'

'Pippa, you've organised today. What exactly do we have to do?' asked Alex.

'Well,' she giggled, 'the first task involves driving a tractor.'

'Piece of cake,' said James, who fancied himself as the country squire.

Kitted out in green wellies, they headed outside

where they were greeted by a girl from Marketing who was running the event along with Miles, a professional instructor. It seemed that the challenge was to drive a tractor down a straight path balancing a tray of pint glasses dangling from the front loader without spilling any of the contents. They then had to lower the tray onto a table and reverse back up the path. James was very keen to go first. He hauled himself up into the cabin. The others watched as he took instruction from Miles and then turned the keys in the ignition.

'Well, he looks the part,' said Lisa as they watched James concentrating on moving the vehicle as precisely as possible. James had a ruddy face and a short-sleeved checked shirt and chinos.

'Short-sleeved shirt, though. Nul point for style,' said Jenny.

'Here he comes. Watch out for spillage,' said Alex as James picked up speed and headed towards them, the tray of beer now swinging from side to side. They stepped back as the first beer glass toppled over.

'Come on, James. Take it steady,' Pippa shouted.

James took his hand off the wheel to give Pippa a thumbs up and another glass lurched off the edge of the tray. He refocused his efforts and slowly lowered the front loader towards the table, the tray still swinging.

'Okay, James, you're almost there,' shouted Dan. 'Another ten centimetres.'

'What's that in old money?' James shouted back.

He dropped the tray onto the table and miraculously the remaining glasses stayed upright. He then put the tractor into reverse and manoeuvred at some speed back up the path. Back at the starting point, he jumped out of the cabin and punched the air.

'Not bad for an old timer. Only two glasses down. Come on, Furtado, beat that.' He punched Dan on the shoulder as he passed.

'Here we go. It's testosterone time,' said Lisa as Dan took the driver's seat and started to rev the engine. 'Time for the alpha male of the group to assert himself and my money's on Dan.'

'So how's it going? Your mission to get Dan?' Alex asked as they watched him.

'Slowly, slowly catchy monkey,' said Lisa. 'It's a delicate process.'

'So no joy yet then,' laughed Alex.

'Nope. Not a sausage. I'm still hopeful, though. I think he's programmed not to notice me cause of the "firm rule".' She made pretend speech marks with her fingers as she said this.

'You reckon? My mate Emma says we're probably all fascinated with each other because we're all forbidden fruit.'

'Well, I'm hoping he'll be fascinated with me by the end of today,' said Lisa. 'I've got a knockout outfit for tonight.'

'Seriously, though, what would you do if you did meet someone at work? Would you leave?' said Alex.

'I'd love to think I'd make a massive fuss and take the firm to a tribunal for breaching some human right of mine to have a relationship, but in reality I'd just keep it under wraps until I knew if it was serious or not. If it was, I'd probably leave, I guess. Apparently

James was dating a girl in the litigation department for six years and only 'fessed up to it when they offered him partnership. She left the next day and is now at home with their three kids.'

Lisa nodded towards James who was now jumping up and down and cheering as he watched Dan spill the whole tray of beer. Dan reversed the tractor back up the path and jumped down, laughing.

'You win, Jimbo.' He patted James on the back. 'Unless, of course, Alex or Lisa do better.'

Lisa adopted the bull in china shop approach and raced the tractor down the lane, crashed the tray onto the table and careered wildly in reverse back to the start.

'I beat you, Dan,' she said as they counted the glasses that were still upright.

'But I remain undisputed champion,' crowed James.

It was Alex's turn. She felt very self-conscious as all eyes turned to her. She listened intently to Miles's brief and put the engine into gear. The tractor lurched forwards immediately, spilling one glass. She could hear James cheering. She then got into a groove and reached the table without spilling any more. She carefully moved the lever to lower the loader and the tray practically kissed the table.

'Go girl!' screamed Lisa. 'You did it!'

When Alex jumped down from the cabin Dan ran up to her, beaming. 'Well done! You beat him.' He moved towards her and she thought he was going to hug her but he clearly had second thoughts as he stepped back and Alex was engulfed by Lisa, Pippa and the other girls on the team.

After everyone had taken their turn on the tractor they moved onto a clay pigeon shooting task. They each had three clays to shoot and their collective scores would be totalled up.

James was in his element again and neatly picked out his three clays. The rest of them had mixed results. Alex took three shots in quick succession before the clays had even been released and Pippa fell backwards onto the grass from the force of the gun recoiling.

They were then ushered inside again for the final challenge.

'What's this one then, Pippa?' James asked, rubbing his hands together.

'You'll find out,' she said as they entered a small lounge containing two sofas and two armchairs arranged around a low table. A woman with another clipboard was seated in one of the armchairs.

'Good morning. I'm Miranda and I'll be running the final challenge. Please would you all take a seat?'

Alex was the last to enter the room and found herself sitting on the end of one of the sofas next to Dan.

'This is a tasting challenge,' Miranda continued, 'and involves tasting five different items. Some will be foods and some drinks. I'll need a couple of you to help me hand out the items for tasting and the rest of you will be the tasters. The tasters will all be blindfolded and once you've tasted the item you can discuss amongst the other tasters what you think it is. I'll then take your group answer. Perhaps I could ask you two to help me.' She pointed to Alex and Jenny, who were sitting closest to her. 'The rest of you can put on these.'

She handed round the black blindfolds. 'And no cheating,' she added.

There were lots of giggles from the more junior members of the group as they pulled on their blindfolds.

'This is ruining my hair,' said Pippa.

'Bloody ridiculous if you ask me,' moaned James, who clearly preferred the outdoor pursuits.

Once the tasters were ready Miranda passed Alex and Jenny some small shot glasses, which they then placed into their team members' waiting hands.

'Ugh, that's disgusting,' said Jo, one of the trainees.

'Mmm, that's a good single malt if I'm not mistaken,' said James.

'Is it Bourbon?' asked Dan.

The tasters argued amongst themselves until they settled on Jack Daniels, despite James's protestations. The next item was some kind of jam and came on a teaspoon. Alex and Jenny took the spoons from Miranda. They smiled at each other as they walked round the room feeding the strange jam to their colleagues as if they were toddlers. The door opened while they were doing it. As Alex fed the last spoonful to Dan she heard a cough behind her and saw Margaret Kemp looking directly at her.

'Just wanted to see how the red team were getting on,' she said, her eyes still on Alex.

Alex noticed a line of pigs around the bottom of her jumper.

'Just three items left and then we'll be done,' replied Miranda.

'Okay. We want you back in the function room in ten for the results,' she said and marched out of the room.

When the tasting challenge was over all the teams met up again for the scores to be revealed. The red team had won and James celebrated as though he'd won Wimbledon, falling to his knees and shouting, 'Yes!' The prize was two bottles of champagne and the team headed to the bar to drink it.

The girls sat together sipping their bubbly while comparing notes on what they'd be wearing later in the evening. The boys indulged in a level of post-match analysis that the events of the afternoon hardly merited.

'I have to say, your clay pigeon shooting was inspired,' one of the trainees said, sucking up to James.

'Thanks, years of practice, you know. And Dan's call on the Jack Daniels was spot on,' James continued.

'Bloody hell, anyone would think we'd just beaten Germany in the World Cup on penalties, the way they're going on,' said Lisa to the other girls.

'Come on, ladies, let's finish this before they hog it all,' said Alex, topping up their glasses.

'Yeah and then we should get changed. The other groups will be on their way back down soon and I want to straighten my hair,' said Jenny.

Alex looked at her colleagues as she sipped her champagne and felt herself relax. Despite all the banter she enjoyed these events. It was interesting to see the human side of everyone and it definitely gave the team more cohesion back at the office.

An hour later, after a quick change, everyone started

to drift back into the bar. When Alex came down Lisa, James and Ross were already propping up the bar.

'Here she comes, Queen of the Tractor,' said James as Alex approached. 'I have to say, it's lovely to see a lady who's made a bit of an effort,' he muttered more quietly to her. Alex was in her electric blue silk dress and had put her hair up.

'Thank you, James. The gentleman as always,' she smiled. It was a standing joke between them that she knew he had a tendency to smarm so he always played up to it.

James handed her a gin and tonic as they leant against the bar and people watched.

'Look at Truman.' James nudged her. Truman was in a suit, as always, though he'd daringly discarded his tie. He'd been cornered by Pippa and two other secretaries who were talking him through their gripes about the Word Processing Department.

'Should we save him?' said Alex.

'Nah. He can manage,' said James.

'He looks a bit uncomfortable. Have you seen what Pippa's wearing?' said Alex. Pippa had changed into the shortest skirt with a floaty blouse cinched in with a bright red belt almost as wide as the skirt.

'Bloody marvellous. Though obviously not as classy and sophisticated as you,' James said.

'You silver-tongued devil, you,' she laughed. 'Come on, let me beat you at pool,' she said and dragged him to the games room. 'Are you coming to play pool?' she called to Lisa and Ross as she went.

The pool competition became deadly serious and

before long there were a dozen or so of them playing, breaking only for dinner. The match continued until after midnight by which time only James, Alex, Ross and Lisa were playing. There was one other group still at the bar and Alex couldn't help herself watching Dan chatting to Pippa. They seemed thick as thieves and Pippa seemed to be taking every opportunity to touch him. It didn't take a body language expert to see what she thought of him.

'So we never did get to check out Maggie Kemp's jumper, did we? I saw her from a distance and it looked some hideous golf top,' said Lisa while they watched Ross pot another ball.

'Actually I did see it,' said Alex. 'It was a tank top, and yes, it was hideous. Pigs this time.'

'No! Doesn't that mean I win? Or is it you? Can't remember,' said Lisa.

'I think you win and I have to down the drink of your choice,' said Alex.

Alex's last memories of the evening were standing in the bar being cheered on as she held her nose and drank what looked like neat washing up liquid down in one.

'Quality performance, Fisher,' shouted James as she staggered upstairs to bed.

CHAPTER 15

The banging was getting louder. Alex put the pillow over her head.

'Alex, come on! Breakfast ends in ten minutes,' Lisa shouted from the other side of the door.

'Go without me,' she croaked.

'Are you okay?'

'Never felt worse,' Alex replied. She thought she was going to be sick as she sat up in bed. It was too much sudden movement so she lay back down again and groaned.

'What did you do to me, Lisa? I think I'm going to die.'

'Let me in. I've got paracetamol.'

Alex crawled out of bed, desperately trying not to move her head. 'Okay,' she croaked.

'Wow. You look bad,' said Lisa when she saw Alex slumped on the floor next to the bed.

'Love you too. Come on, where's the drugs? What kind of pusher are you?' Alex said.

Lisa passed her the pills and a glass of water. 'Here you go. Now let's get to breakfast. If you don't turn up you'll get the Spanish inquisition from Maggie Kemp. Come on, it's time for your sixty-second makeover.' Lisa grabbed her hands and pulled her up.

'Okay, okay.' Alex picked her jeans off the floor and put them on. 'I need some slap. I can't go down like this,' she said, looking in the mirror and rummaging in her make-up bag. 'Do you think I can wear sunglasses?' she asked as they left the room. 'I really think I might be sick.'

'Come on, hold it together. You'll be fine.'

Alex grabbed a copy of *The Guardian* from a table by the door as they entered the dining room. Lisa picked up one of the red tops.

'Are you going to read that?' Lisa asked.

'No. But it's the biggest one so I can hide behind it,' Alex replied.

They sat together as far away from the rest of the crowd as they could and ordered some tea. Alex could see Margaret doing the rounds of the tables, pretending to be jolly. Alex knew she was keeping a check on who'd made it downstairs. She had decided to pass on breakfast while Lisa tucked into a full English.

'Mmm, I just love black pudding,' she said. 'It's not the sort of thing I'd ever buy but I love it when I'm on holiday or in these sorts of places.'

'I'll take your word for it,' said Alex, holding her teacup with both hands and taking tiny sips. 'What's the gossip then?' she asked, pointing at the tabloid paper.

'Some footballer has been signed for a squillion pounds, that Tory politician with the ginger hair has been caught with his pants down again — ooh and what's this here?' said Lisa, folding the paper in half and holding it closer to her face.

'What is it?' asked Alex, disinterested.

'It's Gemma, Gemma Kirk — you know, Chris's fiancée,' said Lisa.

'What about her? Is she leaving the soap?'

'No. Oh it's awful. Someone has really stitched her up. Listen to this.' Lisa read aloud, 'Gemma Kirk, soap actress and blonde beauty, has been exposed as being less than truthful about her age. According to her website she's twenty-seven but according to our source she's thirty-three. This may be news to her twenty-nine-year-old fiancé, top lawyer Chris Arrowsmith.'

'For God's sake, does it really matter?' said Alex.

'It gets worse,' said Lisa. She continued, 'Kirk, who's due to wed in the autumn, is alleged to have had some major cosmetic surgery to maintain her youthful appearance, including work on her eyes and regular Botox and fillers. A source has told this column she's a regular client at the Beau Street clinic off Harley Street.'

Alex put down her teacup. 'Shit! That bitch!' she said.

'That's a bit harsh, isn't it? She's only had some work done. I'm sure Chris will get over it,' said Lisa.

'Not Gemma. Someone else. It's to do with the deal I'm on.'

'Ah, Beau Street,' said Lisa. 'Where are you off to?'

Alex had already got up and was trying to find her

phone at the bottom of her bag. 'Need to make some calls,' she replied as she finally located her phone. 'See you later.'

Alex ran up the stairs to her room two at a time. She dialled the number, still panting and feeling even more nauseous than before.

'Felicia? It's Alex Fisher. What's going on? I thought you were going to give us forty-eight hours to get back to you? We still have until later today.'

'Ms Fisher? What are you talking about?' said Felicia.

'You know perfectly well. You told me Beau Street had two days to make you an offer and it's all over the papers this morning about Gemma Kirk, who by the way just happens to be a friend of mine, which no doubt you already know,' Alex replied.

'Hey, hey, steady on there! I don't know what you're talking about. I know Gemma. I worked with her a couple of years ago. It was Gemma who recommended Cassidy to me, but I haven't said anything about her to the papers or anyone else.'

'What?'

'I haven't told anyone about Gemma. She only had a bit of Botox as far as I knew. She's a lovely girl. If I'd carried out my threat I wouldn't have spilled the beans on her. Believe me, I've lots of real nasty pieces of work I'd shop before her. We had a deal, Alex. I haven't gone back on it. I thought you were calling me now with Beau Street's proposal.'

'Oh. Well, if it wasn't you who, was it?' said Alex, rubbing her forehead.

'I've no idea but it wasn't me. You've got the rest of

the morning, Alex, and the next story could be from me. Goodbye.' Felicia hung up.

Alex lay back on the bed and groaned. Within seconds her phone was ringing again.

'Hi, Tom. Let me guess, you've seen the papers,' she said.

'Good morning, Alex. Actually I've only read the sports section this morning but my son is home from university and he has one of the tabloids and he's shown me an article about Gemma Kirk. I thought you said we had forty-eight hours to respond to that woman?'

Alex told him all about her conversation with Felicia.

'And you believe her?' Tom asked.

'Yes, I do, Tom. I really do. I trust her for some reason. Look, it's not a damaging piece for Beau Street, so I don't think it affects the deal. I mean, Gemma Kirk looks great, so it's probably positive in one way.'

'Yes, but what does it say about our client confidentiality? I bet it's Cassidy. The slimeball,' he said.

'Do you think so?'

'Well, if you're sure it's not Felicia. It is a bit of a coincidence, isn't it? He gets fired and I smash his precious trophy and the next morning there's a leak to the papers. I bet he did the work on that girl too.'

'Yes, I think you're probably right,' said Alex, remembering what Felicia had said about Gemma recommending Cassidy to her.

'So not only have we got to do the deal with this Felicia woman, but we need to keep Lloyd quiet too.' Tom sounded panicky.

'Look, I can deal with Cassidy. I know a litigator back at the office who'll be more than happy to get an injunction to keep him quiet. He just happens to be Gemma Kirk's fiancé. But we need to act fast before tomorrow's papers go to print.'

'Okay, you talk to your chap about Lloyd. I think I should call Felicia and make her an offer. Is that okay with you?' he asked.

'Of course. I think she'd appreciate a call from you. I'll draft up an agreement for you and her to sign. Maybe you could suggest she meets with you tomorrow to tie up the legals.'

'All right. I just need to keep Equinox sweet now. The accountants are telling me that this whole Cassidy business leaves us with a big hole in the numbers. I need to come up with some bullshit to keep this deal on track. I also have the small matter of one less surgeon at the clinic to deal with,' Tom said. 'Oh and one more thing, Alex. I've had some lawyer guy calling me. Stupid name. Wally someone?'

'Warren? Warren Wickens?' she said.

'Yeah, that's him. He wants to know when we'll get our comments on the sale contract to him.'

'Idiot.'

'Excuse me?' said Tom.

'I'm sorry, Tom, not you — the Wickens guy. He shouldn't be calling you. You're my client, not his. He should have called me.'

'He said he had but that he couldn't reach you. Anyway, can you give him a call?'

'Yes, of course, Tom. I'll do that right away.'

Tom had already hung up. Alex lay back on the quilted bed cover and curled up in the foetal position. She felt awful. All she wanted was to go home to bed and start again tomorrow but she knew the call to Wickens couldn't wait. Her phone vibrated. It was a text from her mother asking her to call her. She must be getting desperate; Alex knew she hated texting with a passion. As she looked at her phone she checked her electronic diary. Maybe she could do the call with the US lawyer, speak to Chris about Lloyd and then go back home for a duvet day. Then she saw the diary entry for the afternoon. It was blanked out already for her appointment at the STD clinic.

'Fantastic,' she said out loud.

By early afternoon she was back in London and sitting in a soulless waiting room at the STD clinic. She'd spoken to Chris on the train. He was pretty angry about the whole Gemma exposure and had been delighted when she'd given him the opportunity to get some revenge on Lloyd. She'd tried to call Warren Wickens but had forgotten about the time difference again. That call would have to wait until the joys of the STD clinic were over. She cursed Elliott as she sat there amongst a group of students who were discussing the route of their forthcoming world tour. It was a game of geographical one-upmanship.

'I'm so looking forward to Belize. Jezza says it's the DBs,' said a skinny girl in harem pants and a vest top.

'Yeah and then Guatemala,' said the girl next to her.

'Are you guys doing Southeast Asia?' asked a boy in full goth gear and make-up.

'A bit last season. My mum went there when she was at uni,' said the skinny girl, pulling a face.

Great, thought Alex. Even my backpacking days weren't cool.

'Oh I know. Thailand is totally mainstream but what about Cambodia and Laos? They haven't been globalised yet.'

Alex leant her head against the wall and read the HIV, chlamydia and genital warts posters. She prayed that Elliott's groupie was as clean as a whistle but she wouldn't mind if she was struck down with a nasty case of herpes next week.

'Number thirty-seven, please,' said a nurse in a bored tone.

It was Alex's turn. She felt like she was buying olives at the deli counter for a moment as she handed in the tear-off slip with her number on it. That thought soon faded as she was ushered into a consulting room containing a thin bed with an ominous set of stirrups hanging over it.

'Okay. Is there anything specific you need testing for today?' asked the nurse in a manner that suggested that Alex might be back next week with a different set of requirements.

'Er, well, it's my first time here and really I just wanted a general MOT,' said Alex. Elliott's groupie had been very vague about her affliction.

'Okay. So we'll test you for everything. That means we'll need to take some blood, a urine sample and a swab,' the nurse continued.

It didn't sound too bad, Alex thought; no need for the stirrups hopefully.

The nurse handed her a small plastic cup. 'Please could you pop next door and provide the urine sample,' she asked. 'We only need a small amount. No need to fill it to the top.'

'Right, okay. Won't be a moment.'

Alex opened what looked like a cupboard door into a small windowless toilet that smelt of disinfectant. She managed to pee all over her hand as well as the beaker. She then spent what seemed like an eternity washing her hands and the outside of the beaker, which she'd managed to fill to overflowing. She tipped some pee out, splashing her shoes in the process. Finally she left the bathroom and handed the container to the nurse.

'Just put it on there, please,' said the nurse, pointing to a tray. 'Okay, now I need to take some bloods. Roll up your sleeve, please.'

Once she'd labelled the phials of blood and filled in some more paperwork she turned again to Alex.

'This is the last thing now. Please could you hop up onto the bed and I'll do the swab. Remove your trousers and underwear, please.'

Oh great, the stirrups, thought Alex.

She lay on the bed, her legs apart, while the nurse examined her and then took the swab. Although it was the height of summer, she shivered. It was even worse than a smear test and for some reason she was tearful.

'Are you okay?' the nurse asked, not unsympathetically.

'Yeah. I'm fine,' Alex sniffed. She tried to pull herself together but couldn't help thinking of Elliott and why she was there in the first place.

'Okay, all done now,' said the nurse.

Alex was off the bed and dressed again in seconds.

'Your results will be ready in two to three days,' said the nurse, smiling now.

'Thanks.' Alex ran out of the clinic and didn't stop running until she found herself outside a coffee shop. She went in and ordered a huge iced coffee. She would make the call to the US lawyer from here.

'Hello, please can I speak to Warren Wickens?' she asked before the woman at the other end could recite the name of the firm at her.

'Warren Wickens.'

'Warren, it's Alex Fisher, MacArthur Warren.'

'I wondered when you would call. Do you have your comments on the sale documents?' he asked in an aggressive bark.

'I do. We can discuss them now or I can email them. I suggest we deal with the big issues on the phone and I send you a mark-up with the others,' she replied.

'Okay. I've got ten minutes.'

'The first issue is the price. My client expects the full amount on signing. They're not prepared to accept your client's proposal to retain twenty per cent of the purchase price for twelve months.' Alex knew why they'd suggested this. They wanted to hold on to the money in case any problems with the deal surfaced later. It would save them having to try to claw back compensation.

'After the recent revelations at the business, twenty per cent is more than reasonable,' he countered.

'That's unfair. My client has been full and frank with your client and has dealt promptly with the issues surrounding Lloyd Cassidy's practice.'

'Yeah but how do we know there isn't another smoking gun somewhere? It's a dealbreaker and you can tell your client that,' he said.

'And you can tell your client that the principle of a retention is not acceptable to my client. It was never part of the deal.'

'Are you going to be this difficult about everything?' he asked.

'I'm not being difficult. I'm putting across my client's position,' she said, her head throbbing.

'Which from where I'm sitting doesn't look good. Look, Ms Fisher, you send me your mark-up and let's not waste each other's time. Frankly I'll be amazed if this deal ever happens. Good morning.'

'It's the afternoon here,' she replied, but he'd already hung up.

The irritating, arrogant tosser, she thought. She finished her drink and watched the yummy mummy on the next table drinking some skinny, one shot, decaf waste of a drink and chatting to her friend while their two toddlers wiped chocolate over each other's faces. The children stared at Alex and she half smiled back. As she got up to leave one of them said, 'Mummy, why is that lady so sad?'

Alex wanted to scream, 'Because I'm hungover, the deal on which my career depends is crumbling big style, I've just had some woman in a miner's helmet exploring my bits because my fiancé slept with some whore and I have a crazed mother harassing me every hour of the day.' Instead she just smiled at the mother, who was now staring at her too, and left.

As she walked she realised she was close to the jewellery shop for the bridesmaids' bracelets. She decided to pop in and get that sorted once and for all.

The bell rang as she opened the door and she saw the same shop assistant behind the desk.

'Can I help you?' she asked as she stood up. 'Ah, it's you again. I'm afraid I couldn't hold onto your package any longer but we have had some new deliveries since you were last in so you might be in luck.'

'Thanks,' said Alex. 'It's just one adult and two children's charm bracelets, please. I'll pick out the charms again.'

She was in luck. They had everything she needed and the assistant packaged it all beautifully in three neatly wrapped boxes with white ribbons.

Alex handed over her credit card. 'Hope it works this time,' she said, remembering that she hadn't phoned the bank or checked any statements recently.

'So do I,' said the assistant.

Alex stared at the card machine, willing it to work.

'Madam, it has been referred to security,' said the girl, rolling her eyes.

'What does that mean?' asked Alex.

'I need to call the issuer and you'll need to talk to them.'

Alex stood there while the girl made a song and dance of looking up the number, calling the issuer and giving them details of the sale. She finally handed the phone to Alex with an exaggerated sigh. Alex went through the ritual of mother's maiden name, first pet and inside leg measurement before the man believed she wasn't some international fraudster. As it finally seemed they might let her buy the bracelets, she asked why the purchase had been referred in the first place.

'It's just that we've noticed unusual spending patterns on your card recently so it's standard procedure to check up,' the man replied. He wouldn't give Alex any details of what the so-called unusual spending patterns were for 'security reasons'.

'But you know who I am! You know that my first cat was Hong Kong Phooey, for heaven's sake.'

'Sorry, madam. You'll have to check your statements.'

'I thought Hong Kong Phooey was a dog,' muttered the shop assistant.

CHAPTER 16

'Hi, I'm home,' shouted Alex as she slammed the door behind her and hung her coat up.

There was no sign of Elliott but there was a note on the kitchen table. He was rehearsing at the Scout hut. Barney's wife was Brown Owl and sometimes let them have the key. Alex made herself a cup of tea and gathered up the post before collapsing on the sofa with the phone. She decided there was no time like the present. She ripped open the latest credit card bill. There was nothing unusual on it, just the usual lunch at Bar Q that probably featured on every card statement for the past five years, a new pair of shoes and the train ticket from when she'd gone home the other weekend. She was about to phone the credit card company to complain when she noticed the outstanding balance on the account. It was almost ten thousand pounds. That was impossible because she automatically cleared the balance every month by standing order from her bank account. Ever since she'd cleared her student debt she'd been religious about it. How could the balance have accrued to such a sum?

She phoned the bank and, after pressing various options and listening to 'Greensleeves' on a synthesizer for five minutes, got through to a human being.

'And finally, the name of your first pet?' asked the call centre operative.

'Hong Kong Phooey,' she replied.

'Ooh, I used to love that show. Henry the mild mannered janitor and number one superguy. Anyway, how may I help you today?' said the girl, remembering her script.

Alex talked her through the issue with her credit card.

'Well, I can see what's happened. You made a very large purchase the previous month and it looks as though your bank refused to pay off the balance as usual. It probably exceeded a limit you'd set on your account. As a result the balance on your credit card is almost at our pre-agreed limit with you, which is probably why your purchase was referred.'

'What very large purchase did I make last month?' Alex asked.

'Well, let me see. It was for nine thousand four hundred and ninety-five pounds and all I know is that it was to a company called Fulham Fantasy Flights. I have their number if you'd like to call them.'

'Yes, I would. Look, this sounds like someone has been using my card fraudulently,' said Alex.

'What about someone else who has a card on your account?' said the girl, whose tone of voice suggested she heard this allegation hundreds of times a day.

'Who? There's only me.'

'Only our records show that a Mr Elliott Scott is a named cardholder.'

Shit! Elliott. She'd forgotten she'd given him a card on the account. It was supposed to be for shared items like furniture or food. What had he spent the best part of ten grand on? Surely not the honeymoon? That was supposed to be his treat.

'Look, let me call this company in Fulham first and if that doesn't check out I'll call you straight back,' said Alex.

She was panicking as she dialled the number.

'Good afternoon, Fulham Fantasy Flights, let us fly you to your fantasy,' said an impossibly chirpy woman.

'I have a query,' said Alex and told the whole sorry tale again. 'Please could you confirm what exactly was bought on that date with that card and in my name?'

After a long discussion with her manager the girl decided to play ball. 'Apparently as it's your credit card I have to tell you.'

'I should bloody well think so,' Alex muttered.

'Ahem. It was for five airline tickets to Goa plus accommodation for two people at Varca Beach in a lovely hotel.'

'Let me get this right. There are five tickets and accommodation for two.'

'Yes. Sounds a bit odd, I know, but that's correct. Oh and it's such a lovely resort. Sophie in the office went there last year. Raved about it.'

'Thanks for your help.' Alex hung up.

She stared at the framed Rolling Stones poster on the wall as everything sank in. After everything he'd said and done he'd gone ahead and booked the band on her honeymoon and on her credit card. He was still doing the tour. She ran to the door and pulled her jacket off the peg. As she did so she dislodged the large Chinese jar they kept on the low window shelf next to the front door. It was teetering on the edge of the window ledge as she left, slamming the door behind her. She heard it crash to the floor as the door closed. She didn't care.

She ran the short distance to the Scout hut, the adrenaline pumping through her and the tears that had been threatening to come all day now coursing down her cheeks. She could hear the muffled sound of the music as she approached. She flung open the double doors to the hall, leaving them flapping behind her, and ran across the parquet floor to the stage where the band were practising some dreadful old Animals cover. She couldn't see Elliott.

'Where is he?' she screeched.

They saw her but couldn't hear her.

'Where is Elliott!' she screamed so loud that they stopped playing.

'Hey, Alex. What's up?' asked Barney, not remotely concerned.

'I'm going to kill that lying, cheating, thieving little shit. Where is he!' she screamed again.

'Hey, hey, chill. Come on, what's he done this time?' said Barney, rolling his eyes at the other two who looked faintly embarrassed.

'What's he done?' she mimicked. 'He's ruined everything, that's what. He's stolen ten grand from me to pay for you lot to go to Goa on my fucking honeymoon. If it wasn't so sad it would be funny. He wants me to spend what's supposed to be the happiest, most romantic two weeks of my life with you. Oh and to pay for it. And do you know where I spent the afternoon today for that shit? Do you?'

They all watched her uneasily now.

'With my legs in stirrups while some poor woman checked me out for every STD under the sun because of him. That's where!'

She began to sob even harder. Apart from her sobs there was silence until she heard his voice behind her.

'Look, I was going to tell you. I'm really sorry.'

She spun round to face him. 'When? On the plane when I'm sat next to Rory? Or perhaps at dinner on the first night when you ask for a table for five?'

'I don't know. I was, though. I promise,' he shrugged.

'And what about the money? I thought you were paying for the honeymoon?' she asked, still crying.

'I know. I'm sorry. I just had a bit of a cash flow crisis and we needed to confirm our flights were booked before they'd confirm the band on the tour.'

'What? So it was all for them? What about me? What about us? Elliott, it's a joke. We're a joke. I am nothing to you but a meal ticket. You don't love me, you love them.' She pointed at the three band members who were edging further and further away. 'You've made your choice now. That's it. We're over.' She looked at him directly and said more quietly. 'So over.'

With that, she turned and walked away.

He tried to stop her but she shrugged his hand off her, her shoulders shaking from the sobs that now sounded like they were coming from a wounded animal.

'I'm really, really sorry, Alex. Please,' he called after her. He actually sounded sorry.

She turned back to look at him one last time. 'No, Elliott, I'm done. It's been the longest holiday romance in history and I need so much more.'

She went to take her engagement ring off to throw at him. That was what you were supposed to do, she thought, but then remembered that she'd paid for it and shoved it firmly back on her finger. She pushed her way through the heavy doors. He didn't follow her.

She walked the streets aimlessly as the sobs gradually subsided. She felt absolutely drained. About an hour after she'd left it she returned to the house. As she pushed the door open she saw the contents of the Chinese jar strewn across the hall. Hundreds of coins of every denomination and currency were everywhere. Some had rolled down the wooden floor all the way into the kitchen, others were lodged in the gap between the polished boards. Amongst the coins were scraps of paper: pizza delivery receipts, bus tickets and business cards that they'd both shoved into the jar over the years as they'd come in and out of the house.

She sat down amongst it all and cried again, more gently this time. She looked at the Thai baht and Singapore dollars and the pennies and change they'd planned to cash in one day to pay for her outfit at Elliott's first awards dinner. That day would never come now.

She started to collect together all the scraps of paper and put them in a neat pile and went to get a plastic bag to put all the money in. As she sat on the wooden floor carefully bagging up the money the enormity of what had just happened hit her. She wasn't getting married. She needed to tell her parents, Emma, the caterers, the cars, the damn unicorns, everybody.

She took her mobile from her pocket and called Emma.

'Hi, Em.'

'Hi. You okay?' Emma asked.

'Kind of. Look, the wedding's off.'

'Sorry, can't hear you. On a train. Just went through a tunnel.'

'The wedding's off. I just broke up with Elliott.'

'Okay, what was it this time?' Emma asked.

'Emma, I'm serious. I just came to my senses, that's all. I can't do it. I want someone who wants me, not an idea of me. I'm just a habit for Elliott, nothing more.'

'Shit. What's brought this on?'

'Long story involving him stealing money, booking the band on our honeymoon, the usual Elliott inconsiderate crap. It was the final straw really. I should have done it months ago.'

Alex absentmindedly started to flick through the pile of assorted bits of paper she'd assembled next to the broken pieces of the jar.

'Okay. Where are you? I'm coming to see you.'

'I'm at home, but honestly, Em, I'll be fine.'

Alex stared at the piece of paper in her hand. It had a childish scribble on it that said 'Thanks for last night. See you next time you're in Coventry' and a girl's name and phone number. She picked up another scrap. It had a different girl's number on it. There was yet another one with another note, 'Thanks for everything, your greatest fan, Shelly xxxx'. There were more, lots more. Alex picked up the remnants of the jar and threw them against the wall and wailed.

'Alex? What's the matter? Alex?' Emma was worried now.

'The bastard,' Alex sobbed. 'The total bastard.' She was doubled up on the floor sobbing more violently than before.

'I'm on my way. Stay where you are. Hold it together, darling,' said Emma.

Two hours later, by the time they opened the third bottle of wine, they'd both started laughing.

'Look at this one,' said Emma, slurring. 'You rock! In bed and on stage! Mandi, kiss kiss kiss kiss.'

Alex giggled. 'I still love the one from Bo — I am the Paula Yates to your Bob Geldof.'

'She obviously hadn't heard of Michael Hutchence,' said Emma.

They'd been on the sofa under Alex's best cashmere blanket for the entire evening, hugging, laughing and crying (in Alex's case).

Alex felt a sad sense of relief. 'I am so glad this happened before the wedding,' she said.

'Yeah, otherwise that bastard could have gone after your house,' said Emma.

'But I would have gone after his guitars and his tour t-shirts. No, I'm not glad because of that, but because I want to marry the right person and I want it to feel right. And it didn't. Ever. Not really. I was in denial.'

'I know.'

'You've never liked him, have you?' Alex asked her friend.

'That's not true. He was great craic when he was on form and you could tell he loved you in his way. But Alex, he's an obsessive, and it's all about the band, not you. Oh and he's also a selfish good-for-nothing toe-rag who gave you bugger all emotional support or practical help.'

'So on balance you hate him then.'

'Pretty much!' Emma laughed.

'What am I going to do about the wedding?'

'Cancel it would be my call, unless you can line up a replacement in the next few weeks.'

'I know. It's my mother I'm dreading telling.'

'She'll get over it,' said Emma, knocking back her wine.

'God, I hope so. She won't know how to fill her day without organising unicorns and flowers and buying outfits.'

'Book her on another course. Has she done reiki yet? Anyway, more importantly, what shall we do about the hen do? I've spent at least half an hour organising it.'

'Let's do it anyway,' Alex said.

'Really? Wont that be a bit sad?'

'No! We'll make it a celebration of a lucky escape.

Come on, it'll be a great girls' night out. But please, no L plates or nurses' outfits.'

'Okay, it's a date. Yeah, why not.' Emma got up from the sofa. 'Fancy a hot chocolate?'

'Mmm, please. I think we've got some in the cupboard. Are you staying then?'

'Of course I am. I'm not leaving you on your own. Anyway, it's midnight and I'm well over the limit. Do you think he'll come back tonight?'

'Not if he's got any sense. You make the chocolate and I'll set up the spare bed. Oh and thanks, Em. You're a top mate.' Alex got up and hugged Emma.

'Hey, no worries.' Emma held her as she started crying again. 'I hope he doesn't come back or I'll kill him. I knew those taekwondo classes would come in useful one day,' Emma muttered.

'I can see the headline: Cheating fiancé found dead in pool of hot chocolate, police suspect taekwondo and PR genius,' Alex said between sobs. 'At least a good spell inside would keep Olivia Meddoes off your back.'

'I wouldn't bank on it,' Emma replied.

CHAPTER 17

Alex arrived at the office the next day with no recollection of the journey. She'd been lost in her own thoughts and had taken the tube and made the necessary changes on automatic pilot. She'd been determined to make it into work and not to hibernate in a pit of self-indulgence. Her engagement was off. Nobody had died. Nevertheless, she felt raw and isolated and wondered if it showed.

She put her head around Chris Arrowsmith's door on the way to her office.

'Hi. How's Gemma?' she asked.

'Hi, Alex. She's okay, thanks. The PR people at work have gone into overdrive. She's thinking of suing but probably won't. Some of the stuff in the article was bang on. She's mainly just embarrassed.'

'What about Cassidy? Did you get anywhere with him?'

'We had a bit of an issue demonstrating that there was a real likelihood he would make further disclosures but we got there in the end. The judge granted us an injunction so with a bit of luck he won't be dishing the dirt on any other clients of Beau Street,' he replied.

'Well done. That's great news. Have you told Tom Duffy?'

'He was really relieved, I think. He seemed very grateful,' said Chris.

'Good job, Chris, and thanks. That makes my life easier too. Hopefully I can start to focus on the nuts and bolts of the deal rather than worrying about what further trouble that joker Cassidy can cause us. Give Gemma my love, won't you.'

Alex reached her desk and settled in to catch up on her emails. As she worked her way through the backlog, Ross arrived.

'Morning, Alex. Have you recovered?' he asked.

'What do you mean?' she asked. How did he know about Elliott?

'From the away day.'

'Oh! Yes. I was fine. I just had a bit of a bug. Dodgy prawn at dinner, I reckon.'

'Yeah right! I took a call from Warren Wickens from the US late last night. He said he wanted to speak to you this afternoon and that he'd then be flying over to nail the deal. He sounded like a bit of an arse, to be honest.'

'He's a total arse. I can hardly wait to meet him.'

Despite the bravado she was nervous about meeting Wickens. Their negotiations had hardly been constructive so far and Alex's experience of playing hardball was limited. Most lawyers were helpful and agreeing the sale contract was a ritual dance that was usually pretty smooth. She was beginning to think Wickens was a maverick. Either that or he'd been watching too many re-runs of LA Law.

Alex spent the rest of the morning catching up. She called Felicia, who'd reached an agreement with Tom and seemed to be more than happy with it. Alex mentioned Bex's TV show to her, which didn't seem to excite her too much, but she did say she'd talk to her agent about it. Then Alex spoke to Tom about the forthcoming call with Warren Wickens and Tom confirmed that a meeting with the Equinox lawyers was scheduled for next week. She got up to get a coffee and noticed the picture frame on the corner of her desk. Elliott smiled back at her through his fringe. She carefully removed the photo from the frame and put it in her top drawer.

'Coffee?' she asked Ross.

'Please, the usual,' he said.

'Okay. Oh and Ross, I've just spoken to Tom and there's a meeting with the US lawyers on Thursday. You need to blank out the whole day. Please could you mention it to Dan too?' She'd let him deal with Dan.

As she waited for the kettle to boil she heard the unmistakable sound of Margaret Kemp berating some poor secretary about something. She made the coffees as quietly as possible, closing the fridge door as she returned the milk as gently as she could. Margaret was standing at the workstation immediately next to the small kitchen and she was the last person Alex wanted to chat to.

'Next time check the client's details first. It's bad enough that he got it late, but the fact that it was emailed to someone else is unforgivable. I expect better than this,' Margeret shouted.

'Of course,' came the meek response.

'Right, now I want to go through the completion documents with you,' Margaret continued.

This is ridiculous, thought Alex. She couldn't skulk around in the kitchen for the next ten minutes while Margaret gave some poor employee a hard time. She walked out, a mug in each hand.

'Ah, Ms Fisher, I need a word with you. No time like the present. My office?' Margaret called across the partition.

'Er, okay,' said Alex, wishing she'd stayed in the kitchen and cleaned out the office fridge instead. She followed Margaret into her office, putting down the two mugs on her secretary's desk as she passed. Margaret's office was tidy to the point of obsessive. There was no evidence that any work went on here at all. The only personal paraphernalia was a framed degree certificate and a picture of an elderly couple; her parents, Alex guessed.

'Right. How's your deal going? I heard a rumour you'd got into difficulties,' Margaret asked.

'Well, Margaret, we did uncover some problems but we're trying to manage them,' Alex replied.

'Hmm. What does the purchaser think? Are these problems terminal?'

'I've only just opened negotiations with their lawyer but I do think they might drop the price. A significant revenue stream has been knocked out by our findings so the forecasted profits won't be as good as they'd hoped,' Alex replied.

'Look, Alex, you need to do everything from our end of the deal to keep this on track. Despite my concerns Truman has already banked your deal. You probably noticed that the figures at the away day assumed the deal would be done. It has to happen or Truman will lose face with the management committee and we all miss out on our bonuses.'

'I'll do the best I can, but at the end of the day it's not up to me if Equinox want to proceed.'

'Oh and one more thing,' Margaret said as Alex turned to leave. 'I was watching you at the away day.'

'Really?' said Alex. And? she thought.

'That was all. Can you get Jane to come in now.' Margaret was already looking at the document in her hands.

Alex stood still. 'So come on Margaret, did I pass?'

Margaret looked up from the document, confused.

'Did I pass? Whatever stupid test you'd set for me? I'm sick of you watching my every move, Margaret. Come on, spit it out. You think I'm having an affair with Dan Furtado, don't you?'

'Alex, I've never said anything of the sort. I'm merely monitoring your behaviour like I do with everyone. But Alex, if there is something you need to tell me…?'

'There isn't. Well, nothing that's repeatable. There's nothing going on with me and Dan or anyone else for that matter. Will you just back off? Please.'

Margaret slowly put the document down on her

desk and then spoke slowly and quietly. 'Listen to me, young lady. I've worked for years to reach the position I'm in today and I will not take that tone from you. I will not "back off", as you so delightfully put it, from you or any other lawyer in this firm. You'd better get used to that. I'll be watching you every step of the way to that partnership, which Truman in his wisdom seems to think you deserve.' Margaret picked up the document again.

Alex returned to her office and handed Ross his coffee. 'I'm just popping out for a minute,' she said, grabbing her bag.

She left the office and walked. She wasn't heading anywhere; she just needed to walk. It was a beautiful sunny day and City workers in their suits and sunglasses were out in force, making excuses to be away from their desks to savour the summer's day. She walked up Cheapside into the depths of the City. A fat man carrying a huge document case rushed past, brushing against her as he went and catching her off balance. She put her arms out to steady herself and knocked into a City trader in his pyjama-striped jacket.

'Oi! Watch it!' he snarled as he fended her off.

The tears came easily now. She found a bench in the grounds of St Paul's Cathedral and sat and wept. It wasn't anger now but tears for the lost future she'd spent the last few years constructing. The wedding, the house, the fabulous career, even the breakthrough for the band and, of course, babies. She'd dreamt up the whole package so many times and now she felt like she'd fallen down the longest snake on the penultimate square on the snakes and ladders board.

She was wondering how long she could sit crying on a bench in central London before someone asked her how she was when her phone rang.

'You okay today?' It was Emma.

'Hi, hun,' Alex laughed.

'You sound odd. Where are you?'

'I'm at St Paul's Cathedral. I had to get out of the office,' Alex replied.

'Oh no, it's worse than I thought. You've turned to God.'

'No. I'm outside on a bench. Can you meet up? Early lunch? I need a friendly face,' she asked.

Alex watched Emma and Bex walking towards her, both searching for her through the crowds of tourists queuing up for a tour of the cathedral. Emma was taller, fairer and skinnier than her sister. From a distance they looked nothing like sisters but they both had the same unforced smile that wrinkled the side of their nose and the laugh that guaranteed that whenever they went out for dinner together the next table would be asking to move by the end of the evening. They saw Alex and waved.

'Hi, Alex. Sorry to hear about what happened,' said Bex, hugging her.

'Thanks. Not sure I'm ready to say it's for the best but it probably is,' Alex replied.

'You bet it is. You can do so much better,' said Emma.

'Good to see you've finally got off the fence!' said Bex.

'Yeah well, he's a tosser and I'm glad Alex has finally realised it. I'm so relieved, to be honest.'

'So now's not the time to tell you we had an emotional reunion this morning and the wedding's back on?' said Alex.

'Really?' said Bex as Emma went white.

'No! I just wanted to see Emma's face. No, it's most definitely off and won't ever be back on, but it doesn't stop me feeling sorry for myself. I don't know what to do with myself. I haven't told Mum and Dad yet. You guys are the only people who know.'

'Hey, there's no rush. Take your time,' said Emma.

'Well, Mum has tried to get me twice this morning. I'm supposed to be going home this weekend and the invitations are due to go out next week, so I've got two days at the most before all hell breaks loose.'

'Do you want me to come home with you for moral support?' Emma asked.

'That's really sweet, Em, but no. I'll be fine. Think I'll phone my dad and warn him. He can book Mum in for some emergency crystal healing or something.'

Bex took the sandwich order and disappeared to a local deli, returning with their lunch.

'Tuna mayo for you, Em, and chicken salad for Alex.' She handed out the sandwiches and then joined them on the bench with a tiny pot of cereal and yogurt.

'So what's happening to the honeymoon then? Can we come with you instead?' Emma asked, taking a huge sideways bite of her sandwich.

'Gosh, I hadn't really thought about it. I need to

cancel the flights and try to get my money back, I suppose,' said Alex.

'Ah. I thought we could go off on a girls' holiday,' said Emma, still chewing.

'I don't fancy it, Em. Elliott and the band will probably still be going on the tour. It would be bad enough going on my honeymoon with my friends, but bumping into the ex-groom and his band would be a nightmare.'

'Fair point,' Emma replied.

'How's things with you guys? How come you're up our end of town, Bex?' Alex asked.

'Em's got me a gig with Olivia Meddoes. More like a hospital pass really,' Bex replied.

Emma added, 'She fired her make-up woman so I put Bex in the frame. She's been really twitchy lately. She's obsessed with the tabloids. She has one poor girl read all the red tops every morning and highlight anything remotely to do with her. The make-up girl's brother was a journalist so she got the boot.'

'I'm not sure I want to work for her but it'll look good on my CV and I'm not that busy at the moment. The hospital drama has finished and the cosmetic surgery thing is still in development.' Bex picked at her yogurt and granola.

'What is that shit you're eating?' asked Emma.

'I wasn't that hungry. Just fancied some yogurt,' said Bex.

'You're not on another stupid diet, are you? Honestly, Bex, just eat normally and do some exercise for a change,' said Emma.

'Easy for you to say when you're five foot nine and eight and a half stone wet through,' Bex retorted.

'Hey, guys, calm it down. Bex, you're beautiful, and Emma, give her a break.' Alex changed the subject as the sisters sulked. 'Is that cosmetic surgery show definitely on then? I mentioned it to Felicia so you're free to call her about it if you want. You need to get moving, though, 'cause I think she's booked in now to sort out her boobs.'

'Great, thanks, Alex. I'll call her. The broadcaster looks like it's going to commission the show but we still haven't sorted all the logistics yet. The producer's a bit scatty.'

Emma's ringtone started up. It was Olivia.

'Shit. I need to go. Sorry, guys.' Emma wiped sandwich from her face and swallowed her last mouthful before answering the phone. 'Olivia. I'm sorry, I was just on the other line,' she said as she walked off, waving to Alex and Bex.

'I'd better get going too,' Bex said, throwing her yogurt pot into the bin next to the bench. 'Are you going to be okay?'

'Of course. I'll be fine.'

They hugged each other and went their separate ways back to work.

When Alex got back to her desk there were several phone messages that Ross had taken for her. She worked through them one by one, returning the calls, until she got to her mum's message. It was something about the bay trees for the marquee. She closed her office door before phoning her dad.

'Hi, sweetheart. How nice to hear from you. I never speak to you nowadays. Your mother monopolises you.'

'Hi, Dad. Look, I don't know how to say this but I've got some bad news. The wedding's off.'

There was silence.

'Dad? Are you still there? Did you hear me?'

'Yes. What's he done?' he said slowly.

'Dad, it was me who called it off. It's a long story but it just isn't right.'

She filled him in on the honeymoon debacle and gave an edited version of Elliott's infidelities.

'I'm going to kill that bloody hippy.'

'Dad, watch your blood pressure. Look, please don't get upset. I just need you to know before I come home. It's Mum I'm worried about. She'll go spare.'

'Darling, she'll be distraught, but I can manage her. What about you? Are you sure you're okay? Do you want me to come and stay?' her dad asked.

Alex was touched but managed to persuade him she could cope until the weekend.

'I'm so sorry, Dad, about the wedding and everything. I thought maybe we could go to the hotel and explain everything on Saturday. Hopefully we'll only lose the deposit.'

'Alex, don't worry about the money. I took out wedding insurance anyway.'

'Oh. Did you?' Alex was a little offended. 'Didn't you think it would last then?'

'Put it this way, I always thought Elliott was a bit – what's that word you use? – flaky, isn't it?'

'Yeah,' she laughed.

'But I'll kill the little shit, though, if I ever get my hands on him. He didn't realise how lucky he was.'

'Well, Dad, maybe it's for the best, but please don't kill him. The band will only come after you. Look, are you going to tell Mum?'

'I'll sit her down with a sherry tonight and break it to her. No doubt she'll call Beryl for an emergency summit and I'll be able to watch Midsomer Murders.'

'Thanks, Dad.'

'Look, sweetheart, just you remember you're too good for him and you'll find someone else who deserves you. Now are you sure you're okay?'

'I'm just fine. I promise.'

'Well, you take care. I'll pick you up from the station Saturday morning.'

She hung up and sat at her desk with her head in her hands until Ross came back in the room.

'You okay?' he asked.

'Fine,' she said. 'Just mustering up the courage to call WW.'

'WW?'

'Yeah Warren Wickens, the Simon Cowell of the legal world. Although that's probably unfair to Simon Cowell.'

She made the call and had another unhelpful conversation. The concept of negotiation seemed to be lost on him.

'Look, if we can't agree anything over the phone we might as well wait until the meeting when both our clients are present. Then we can refer contentious points to them and get their instructions,' Alex said.

'You don't seem to understand that your client has changed the ground rules for this deal and my client needs to get real comfortable again before it will proceed. We need protections in the legal documents and without them this deal won't happen,' he countered.

'My client will give standard warranties and protections to yours about the business, but what you're proposing is extreme and unnecessary,' said Alex.

'You're right. Let's discuss this face to face. Monday, ten a.m., your time, at your offices. I'll see you then.'

She stared at the receiver, which was now emitting a loud dial tone, and then at Ross.

He laughed. 'Good call with Simon?'

'The equivalent of three no's, I think. I did not "nail it", "make it my own" or have the X factor,' she replied.

CHAPTER **18**

Alex leant her face against the train window and stared at the blurred trees and fields that sped past. It was always a wonder to her that there was real countryside so soon after the train left London. But it wasn't very long before the trees gave way to neat red-brick estates and then corrugated warehouses and distribution yards as they neared the station.

Her dad met her as promised and they drove in an awkward silence to the familiar 1930s semi that seemed to get smaller every time she visited. Her mother was waiting for her on the doorstep, looking like a distraught diva with her voluminous dress and pained expression.

'Darling! My poor darling! Come here.' She held out her freckled arms and hugged Alex and kissed her head.

'Hi, Mum,' Alex muttered from the depths of her mother's bosom. To her horror her mother started to sob.

'You poor thing. It's a nightmare. My worst

nightmare,' her mother said, taking her handkerchief from the depths of her dress and dabbing at her eyes. 'Oh Alex, what are we going to do?' She sobbed even more dramatically.

'Hey, hey. It'll all be okay. It's for the best, Mum,' said Alex, hugging her now and patting her gently on the back.

'For heaven's sake, Jean, get inside and stop making a show of yourself,' said her dad as he bundled them both into the house. 'What on earth will the neighbours think? Get a grip, woman. It's Alex who needs looking after, not you.'

Alex sat in the conservatory with tea and chocolate biscuits while her mum, the theatrics over and now keen on getting to the facts, gave her the third degree.

'So what did you say to him? Tell me exactly.'

Alex gave her the blow by blow account of her showdown with Elliott.

'And you are sure it's definitely over? We haven't cancelled the hotel yet, you know.'

'Mum, it's definitely over. There's no way I'm marrying him. I can't actually believe I was marrying him in the first place. I'm really, really sorry. I know how much you were looking forward to it.' Alex dunked her biscuit in her tea.

'Darling, I have to say it did come as a bit of a shock. My chakras were a bit unbalanced yesterday when your father told me. But if it isn't to be then it isn't to be. It's much better to change your mind now than in a year's time. Look at Beryl's Belinda. Divorced with a baby before she's thirty. That's not what I want for you.' Her mum smiled, slightly patronisingly.

'Thanks, Mum. You're right, but I know how much you wanted all this — you know, the wedding — and you'd have made it such a special day,' said Alex, fishing for bit of broken biscuit in her tea.

'Alex, I was carried away by the whole thing, I admit it. At the end of the day it's about your happiness. That's what matters. Though I have to say I was dying to see those unicorns. And I'll have to return at least one of my outfits.'

'Fancy a top up?' Her dad came in with the teapot.

'No thanks, I've had plenty.' Alex put her hand over the top of her teacup.

'Do you fancy a ride out in a bit? I thought we could go and have a word with the hotel. Don't worry if you're not up to it. I can go by myself,' her dad said.

'Yeah. Good idea, Dad. I'll come along,' said Alex, thankful for the opportunity to get away from her surprisingly sympathetic mother.

'Yes, you do that. I'll call the florists and the unicorn man,' her mother said. 'And then I'll make us a casserole for tonight.'

As Alex and her father pulled up outside the hotel a bride and groom were posing next to a vintage car for their photographer. Her dad looked at Alex.

'Are you sure you want to do this now?' he asked quietly.

'Yes. No time like the present.' She grabbed her handbag and opened the car door.

They walked into the hotel and took the familiar corridor to the hospitality office. The bridesmaids from the wedding party were in front of them, searching for the toilets. Alex couldn't help analysing their lilac empire line dresses and making a note to self that the one-style-fits-all approach to bridesmaids' dresses didn't work, especially when, like this lot, one of them was a flat-chested stick, one was a voluptuous size eighteen and one was Amazonian.

Her dad was explaining to the events lady that the wedding wouldn't be taking place.

'So you see, we're terribly sorry but we'll have to cancel,' he said in his best telephone voice.

The girl failed to keep the gleam of excitement from her eyes as she filled in the cancellation form. She'd clearly never had to do it before.

'I'm so sorry,' she said, looking at Alex. 'A friend of mine was jilted. It took her ages to recover. She moved to Australia in the end.'

Alex smiled weakly. Christ, she was like a vulture on speed.

'What will you do with your dress?' the girl asked.

'I'll probably wear it every year on our anniversary. Look, Dad, I think I'll wait for you in reception,' Alex said.

'Ooh, I'm sorry if I upset her,' Alex heard the girl say to her dad as she walked slowly back to the hotel reception.

She sat on one of the sofas by the check-in desk, watching the wedding party milling around while the photos were being taken. An orange girl in a black bandeau style mini dress and a bright red fascinator was giving her boyfriend an ear bashing.

'Shelley is eighteen months younger than me and she's only been with Steve for two years. We've been together for nearly four years now and I haven't got a ring. Christmas: that's your deadline, Daryl, or I'm off.' The girl knocked back what was clearly not her first glass of champagne.

Alex smiled to herself. That was another mistake she wouldn't make again. She'd badgered Elliott into getting engaged and then married. He hadn't stood a chance.

Eventually her dad reappeared. 'Come on, love. That's all sorted. Let's go and get a pub lunch.'

He escorted her to the car, opening the door for her to get in. He walked round to the driver's side and settled himself in.

'The Bull's Head does a good lunch. Let's go there for a treat.' He smiled at her and put his hand on hers. 'I'm sorry about that stupid girl. I put her in her place, I can tell you. I told her you'd had a better offer and dumped Elliott. You should've seen her face.'

It was a traditional pub with a thatched roof and tables with umbrellas outside. Her dad directed her to the beer garden, which looked onto a bowling green where two elderly couples dressed head to toe in white were playing a match. She sat down and watched the bowls until her father returned with their drinks and the menus.

'Looks like a serious game,' he said.

'You bet. That blonde woman with the bright pink lipstick takes no prisoners.'

They sat and watched the game for a few minutes until her dad coughed and then spoke.

'Look, Alex, I'm not one to get all soppy but I just want you to know that your mum and I are very proud of you. I know you think all we wanted was for you to get married and have babies but that's not the case. To be honest, we're both a bit worried that we pressurised you into it when you weren't ready.' He sipped his shandy.

'Dad, it wasn't you, honest,' she said.

'Let me finish, love. I just want you to know that we've been constantly amazed by what you've achieved. We don't know much about what you do really, but to make your way as a lawyer in the City when we haven't pushed you and we don't know the first thing about the law – that's something, Alex. You've done it all on your own and we're very proud of you. Your mum especially. I think she's almost jealous in a way and wishes she'd done more with her career.

'And as for Elliott, well, to be honest I never thought he was good enough for you. But then I'm your dad and I don't suppose anyone ever will be in my eyes. You're young, you're beautiful. You've got everything going for you. For what it's worth, I'm sure you're doing the right thing. Marriage is a serious business, believe me. You've got to be sure. You've got your whole life in front of you.'

'Thanks, Dad. I think you're a bit biased, though.' She smiled and kissed him on the cheek.

'Maybe a bit. But I mean it.' He smiled back. 'Right, what are you having? Think I'll have the ploughman's.' The pep talk was over.

She smiled as he busied himself placing their order

and picking up the cutlery. She was touched. It was the longest speech he'd made to her since the 'I know what fourteen-year-old boys are like because I used to be one' lecture many years ago.

Alex spent the afternoon with her mother going through the wedding file, calling caterers, stationers, tea-light suppliers, florists and most importantly Beryl. With the exception of Beryl, they all took it in their stride. Alex was amazed how easy it was to cancel something that had taken over so much of her life and with which her mother had been obsessed for the past six months. Her mother spent at least an hour comforting Beryl, who seemed to have taken the news worse than anyone, if only because she wished her own daughter had had the cojones to cancel her own wedding before she'd saddled herself with that 'bloody philanderer who couldn't even change a light bulb'.

The next morning Alex was up early and joined her parents for the traditional Fisher Sunday breakfast of croissants, orange juice and crispy bacon at the kitchen table. The Sunday papers were piled up and her dad was methodically checking the sports section of each publication for the golf scores. Alex nibbled her croissant while flicking through one of the broadsheets. Her mum had commandeered the tabloids and was busy reading all the trashy celebrity gossip, punctuated by her running commentary and opinion.

'Listen to this one, Alex: My three in a bed romp with rock star bad boy. Mark my words, that's where Elliott's heading. It won't bring him happiness, you know.'

Alex tried not to choke on her croissant as she caught her dad's eye.

'Ooh, I don't know,' her dad said.

'John!' Her mum reprimanded. She turned the page and continued, 'And here's another girl been fired from one of the soaps. It says here she had so much time off as a result of cosmetic surgery she kept missing her scenes. I would never have thought she wasn't real,' she said, peering at the picture of the young actress.

'Mum, just because she's had a bit of work done doesn't mean she's not real.'

'Well, all I know is that she isn't as nature intended,' her mum replied.

'Yeah well, neither is Uncle Maurice. His kidney came from some poor sod who died in a car accident but you don't give him a hard time,' said Alex.

'That's totally different and you know it. These people are choosing to mess with themselves. It's not natural.'

'I think they're just being open to using technology to make the best of themselves. It's very common now, you know.'

'Yes and so are tattoos, but it doesn't make them right. And since when have you become the authority on plastic surgery, Alex? You're not thinking of having anything done, are you?' Her mother asked the question in a manner that suggested Alex was thinking of joining a devil worshipping cult.

'It's just a deal I'm working on, that's all. We're selling a cosmetic surgery business. All I know is that there seems to be a lot of demand for what they do,' she replied.

'Well, this poor girl has spent more than ten thousand pounds on a breast augmentation, liposuction and some filler thing I can't pronounce. What's that then?' her mother showed the article to Alex.

Alex froze when she saw Gemma Kirk's name again. According to the article the actress in question had gone to the Beau Street surgery on the recommendation of her great friend and colleague Gemma Kirk, and she'd had numerous procedures there over several months.

'It's the product name for an injectable filler, Mum. Excuse me,' said Alex, scraping back her chair. 'Can I borrow this?'

She ran upstairs carrying the paper and closed her bedroom door behind her. She needed to call Tom.

'Tom? It's Alex Fisher. I'm so sorry to bother you on a Sunday but have you seen the *Sunday Journal*?'

'Alex? What is it?' a voice like Barry White responded. 'I was, er, asleep.'

'I'm really sorry, Tom. I forgot it was still early but I saw this article and I panicked.'

'Okay, okay, bear with me. Speak slowly and not too loudly. I was at a friend's fiftieth last night and I'm feeling a bit fragile.'

'Okay, sorry. Well, there's an article about Sarah Bellamy, the soap actress — you might have heard of her? Anyway, she's supposedly had ten grand's worth of treatment at Beau Street and has been sacked from the soap she stars in for taking too much time off work.'

'And that's it? Is there anything derogatory about us?' he asked.

'No. But Tom, it means someone is still leaking stuff to the papers. It's not great for client confidentiality. No one with a profile is going to come to Beau Street if details of what they've had done are going to end up all over the papers. And what if they leak the story about Felicia and the state of her boobs? Then they'll make Beau Street look like cowboys.'

'I know, Alex. Mmm, it's funny how we've not read about Felicia yet. But if it was her doing the leaking, we wouldn't, would we?' he croaked.

'Tom, why would she do that? You've reached a deal with her, haven't you?'

'I know, but she's very manipulative. I just get the impression that she's desperate to make money and might not be too bothered how she does it.'

'I don't think so. It's more likely to be Lloyd,' said Alex.

'But haven't we got some injunction against him, or are you telling me that isn't worth the paper it's written on?'

'I know. It seems unlikely it's him. But who else could it be?'

'I've no idea. No one else knows Cassidy's client list except that Chris chap who works with you, the accountants and of course Audrey Fox.'

'Could it be her?'

'I suppose so. But what's in it for her?' he said.

'Cash? Loyalty to Cassidy? Isn't she supposed to be very close to Cassidy, if you know what I mean? If he's not allowed to leak because of the injunction there's nothing to stop her.'

'Except ethics and professionalism, Alex.'

'And what about the theatrical agent that works for Felicia? She said lots of Cassidy's clients came through the agency. They'd know about a lot of the work being done. They'd have to schedule their clients' work around the surgery.' Alex was clutching at straws.

'Look, Alex, I don't know, but we need to stop it if we can. I'll have a conversation with Cassidy, Audrey and Felicia. In the meantime can you look into the agency angle and maybe send them some sort of scary legal letter. The best thing we can do is get this deal done and dusted as soon as possible. I'll see you in the morning at the meeting. Perhaps we could have an hour together first?' he suggested.

'Okay, Tom. Good plan. Hope you feel better.'

'Nothing a good rest and a few pints of water can't sort. I'll see you tomorrow.'

Alex made her excuses and left her parents after breakfast, despite their protestations, and spent most of the afternoon removing every trace of Elliott from the house. Four boxes, two guitar cases and three bin bags later she was done. Taking down the framed album covers and tour posters from the walls had been satisfactorily cathartic. She decided she needed to give her house a makeover and, as she removed the last pair of jeans from his wardrobe, she realised she had lots of hanging space to fill. She needed some retail therapy with Emma very soon.

That evening she spent several hours drafting a letter to the theatrical agency and reviewing the sale and purchase documents. She was determined to hold her own against Warren Wickens and to show Tom that she could nail down the deal for him.

CHAPTER 19

It was before eight in the morning and Alex, Dan and Ross were gathered in Alex's office, discussing the game plan for the meeting.

'Tom should be here any minute now and then we'll take him through the documents and get a feel for what issues are non-negotiable for him and in which areas we can concede points. Wickens isn't going to be a pushover and the whole Cassidy fiasco puts us in a weaker bargaining position,' Alex was saying. 'The main issues, as I see them, are that we need to get the sale monies through when we sign the deal and without them holding any of it back, we need to avoid giving too much comfort on the Cassidy problems and we need to make sure there's no long gap between exchange and completion, when they can wriggle out. Any other issues we should be worried about, guys?'

'Well, Equinox seem to be keen to rebrand the business and lose the Beau Street name. We should check with Tom whether he cares about that,' said Dan.

'Okay. Though with all the leaks to the press at the moment it might not be a bad idea to rebrand the business,' muttered Alex.

'I know but we need to make sure that they'll still pay a full price for the goodwill attached to the current brand,' said Dan. 'A certain amount of their valuation of the business will relate to what the Beau Street name is worth in the marketplace,' he explained to Ross.

'Dan, do you know anything about this Wickens guy? I don't know if Ross has mentioned him to you but so far he's been a nightmare to deal with,' said Alex.

'One of my sister's college friends works at Beckmann, Grossberg, Fitzpatrick and Hale in New York. I could speak with her.'

Alex's phone rang. Tom had arrived.

They trooped to reception to collect Tom and then all took the lift to the meeting rooms on the top floor. They'd been assigned the corner room, which was the most impressive. Alex had been conscious she had a New York hot shot to impress. After sorting the coffee order they got down to business.

'Okay, Tom, I suggest we turn pages on the agreement and I flag up areas of concern, either where we have an issue with what they've drafted or where we want to insert something new. Then we can draw up a list of key issues for the negotiation. There'll be issues that will be non-negotiable but there'll be others that we're more relaxed about and that we can concede if necessary so that we don't have to move our position on the deal breakers.'

'Sounds like a sensible strategy,' Tom agreed.

The four of them turned each page of the thick document and at each point where Alex had made notes they discussed the implications for Beau Street if they agreed to the drafting. Where Tom wasn't happy or where something was a deal breaker Ross made a note. He also made a note of the all the issues they were prepared to trade if they had to. They were just finishing the exercise as Ross took the call to announce that the Equinox team had arrived. Alex stood up.

She took the lift down to reception, appraising herself in the mirror as she went. She'd worn a black shift dress with a stripy fitted shirt underneath and had secured her hair in a half up, half down style. She started to suck nervously on the end of the pen she was carrying, suddenly panicking, as the lift doors started to open, that she might have ink on her mouth. She wiped her mouth frantically with the back of her hand before turning to greet the US team.

'Good morning, gentlemen,' she began.

'Ah, good morning. I'm Warren Wickens and this is my client, Ryan Miller. We're here to meet Alex Fisher and her client.'

'I'm Alex Fisher.' She extended her hand towards the American.

'Really?' Wickens said, looking her up and down.

'Really. Pleased to meet you at last, Warren, and you too, Mr Miller. If you'd like to follow me to the meeting room.'

She led them to the lift where they stood in silence. She sneaked a glance at Wickens. He was slightly on the short side but good looking, with dark hair showing hints of silver at the temples, olive skin and a heavy brow. He was extremely well groomed in an understated but expensive suit, shiny black loafers and striped shirt. He had a discreet gold tie pin and she was sure he would have a set of braces on under his jacket. Ryan was in his late thirties, tanned and quite athletic looking. He was self-assured without the cocky edge of his lawyer. The lift reached the top floor and she held the door as they got out.

'You have ink on your mouth,' Wickens said loudly as they walked to the meeting room.

'Thanks,' she said, rubbing at her mouth again.

Alex introduced everyone. Tom and Ryan had met before and were already talking together. She heard Cassidy's name and something about the fall in turnover. Shit. This Cassidy issue was hanging like a cloud over the whole transaction. She had to steer the conversation away from it otherwise Wickens would use it to undermine their position on every aspect of the deal.

'I'd like an espresso, no sugar,' said Wickens, looking at Alex.

Yeah, would you? she thought. Then get your silky lawyer's ass to Starbucks.

'I'll call catering,' she said, reaching for the buzzer to summon someone.

After the refreshments arrived they arranged themselves around the oval table with Wickens and Ryan facing Tom and his lawyers. The US lawyer removed his jacket as he sat down and hung it fastidiously on the back of his chair, revealing a set of red braces. Alex almost laughed out loud.

'Okay, Ms Fisher, perhaps you could talk us through the agenda for today,' he said.

'Of course. I think the priority for us today is to make some progress on the sale and purchase agreement. I suggest we thrash out the issues on that and then later if we have time we can look at the other documents.'

'I agree. But rather than turning pages we need to deal with the big points up front. There are some key issues that my client would like to deal with first,' he said.

'I'm sure that would work for us too. Tom, are you happy with that approach?' She turned to Tom.

He smiled back at her. 'Of course,' he said.

She could sense he was uneasy now. Sometimes she forgot that even for the most confident and urbane of clients, these kinds of meetings weren't their day job. She smiled back at him in what she hoped was a reassuring way.

'Great. That's agreed. We have at least three major issues we'd like to table,' she continued.

Tom leant towards her and whispered, 'You've got ink on your mouth.'

Predictably, Ryan and Wickens opened the discussion with the Lloyd Cassidy issue.

'There are several issues that are causing us concern,' started Ryan. 'First there's the fact that a fraudulent covert practice was able to function within the business without being detected. Then there's the lack of confidentiality. Our UK PR guys are telling us that there have been several stories in the press recently that have been leaked from the business. Then there's the hit on the revenues. The finance guys reckon the figures in the business plan could be out by up to half a million dollars.'

'First, can I just say that the issue with Dr Cassidy has been disclosed promptly and in full to you and no one is denying it's a big shock to everyone,' said Alex.

'Not least me,' Tom interjected. 'That slimeball founded the business with Charles Sutton. I'm afraid he was always attracted to the glamour side of the business and courted the celebrity client base. Unfortunately he got greedy too. No one's suggesting he's been doing this from the start, but Ryan, you've seen the size of our operation. It's a big place. I'm not making any excuses but the man took advantage of his position. We're not the first and we won't be the last business this kind of thing happens to. The good news is that the lawyers and accountants found out about it. As for the revenue, Ryan, we're interviewing several doctors at the moment who have their own practices they could bring with them.'

'Has Cassidy been fired yet?' Wickens interrupted.

'He's been dismissed. It seems that not only was he running his own unregulated practice but that he was defrauding the business by skimming monies off the top. Now, let's move on, shall we,' said Alex.

'But Ms Fisher, that's the whole point. The Cassidy problem clouds everything. It comes down to trust. How can my client trust yours when an issue as big as this can come onto the table a few weeks before they're due to sign the deal?' said Wickens.

The debate went round in circles for most of the morning. Every time Alex tried to get them to focus on the agreement Wickens waved his ruler at her and rambled on about Cassidy.

They decided to break for lunch. Ross went to sort out the sandwiches with the kitchen and Tom and Ryan went for a comfort break.

'Do you have any sushi?' Wickens asked, pointing his ruler towards Alex.

'Er, we were planning on a sandwich lunch, Warren,' said Alex.

'I'm wheat intolerant. Could you get me some sushi?' he asked again.

'Well, we'll see what we can do,' she said through gritted teeth. 'Dan, perhaps you could come with me.'

They left the room together.

'What an asshole,' said Dan. 'If he waves that ruler again I'll snap it.'

'Look, can you get one of the trainees to run down to the sushi place round the corner? I'll see how Ross is getting on with the caterers. He's been gone for ages now.'

'Are you okay, Alex?' Dan asked.

'Yeah, I'm fine. I've dealt with worse than Mr Wickens,' she said, thinking that actually she probably hadn't.

If the morning had been bad then the afternoon proved to be an unmitigated disaster. Warren pronounced his sushi to be the worst he'd ever had, even by European standards. Ryan and Tom seemed to make some informal progress over lunch, but as soon as everyone resumed the formal meeting they took three steps back for the two steps forward they'd made.

Every time Alex attempted to win a point for Beau Street Wickens demanded she make a concession. Once she'd conceded a point he then moved the goalposts on the original point they'd been discussing. By mid afternoon Beau Street had conceded almost all the points on Ross's list of issues they were happy to give up and only secured one of the three deal breakers that were essential for them. Alex felt like she was going into battle with no ammunition. She had nothing left to trade with.

Wickens, on the other hand, was clearly enjoying himself. He'd started to pace the room during the negotiations, still holding his ruler and occasionally threading it through his braces with one hand and retrieving it with the other.

It was Tom who eventually called for a break. 'Look, Ryan, Warren, would you mind if we stopped for a coffee and maybe Alex, you and I, and Ross and Dan of course, could have five minutes on our own?'

'That's cool,' said Ryan. 'I'd like to talk to Warren as well.'

'Okay. I suggest we move to the meeting room next door and you and Warren stay here,' said Alex. 'I'll get someone to come and take your drinks order.' She got up from the table and followed Tom and the others out of the room.

'Look, Alex, I'm no lawyer but that didn't seem to go too well in there,' said Tom.

'Tom, I'm sorry, you're right. He's a slippery

customer and he's using the whole Cassidy thing to spook Ryan and to undermine every point we make,' she said.

'I think he's up to something,' said Dan.

'What do you mean?' asked Alex.

'Well, I just don't trust him,' Dan muttered.

'Look, we have two more key issues we need to nail. Do you think we can do that tonight or do you think we should park them for another day?' said Tom.

'I think we should leave the sale and purchase agreement for today. We've got plenty of other issues to discuss, such as your employment contract, Tom. Your contract will be the template for Stella, Charles Sutton and the other doctors on the management team. It's also less contentious. I suggest we spend some time on that,' she said.

Warren didn't like the idea when they floated it. He was on a roll and he knew it. However, for once his client overruled him and he sulkily agreed to look at the other contracts. Although they were much less contentious, Wickens made it hard going. In Alex's experience lawyers fell into two categories: some were keen to get the deal done and draft the wording at a later stage; others were anal about every last bit of wording, down to the grammar and the punctuation. Wickens fell into the second category. He underlined every point he wasn't happy with in red ink and argued about every bit of drafting. Somehow he managed to debate the positioning of a semi-colon for twenty minutes, costing his client two hundred and fifty dollars of his time in the process.

Alex hoped she'd performed better later in the day. She was well aware she hadn't exactly covered herself in glory earlier. It was getting late now and both clients were starting to look at their watches. It was Ryan who broke first.

'Okay, guys, I think I can feel the jet lag kicking in. Warren, can we quit for the day?' he said.

'Well, Ryan, there's still plenty of work to be done on these agreements and there's still some distance between us on the sale contract.'

'Warren, I'm done. We need to finish this another time. Maybe you and Alex can progress things the next couple of days. I've got back-to-back meetings tomorrow with the bankers and then with Charles, Tom and the guys from Beau Street Wednesday. We could all get together on Thursday if people can do that?' Ryan looked around the room.

The thought of two days dealing one to one with Warren didn't appeal to Alex.

'I'm tied up with Brenda tomorrow,' said Warren.

'Brenda Martinez is Equinox's in-house lawyer,' Tom explained to Alex. 'As Ryan said, we're meeting on Wednesday and I have the interviews for our in-house legal position tomorrow. Thursday is good for me. Can you do that, Alex?'

'Absolutely. Shall we say nine a.m. here on Thursday, and in the meantime perhaps Warren can arrange for a revised set of documents to be circulated.'

'Sure. I'll get our London people to sort that,' Warren said as he put on his jacket and brushed it down.

Ryan and Warren left and the rest of them visibly relaxed.

'Was it me or was that hard going?' asked Ross.

'It was. Please excuse my language, Tom, but that Wickens guy is an A1 asshole, as I believe his fellow countrymen would call him. We know the Cassidy issue is a problem but we've told them everything about it, we've sacked the guy and we're looking at ways to fill the revenue hole. Tom, I think it's very likely the price will be chipped at but it shouldn't affect every clause of every contract. Wickens is trying to paint us as some kind of sneaky, back street, off-the-back-of-a-lorry kind of operation,' said Alex.

'Look, don't worry, Alex. Ryan seems more relaxed about it. I'll talk to him tomorrow,' Tom replied. 'Do any of you fancy a drink?'

'Count me in,' said Dan.

'Me too,' said Ross.

'Okay, you twisted my arm,' smiled Alex. 'I'll meet you all downstairs in five. Dan, could you show Tom back downstairs to reception.'

Alex raced back to her desk, ignoring the flashing light indicating zillions of voicemail messages, and grabbed her handbag from under her desk. She saw handwritten messages on her desk from her secretary. Bex and Emma had both called. So had Elliott. She sighed and sat down. She'd wondered how long it would take for him to get in touch. He hadn't been home since the Scout hut showdown, no doubt kipping on a band mate's floor. She called him and got through to his message system. It was seven o'clock. He was probably gigging somewhere.

She went to the toilets to reapply her make-up and noticed the blue ink still smeared across her top lip. Great! Not only had she taken a kicking from Wickens but she'd looked a muppet in the process.

She took the lift down with Ross and found Dan and Tom already chatting in reception. They stopped talking as they arrived. Was it her or did they look uneasy?

'Okay, where do you suggest? I'm a stranger in these parts,' said Tom.

'Bar Q,' they all said in unison and then laughed.

As they arrived at the waterfront Alex's phone rang. It was Bex.

'Do you mind if I take this?' she asked Tom.

'Not at all. What shall I get you?' he asked.

'A glass of white wine, please,' Alex asked. She answered the phone and stood outside the bar as the men filed in.

'Hi, Bex. You okay?' she said.

'Yeah, great. Sorry to hassle you, Alex, but I need to speak to you about this TV show — you know, the cosmetic surgery one. It's really taking off.'

'Er, okay. But why me?'

'Well, that Felicia woman is really hot to trot. Her agent thinks it's a fab idea. Great way to relaunch her, apparently. Anyway, it's all racing ahead and with all your contacts I thought you might be able to help. We might need to talk to that Rob guy. We don't even have a surgeon lined up. Can we meet up?'

'Sure. Not sure I'll be much help, though. When were you thinking of?' she asked.

'Don't suppose you could do a quick meeting tomorrow? I know it's short notice. I've been trying to track you down all day.'

Shit, thought Alex. She had so much stuff on the deal to do.

'What time and where?'

'About three? We could come to you if that helps?'

'Okay. I'll make it a late lunch but I can only spare an hour. Could you meet at Bar Q? Not sure I can wangle a meeting room at work for this one.'

'Yeah, sure. It'll be me, Felicia and the producer,' said Bex.

'Do you want me to call Rob for you?' Alex asked. 'You never know, he might be able to make the meeting.'

'Ah would you? That would be fantastic. You're a star.'

'No probs. See you then.'

CHAPTER 20

Alex was late for work. She half-ran half-walked from the tube, trying not to trip in her pencil skirt and heels. She put her face up to the sun to feel its warmth before entering the office and came perilously close to tripping over a sandwich board outside a coffee shop. As she composed herself she almost bumped into Truman.

'Ah, good morning, Alex,' he boomed, rearranging his combover.

'Morning, Truman,' she said, wondering why she only came across him when she was late.

'How's the deal? Must be almost there by now,' he said, clearly not expecting an answer as he strode off and hailed a cab.

I wish, she thought.

It was another day on Project Pout. By three she'd already had two difficult calls with Wickens in which he tried to unravel some of the deal agreed on the previous day because he'd now had the chance to speak to Brenda Martinez, the lawyer at Equinox.

'I'd assumed you already had your client's instructions seeing as Ryan Miller was in the meeting with us,' she'd told him.

The way he'd talked about Brenda it was clear he had her on some kind of pedestal. Alex realised he was scared of her. She filed that fact away. It would be useful at the next meeting and she might be able to use it to her advantage.

At just before three she left the office, telling Ross she was going to grab a sandwich and some fresh air. She'd just taken a call from the STD clinic. Her results were clear, so she was feeling a lot more positive than she had for a few days when she opened the door to Bar Q. Bex and her group were already there. The smell of stale beer hit her as she walked past the bar to their table. Why did the place smell so different in the daytime, she wondered?

'Hi,' said Bex, standing up. 'This is Ben, the producer,' she gestured towards a tall, slim, twenty-something man in a loose-fitting t-shirt, baggy jeans and baseball boots.

Very media, Alex thought.

'And Felicia you already know, I believe.'

'Hi, Ben. Hi, Felicia. How's things?' she asked.

They made small talk while Alex ordered a sandwich. No one else was eating.

'The good news is that I've spoken to Rob Sweeney and he's hoping to join us,' said Alex.

'That's great,' said Ben.

He went on to describe the format of the show. As Bex had said, it was a makeover show for former celebrities that would involve cosmetic surgery of some sort.

'It's not going to be seedy or unrealistic. It's not one of those extreme makeover type shows but more subtle than that. It will almost be a documentary series showing how good surgery can positively improve someone's looks and prospects,' Ben explained.

Yeah right, thought Alex. But Felicia and Bex were nodding along and had clearly bought it.

'The gaps in the plan at the moment are the surgeon and the clinic. Ideally we'll find a clinic that wants the free publicity and a TV-friendly surgeon who works there. At the moment we've found a clinic but none of their surgeons are up for it. We already have our first celebrity,' he said, smiling at Felicia. 'And Felicia's agency seems confident there will be plenty more of its clients who'd be keen to take part.'

As he spoke Alex watched Rob glide in, his white veneers already fixed in a smile. He would be so perfect for TV.

'Ben, Bex, Felicia, this is Rob,' she said, standing up as he approached.

'Hi, everyone. Lovely to meet you,' he said, shaking all their hands.

In less than ten minutes he'd charmed the pants off everyone. Alex had to hand it to him: his bedside manner was impressive.

'So how do we get you to sign up for it? Do you think your clinic would let us film there?' Ben was already asking.

'Well, that's the only teeny fly in the ointment.

They seem to have a bit of a problem with it. You see, it's a very small clinic and they seem to think that having your cameras and crew and entourage would disrupt the day to day operation. But believe me, I'm working on them. They're a bunch of dinosaurs really. They don't understand the media age we live in,' Rob said.

They don't understand the size of your ego more like, Alex thought.

Suddenly she had an idea. 'Rob, have you ever considered moving practices?' she asked.

'Well, obviously I've been headhunted from time to time, but I'm very loyal, you know,' he said.

'Look, excuse me, guys, but would you mind if I had a chat with Rob in private?' she asked.

Alex ushered Rob outside and they sat at one of the tables overlooking the Thames.

'Look, Rob, I don't know if Tom Duffy has been in touch but they need a new surgeon at Beau Street. It could be right up your street. The only issue is whether they'd be up for the filming side of it, but it's an enormous building; I'm sure they could ring fence an area where the cameras couldn't go to keep normal clients away from the media circus,' Alex said.

Rob's eyes lit up. 'Wow, that would be fantastic, Alex. Look, I really want this gig. I'd be great at it, I know I would. The publicity would be fantastic.'

'For you or the practice?' she asked, smiling.

'Both,' he smiled back.

'Look, leave it with me. I'll talk to Tom and see if he'd be interested in principle. Don't call him yet. Okay?'

'Yeah sure, Alex, whatever you say,' he replied. 'Oh and thanks, I owe you this time.'

They rejoined the others inside.

'Look, guys, there's a chance that I may be able to deliver you Rob and the clinic, but you need to leave it with me for a few days,' said Alex.

'If you could that would be fantastic,' said Ben. 'Here's my card.'

As Alex took the card Ben, Bex and Rob got up to leave.

'Let's leave you to your lunch!' Ben said, pointing at Alex's untouched sandwich.

They said their goodbyes and Alex found herself left with Felicia while she stuffed down her late lunch.

'Look, Alex, I just wanted to thank you for your help with Beau Street.'

'Not at all,' she said through a mouthful of cheese and pickle.

'If the show goes ahead I want you to know I won't cause any trouble for Beau Street.'

'That's good to know.'

'Look, you know these leaks to the papers? Tom phoned me about them and I swear it isn't me,' she said, appealing to Alex.

'Felicia,' Alex said, wiping her mouth with her napkin, 'I never thought they were. I guess it must be Cassidy.'

'Yeah, but I don't think it's him either. Why would it be?'

'Don't you know he's been sacked? He's in big trouble with the General Medical Council too.'

'Tom did mention something. But Alex, he'll resurface somewhere eventually. He's a clever guy. Why would he make things worse for himself? Clients won't want to go to him again if they think he's indiscreet. That Audrey woman says he's fuming about it.'

'You've spoken to Audrey Fox?' Alex asked. Bloody hell, what was Felicia up to?

'Well, yes. Look, I didn't want my name blackened by all this. I wanted to find out if it was Cassidy. He's caused me enough grief without dragging me into his media expose. To be honest, I thought he might spill the beans on me to the papers and that could ruin my chances of doing this TV show.'

'Okay. Fair point. So what did she say?'

'She said Cassidy was incandescent. Not only had he been kicked out of Beau Street but his precious private practice was threatened by whoever was doing the leaking. I don't think for a minute it's either of them.'

'So who the hell is it?'

'Audrey said she thought it was someone with a grudge. She wouldn't say who.'

'So she has her suspicions, does she?' said Alex.

'It seemed like it.'

'Well, I think I might have a word with her. Better still, I'll send in Dan to see her.'

'Good plan. He's really good looking, that Dan guy. Probably a bit young for me, though,' Felicia said wistfully.

'I don't know. Cougars are all the rage now,' said Alex.

Back at the office Alex found Dan waiting for her with Ross.

'The very man,' she said as she walked in.

'Really?'

'Yeah. I've just had a very interesting chat with Felicia Monroe.'

Alex filled Ross and Dan in on Felicia's theory.

'I think you need to speak to Audrey and find out who she thinks is the mole.'

'Okay. I'll do my best. Is tomorrow okay now?' he asked.

'Sure. Okay, so what brings you here? I thought you said you were spending the day at Beau Street?' she asked as she sat down at her desk.

'Mr Wickens,' he said.

'My favourite person,' said Alex.

'The very same. I spoke to my sister's friend, Gina. She didn't seem to like him much.'

'Who could?' said Ross.

'It seems he was trained by a certain Brenda Martinez. She used to be a partner at Beckmann, Grossberg, Fitzpatrick and Hale.'

'Ah that figures,' said Alex to herself.

'According to Gina he was made a partner because he pulled in Equinox as a client after Brenda left to go and work there. They're his biggest client and he's really precious about them. He won't let any other lawyer work on the account. He's desperate not to lose them and he doesn't want anyone poaching them from under his nose.'

'Yeah and he won't want to cock up on any of their

jobs in case they fire him. No wonder he's so scared of Brenda, even if she is a woman,' added Alex.

'Yeah, he's a bit of a misogynist, isn't he?' said Dan.

'He asked me who you'd slept with, Alex, to make associate,' said Ross.

'You're kidding! The creep!' Alex shrieked.

'Oops, sorry. Probably shouldn't have repeated that,' said Ross.

'No, you did the right thing. I'll be even more fired up when I next see him,' she said.

'Anyway, the conclusion is that he's an insecure guy desperate to hang onto his client. No one at the firm likes him much, according to Gina. She said he wasn't to be trusted,' Dan said.

'Well, I didn't expect her to describe him as Mother Teresa but that's pretty damning, especially from a colleague,' Alex commented.

As Dan and Ross left to get a coffee, Alex's phone rang. It was Elliott.

'Hello, Elliott,' she said, waving to Dan to close the door behind him and Ross.

'Hi, Alex. How are you?' he asked.

'Fine in the circumstances. At least the STD results were clear. And you?' she asked, her voice faltering slightly.

'I'm okay, I suppose. Missing you. Look, I'm sorry about everything, Alex.'

'You and me both. You know, I don't think the wedding was a good idea, really. I'm sorry if I pressured you into it in any way,' she said.

'Why are you being so nice? I'm the one who threw it all away. I was a total idiot,' he said.

'Yeah, you were, but maybe you did us both a favour.'

'Do you think so? So you really think there's no hope for us?'

'No, Elliott. No hope whatsoever.'

'I had to ask. We were good together for a long time, you know.'

'I know, Elliott, but we just didn't know how to bring it to an end and we both want different things and different people. I'm not going to change for you and you're not going to change for me.'

There was a silence for a moment.

'I know there were others, Elliott. You swore there was only the one. You lied, big time.'

'What do you mean?'

'Other girls. I found loads of numbers in the Chinese jar. You didn't even hide it very well.'

'Shit.'

'Elliott? Are you still there?' she asked.

'Yes. What can I say, Alex? I'm so sorry. Again.'

'Look, it's over now. I've done my screaming and shouting. But one top tip, Elliott. Get the whole shagging a groupie thing out of your system before you settle down with someone else.'

'You're right. To be honest it was an unimpressive collection of groupies. I was hardly Mick Jagger. Definitely single figures.'

'Spare me the details, please. Look, Elliott, I'm at work and a colleague is waiting for me.' She could see Ross and Dan at the door with the coffee cups. 'I need to go. I've packed up all your stuff. You can come and get it whenever suits and then leave your key.'

'Okay, will do. Look, Alex, about the plane tickets.'

'I'm going to cancel them and try to get my money back,' she said.

'Well, I was going to suggest I bought them off you. I was always going to pay you back. I promise.'

'Okay,' she said, surprised.

'I'll leave you a cheque for half of it when I pick up my stuff. The boys have had a whip round. I'll give you the balance in a couple of months, if that's okay. You might want to cancel the hotel, though. I'm not sure the band will want to squeeze into the honeymoon suite at a five-star hotel.'

'Ooh, I don't know. It's very rock and roll,' she replied.

'I think it'll be a local B and B for us. Look, Alex, thanks for being so amazing.'

'You don't deserve it.'

'I know,' he replied.

As she hung up she signalled for Ross and Dan to come back in. She was surprised at how calm she felt.

'Sorry about that,' she said. 'Okay, so how are we fixed for Thursday's meeting?'

'Well, Wickens has just sent out re-drafts of all the agreements,' said Dan.

'Yeah. I saw the email.'

'The main problem is the Cassidy thing. He's using it to knock us down on every single point,' said Dan.

'Well, it's good ammunition and he knows it,' said Alex. 'What we need is a counterattack.'

'Yeah,' said Dan thoughtfully.

'I could break his ruler,' suggested Ross.

Alex decided to tell Dan and Ross about the reality show idea and the meeting with Bex and the others.

'It might not come to anything, but if we can get Rob on board then that's one more doctor bringing in the cash,' she said.

'I'm pretty sure there was a similar show in the States,' said Dan.

'Yeah, Ben did mention something about an American format. Could you look into that, do you think?' she asked.

'Sure,' said Dan, making notes and flicking his fringe from his eyes.

'Okay. Is that it?' she asked as her phone started ringing again.

'Yeah. Alex, you get that,' Dan said, pointing to the phone.

'Alex Fisher speaking,' Alex said, turning her chair towards her desk as Ross and Dan chatted quietly. It was Emma.

'Hi, Em. What's that? The hen do?'

Dan left the room and closed the door behind him.

'Alex, I'm really sorry but I think I'll have to bail,' said Emma apologetically.

'What do mean you can't make it? You organised it!' Alex said.

'It's a long story but Olivia's got me at the end of my rope. She only wants me to accompany her to her book signing in Scotland,' said Emma.

'Why do you need to be there?'

'God, you know what she's like. She's written some poor me sob story thing about her childhood. That's what I've been so busy on since the perfume launch. I've known about the signing for ages but I haven't been to any of the others so I didn't for a minute think she'd want me at this one, but she seems to be even more of a control freak than ever.'

'Oh, Em. It won't be the same without you. Let's cancel it.'

'Look, I'm really sorry. Don't cancel. Everyone else is all tee'd up for it. I'm looking into flights back. There's a chance I could be at Heathrow for nine so I might be able to get to the club after ten-ish.'

'But you'll miss all the spa stuff. God, I hate that woman,' said Alex.

'You and me both, believe me. Look, are you okay?'

'Surprisingly yes. I spoke to him earlier and it was cool. I actually feel relieved.'

'Wow. Good for you.'

'Yeah. It's weird. You know when you can't make up your mind about something and you toss a coin?'

'Er, yeah,' said Emma.

'Well, when you get the result you don't really want it makes you realise what you really did want. It's a bit like that really. Now it's happened it just feels right,' Alex said.

'As always, clarity is your middle name. As long as you're okay that's all that matters,' said Emma.

CHAPTER 21

'Morning, Ms Fisher,' the security guard called out as she strode into reception.

'Good morning,' she replied.

'Turned out beautiful again.'

He was right; it was another beautiful day.

'Are we still keeping you busy then?' he asked.

'Yes, I'm afraid so, Fred,' she said, noticing his name tag. 'I don't suppose you know which meeting room I'll be in with Tom Duffy and his guests today?' she asked. Alex was meeting Tom, Ryan and Wickens again.

'Let me check for you,' he said. 'Right, Ms Fisher. You're in the main boardroom and Mr Duffy has also reserved the basement meeting room for you and your colleagues. I believe your American colleague is already here. I saw him arriving earlier. Lovely gentlemen he is. Did you know his brother-in-law works for the Weather Channel in the US?'

'I had no idea, Fred. Thanks for your help.'

He was so much more pleasant to deal with than the hard-faced receptionist.

Dan was already engrossed in his work and he didn't notice Alex as she entered the room. He was in his shirt sleeves, his brow furrowed as he concentrated on the document in front of him. She coughed. He jumped. He'd been acting strangely around her for the past week. It was understandable, she supposed, after what had nearly happened between them, and as far as he was concerned she was still getting married. She hadn't been able to bring herself to tell anyone at work about the break-up.

'Hi. I didn't hear you come in.' He picked up the papers in front of him and tapped the bottom of the pile on the table so they all lined up, before putting them into his briefcase.

'Hi. Is everything okay? Have you got hold of Audrey yet?' she asked.

'She doesn't get in until nine, but I'm hoping to get some time with her before the meeting. Alex, can I run something else past you?' he said, watching her unpack her briefcase and sit down.

'Of course. Fire away.' She smiled at him.

'I could be wrong but I've got a theory about Wickens' behaviour at the meeting the other day. Do you remember when we went out to sort out his sushi? Well, Ryan and Ross were both out of the room at that point so Wickens was on his own.'

'So?' Where was he going with this?

'Well, we all left all our paperwork in the meeting room including our list of deal breakers and the points we were happy to give up on.'

'And you think he took a peek,' said Alex, nodding slowly.

'I think it stacks up. It was after lunch when he was really gunning for us. Don't you remember? It was as though he knew exactly which points we were relaxed about.'

'Yeah, you're right. And he kept trying to chip away at our key issues that we were desperate not to concede. It was as though he knew. Well, I wouldn't put it past him. Especially if he's as desperate to impress his client as we think he is,' she said.

'What if we leave a list lying around today, but not the real one, a bogus one?' said Dan.

'I see where you're coming from. Why not? If he's playing dirty then it serves him right. Yeah, okay. Let's draw one up.' She drew her chair forward.

'Here's one I prepared earlier,' he said, smiling as he passed it to her.

She scanned it. 'That's perfect. It's realistic enough to be believable but will really confuse him. If we have to we can concede those issues you've highlighted as deal breakers. That'll really throw him. He'll think he's winning major concessions from us but our reaction won't be what he's expecting. Well done. We just need to manipulate a situation where he's left alone in the meeting room.'

Ross arrived and at nine Dan disappeared for his chat with Audrey. Alex and Ross made their way to the boardroom where Tom was already waiting and Alex took the opportunity to mention the possibility of hiring Rob.

'I'd love to have him on board, but I thought he was settled where he is? The last time I saw him he was raving about how well it was going. It hadn't even crossed my mind to call him,' said Tom.

'Well, I saw him earlier this week and I floated the idea of a move to Beau Street and he seemed quite interested. I don't think it would do any harm to give him a call,' said Alex.

'That's great, Alex. Thanks, I will.' Tom's face brightened.

As they spoke Tom's PA showed Wickens, Ryan and an older woman into the room.

'Ah Tom,' said the woman, striding towards him. 'Good to see you.'

They shook hands and Tom introduced her to Alex.

'Alex, this is Brenda Martinez, global general counsel for Equinox. Brenda, this is Alex Fisher from MacArthur Warren.'

The two women shook hands and appraised each other. Martinez was immaculately dressed in a slightly eighties power suit and big hair. Intimidated, Alex found herself tidying her hair and smoothing her skirt as they made small talk. After the ritual of tea and coffee orders they all sat down as Dan arrived. He nodded at Tom and Warren as he sat down next to Ross. Wickens introduced Dan to Brenda in a half-hearted manner.

Wickens started talking and Alex had to avoid Dan's eyes as the American lawyer picked up his ruler and started conducting the room with it. Dan had positioned the bogus list next to Alex and she and he made pointed references to it throughout the morning.

After a particularly turgid hour of discussing two clauses of the agreement, Brenda called a break. She was looking worriedly at her Blackberry and asked if she could make a call outside. Tom directed her to a spare office. Alex seized her chance.

'Warren, if you don't mind I'd just like to have a quick word with my client in private.'

'Be my guest,' he said, tapping his ruler on the table as he reclined in his chair like a schoolchild. Alex almost wanted to stay and see if he fell backwards as the back of his chair almost became parallel with the floor but she signalled to Ross and Dan to follow her. As they closed the meeting room door behind them Dan explained to Ross what was going on.

Once Tom returned they all gathered in Tom's office on the pretext of discussing Dan's conversation with Audrey.

'She's pretty convinced she knows who the leak is,' he said.

'Yeah, me too,' said Tom. 'It's got to be Cassidy. He's the only one who's got nothing to lose. His name is already mud. He knows he's lost his job. It's just a parting shot.'

'She doesn't think so,' Dan continued.

'She wouldn't. She thinks the sun shines out of his backside. The man's been bankrolling her for years,' Tom said.

'She's convinced he'll want to set up again somewhere. He loves the celeb work and he's distraught his confidentiality is being blown. He can't set up again if his client base doesn't trust him.'

'A fair point, I suppose. But no one in this town will hire him for years to come and that's assuming he doesn't get struck off,' Tom said.

'She thinks he might go back to South America. Apparently there's a growing trend for US celebs to go there,' said Dan.

'Okay, so who does Miss Marple think it is then?' Tom asked.

'Albert Cheung,' said Dan.

'Albert? Why him?' said Alex.

'He's told her. They're friends apparently,' said Dan.

'Great friend she is,' muttered Tom.

'That would make sense. They have coffee together all the time,' Ross chipped in.

'How do you know?' asked Tom.

Ross blushed. 'Well, since the incident in Dr Webb's office I try to keep away from the staff as much as possible and when I get my lunch I always eat in the far corner of the canteen behind the plastic plants near to the entrance to the kitchen. Well, that's where they always sit. I see them nearly every day. They're as thick as thieves.'

'That's right. Apparently Albert referred quite a few patients to Cassidy. Audrey alluded to some kickback arrangement where Cassidy looked after Albert,' said Dan.

'Looked after? What does that mean?' asked Alex.

'Crossed his palm with silver I'll bet,' said Tom.

'Well, obviously that stream of money will have

dried up since Cassidy's gone and Albert's worried it won't come back. Audrey's pretty sure he knows about some of the clients as he's dropped hints, but she doesn't know how,' Dan continued.

'Well, I can guess,' said Alex. 'He's the one who mysteriously came up with the missing file with Felicia's letter in it. He said a temp had found it but I bet he's been having a good look around.'

'But that didn't have the names of any other clients in, did it?' said Dan.

'Good point,' said Alex.

'I don't know how he knows, but Audrey's convinced it's him,' Dan said.

'You leave Albert to me. Well done, Dan. Good work. Okay, we should get back to the meeting now,' said Tom.

Dan and Alex walked side by side down the corridor to the boardroom. 'Let's see if he's taken the bait,' said Dan.

Alex couldn't help giggling.

They returned to the room at the same time as Brenda.

'I'm sorry about that. It was Ryan. He was in a meeting with Clinton Wahlberg,' she said.

'Not a problem,' said Alex.

'Okay, let's get back to business, shall we?' Wickens said and proceeded to open up negotiations on the next issue. 'My client reserves the right to rebrand the business in the UK. You may be attached to the Beau Street name but Equinox is a global brand.'

Alex looked across the table at Wickens. He was

sitting back in his chair holding his ruler in the fingertips of both hands in a horizontal position.

'Well, as you anticipated this is a point of principle for my client and we would resist your proposal. The business has been Beau Street since it was founded and it's a strong name in the UK market,' Alex replied.

'One that's being blackened every day in the media,' Wickens responded, looking sideways at Brenda.

'Hardly. None of the pieces has damaged the brand at all. All the surgery in question has been praised in the media,' Alex said. Then, as though she was really struggling with the possibility, she said, 'I suppose we might be prepared to consider moving on this issue if you were prepared to trade one or two other areas of contention with us.'

'Such as?' asked Wickens, delighted that he seemed to be making some progress.

'Your demand to retain an element of the price for six months post-completion,' said Alex.

They horse-traded for half an hour until she'd agreed to the rebranding and he'd agreed to drop two other demands. Alex and Dan were thrilled. Tom had already agreed he didn't care about the rebranding. Equinox had a great name and once the PR people had run a few ads to tell everyone that Beau Street was now Equinox it wouldn't be a problem. Of course, what Tom didn't know was that the rebranding had featured as a deal breaker on Dan's bogus list.

The afternoon continued in the same vein with Warren Wickens both pleased and confused every time they conceded a point. What he didn't know was that every point they conceded was not a big deal to them and the trade-offs they were getting in return were real achievements. He was starting to look flustered and kept looking sideways at Brenda and running his hands through his hair.

After a couple of hours Wickens turned to Dan. 'You, can you get us some drinks?'

Alex saw Brenda dart a disapproving look at Wickens. Dan raised his eyebrows and smiled. Alex had been watching Dan and Warren all afternoon. There was a definite antipathy between them.

'I'm sure that can be arranged.' He got up and went to find Tom's PA.

He returned a few minutes later and went over to Alex. He looked agitated. 'A quick word?' he whispered to her.

Wickens had disappeared to the bathroom and Brenda was tapping away on her Blackberry.

'What is it?' Alex asked.

'There's another story in tonight's *London News*,' he whispered. 'Albert's been at it again.'

'Oh no!' she said. 'It couldn't be worse timing.'

Alex whispered the news to Tom.

He was livid. 'Look, Alex, I need to speak to a certain Mr Cheung asap. Can we close the meeting for today?' he asked, already getting up.

'I'll give it a go.' Alex coughed and said in a louder voice, 'Er, Brenda? Could I make a suggestion?' she said.

Brenda Martinez looked up from the email she was sending.

'Perhaps we could leave the negotiations at this point. I feel we've made good progress today and Warren and I can resolve the remaining drafting points over the phone. The final points of principle can be dealt with at the all-party meeting next week, don't you think?' Alex smiled at the older woman.

'Well, that would suit me. I have the bankers to see today and some local business to deal with. You're right; we have moved things on. Okay, let's finish it for today.' Brenda started to gather her papers together as Warren returned.

'Warren, we're done here. Let's get over to the bank now,' she said as she put her Blackberry into her black patent bag.

'Okay, sure,' he said, looking around at everyone else packing away their stuff. 'We haven't finished on the documents yet, though.' He looked thoroughly confused.

'We're nearly there, Warren, I think? We'll see you at the all-party meeting,' said Alex.

As soon as Brenda and Warren had left they all descended on Tom's office. Tom was already scouring the pages of the evening paper. The story was front-page news.

'This is the worst yet,' he said. 'This time it's A list.'

'Who is it?' Alex asked.

Tom held up the front page of the paper. Olivia Meddoes' face stared back. 'I had no idea she was ever a client of ours,' he said. 'Listen to this,' he continued as he read from the article. 'Meddoes, the Hollywood darling and undisputed queen of the romantic comedy, is reputed to be a regular at the Beau Street clinic. Our source claims she's had a face lift, boob job, liposuction, fillers and Botox. This will come as a shock to her fans, especially after her recent appearance on TV show *Chat* where she claimed her good looks were down to good genes, yoga and drinking water.'

Alex's first thought was for Emma. What kind of nightmare must she be suffering at the moment?

'This is the worst bit,' Tom continued. 'They've made the link. Look at this bit — "Meddoes is the third celebrity in recent weeks to have been exposed as having work done at the Beau Street clinic. It seems that someone at Beau Street isn't very good at keeping secrets." This is a disaster for us. I just pray the deal goes through and it doesn't scare the Americans off. It's a good job we agreed to the rebranding today. After all this nonsense in the papers this business is going to need a new brand sooner rather than later.'

'I suggest we track down Albert Cheung and find out if Audrey's theory holds up,' said Dan.

'You're right. Let's go and find him,' said Tom, grim faced. He got up from his desk and the rest of them followed him through the corridors like a lynch mob on their way to find their man.

Unsurprisingly, Albert was nowhere to be found. His last appointment had been before lunch and he'd taken a half day. Fred the security guard said he'd left the building at twelve twenty.

'The first edition of the *London News* comes out at about two, so that adds up,' said Tom.

'Tom, do you mind if I have another word with Audrey?' asked Dan.

'Be my guest,' said Tom, heading back to his office.

'Can I come along?' said Alex to Dan after Ross had left.

The two lawyers headed up to Audrey's office.

'You again,' she said, unsmiling, as they approached her desk outside Dr Cassidy's empty office.

'Sorry, Ms Fox, but I just wondered if I could ask you a few more questions about Albert. You know Alex Fisher, I believe?' Dan said.

'Yes, we've met. You'd better come in here,' she said, motioning towards Dr Cassidy's room.

'You've seen the paper, I presume?' Dan asked.

'Yes, I have. Ms Meddoes is going to be furious. She was absolutely paranoid about confidentiality. Quite a stickler that one,' Audrey replied.

'Look, do you have any idea how Albert could know about Olivia Meddoes and the other women? I know he works at the clinic but we can't find any evidence that anyone knew about Dr Cassidy's patients, apart from you, I presume,' said Dan, staring wide-eyed at Audrey.

She looked down. 'Look, I didn't know about Lloyd's practice. Well, not all of it. Of course I saw one or two famous people come in but I assumed all the cloak and dagger stuff was because of confidentiality, not because he was up to something dodgy. I have no idea how Albert knew, especially about the work they'd had done. Even I didn't always know that.'

'What about his expertise advising patients? Couldn't

he look at a before and after picture of someone and work out what they'd had done?' asked Dan.

Good thinking, thought Alex as she watched Dan at work.

'Well, of course Albert is very talented at what he does. He definitely has an eye for work. Yes, perhaps he could have guessed,' she said, her head on one side as she contemplated Dan's suggestion. 'And I've just remembered something,' she said, colouring slightly. 'I think I might have mentioned that actress Gemma Kirk to him once. We were talking about that soap she's in. He's obsessed with them all. He tapes them and watches them back to back at the weekend. Anyway, he said something about her brow looking less mobile and I let slip she'd been in here. But we all sign confidentiality agreements when we join, so I didn't think he'd do anything,' she pleaded.

'Look, Audrey, you're not the one who's gone to the papers. It's him. It's a fact of life that if you work here you're going to meet patients. It's up to staff not to disclose that. Now do you think there's any way you might have mentioned any other names to him in passing?' Dan asked.

Christ, his bedside manner was better than Rob's, Alex thought. He could get anyone to confess to anything when he looked at them like that. She watched him nodding sympathetically as Audrey looked at him through her fluttery false eyelashes.

'You know, I might have mentioned a couple of other names to him. We used to have coffee together most mornings. He was a good friend to me.'

CHAPTER 22

Alex was lying face down on clingfilm, her face poking through a hole in the narrow bed while a woman poured warm mud over her back. Emma was on a bed next to her going through the same ritual.

'She went totally mental. I've never seen histrionics like it,' Emma was saying. 'She ripped the paper up into tiny shreds and threw it everywhere then demanded one of her minions go and buy another copy so she could read it again. Her language was unbelievable. She was threatening to sue everyone in the UK from the prime minister to Paul McCartney. She called her lawyer, her therapist and her agent and screamed at them too. It was so crazy it was funny.'

'So she's gone back to the States then?' mumbled Alex through the hole in the bed.

'Yup. Says she hates the UK. I have to say the feeling's mutual.'

'Well, I'm just glad the book signing is cancelled and you can be here,' said Alex.

'Me too. Though I'm not sure about this mud routine. Excuse me, but what happens next?' Emma asked the beautician.

'Well, I'm going to ask you to turn over in a moment and then we pour the seaweed-infused mud onto your front. Then we wrap you up and leave you with a heated blanket for thirty minutes,' the girl replied.

'God, I feel like a marinated salmon being prepared for the barbeque,' said Emma.

'More like a piece of sushi. It's the smell I can't bear,' said Alex.

'Yeah, but we'll be glowing from top to toe for tonight,' said Emma as she turned over and the girl applied the fishy mud to her front.

Alex tried to relax and enjoy the treatment despite the smell.

Emma broke the silence again. 'Yes, Olivia said she might as well go and book herself in for a face lift in LA now everyone thinks she's had one.'

'Why, hasn't she had one then?' asked Alex.

'She says not. They had her bang to rights on all the other stuff but she claims she's never had a face lift.'

So Albert had called that wrong, Alex thought.

'Will she sue anyone do you think?' Alex fished.

'Nah. Don't think so. Her PR people and her lawyer advised her against it. The article was pretty accurate in general. If they sue then it makes an even bigger deal about it. I think her PR people put loads of pressure on other mags so they wouldn't repeat the story. It seems to have gone away already,' said Emma.

Alex was now being wrapped up in the clingfilm

like some sci-fi mummy. 'This is so weird,' she muttered.

'All in the name of beauty, darling,' said Emma as the beauticians placed heated blankets over them.

'Now leave them to cook in a warm oven for thirty minutes until they're no longer soft in the middle,' said Emma as the two girls gently closed the door behind them.

Alex and Emma lay in silence for a while listening to the whale music. Alex felt herself drifting off to sleep. It was strangely relaxing.

'I'm bored,' said Emma, jolting Alex from her snooze.

'You're supposed to relax. I was almost asleep,' said Alex, yawning.

'You were snoring.'

'Wasn't.'

'Was.'

There was silence again.

'What do you reckon we do after this? I say we get showered and grab some cocktails.'

'Mmm, sounds good,' said Alex.

Suddenly a loud siren sounded.

Alex twisted her head towards Emma. 'What's that?'

The door opened and a girl was shouting at them. 'Quick! Grab some robes! It's the fire alarm. We need to get outside at once!' she shouted.

'I can't fucking move,' said Emma as she flapped about on the bed like a salmon trying to swim upstream.

Alex thrashed about in the clingfilm and managed to release one arm over the top of the layers. With her one hand she manoeuvred herself off the bed, her legs still bound together.

The beautician was trying to unravel Emma, who was still wriggling about like a demented worm.

'Miss, please stop moving so I can unwrap you. We need to go. There's a fire. This is not a drill.'

'Come on, Emma. Help her,' said Alex as she inched her way to the door in miniscule steps.

The girl managed to get Emma's clingfilm off and get her into a robe. She put another robe round Alex and helped them down the corridor.

'Wait for me,' Alex called as she tried to keep up with them, her legs still wrapped up like a mermaid with a bondage fetish. As she moved, the plastic came free round her ankles allowing her to shuffle, penguin style, out of the fire door they were being ushered to.

They came out blinking into the bright summer sunshine. They looked around, trying to work out where they were. They were surrounded by a dozen or so other women, including other members of the hen party, looking distinctly embarrassed to be standing on a back street in Covent Garden on a Saturday afternoon in a bathrobe.

Alex saw Lisa, whose face was puckered and green in an ever-tightening facemask.

'God, my face feels so tight it's going to implode,' she said. 'And what's that awful smell?'

'Me and Emma. We're covered in seaweed,' said Alex, flashing Lisa a glimpse of what was under the robe.

'Omigod, you look like an oven-ready chicken that's gone off,' said Lisa.

'Thanks. And you look like the Wicked Witch of the East,' Alex replied.

They both started giggling.

'Oh shit, Alex, don't look now,' said Lisa. She'd stopped giggling and was looking over Alex's shoulder.

'What is it?' Alex asked, trying to twist her plastic wrapped body round to follow her gaze.

'It's Dan from work with some girl. Who the hell is she? Keep your head down. They're heading this way.'

It was too late. Dan had already seen Lisa and was approaching.

'Lisa, hi. Are you okay?' he asked.

'Oh Dan, hi, yeah, I'm good thanks,' she replied as if it was perfectly normal to be standing in the street on a summer afternoon in a green facemask.

'Er, good,' he said, looking round at the other girls in robes. Then he saw her.

'Alex, hi! Didn't see you there too. What's going on?' he asked.

'Hi, Dan. Great to see you,' she lied. 'It's my hen do.'

'Right. Now I'm even more confused. Is it an English tradition to stand around the street in bathrobes when you're getting married?'

'No, of course not! We were having spa treatments and then the fire alarm went off. Hence Lisa's green face,' said Alex.

'Yeah and her fishy smell,' retorted Lisa.

'Thanks, Lisa,' she said through gritted teeth.

'This is my sister, Kim,' said Dan, pointing towards the blonde girl next to him. 'She's over for a visit.'

'Great to meet you,' said Alex, almost falling over as she shuffled herself round to hold out her free hand. 'I'm Alex Fisher. I work with Dan.'

'Alex, hi. I've heard all about you,' she replied.

'Really?' said Alex.

'And I'm Lisa,' said Lisa, leaning across Alex to introduce herself.

'Well, you guys have a great time. Where are you heading tonight then?' asked Dan.

'Some gay club, I think. Emma's organised it,' said Alex, nodding towards Emma who'd been keeping her head down.

'Oh hi, Dan,' Emma said, pretending to notice him for the first time.

As Dan and Emma were chatting about nightclubs one of the beauticians came over to them full of apologies.

'We're so sorry, ladies. It seems someone left a towel hanging over one of the candles and it caused a small fire. Everything's sorted now and we can go back in,' she said.

'Okay, guys, let's get back in and get our dignity back,' said Alex. 'Bye, Dan. Bye, Kim. Nice to meet you.'

Dan was looking straight at her as Emma was still chatting away to his sister. For one moment she was back in the taxi with him. She felt herself blushing and turned to go inside.

'Let me get this mask off before my face snaps off,' said Lisa, leading the way.

Several hours and a couple of cocktails later they were all laughing about it.

'The worst thing is I was desperate for a pee but I was covered in clingfilm,' Alex said.

'You should have gone anyway. It would have been like wearing a wetsuit. It would have warmed you up,' screeched Lisa.

They were in a cocktail bar that was already heaving with life. They had a pre-booked booth and the jugs of Long Island iced tea were going down at an alarming rate.

'How's your leg now?' Alex asked Bex, who'd been half way through a leg wax when she'd had to go outside.

'Sore. That poor girl's face when she pulled off half my skin. The wax was practically grafted to my leg by the time she got at it. Still, not as bad as that Shelley girl.' Bex lowered her voice. 'Have you seen her eyebrows?'

Shelley was a friend of Alex's from law school. Alex glanced over at her. She looked like she was balancing two large African slugs on her eyelids.

'I can't believe she stood out there all that time with the tint still on,' said Bex. 'I'd have got you to lick it off if it'd been me.'

'Yeah and then I would've had a black tongue to go with my green fishy body,' said Alex.

As they left the bar and staggered to the nightclub Emma linked arms with Alex.

'Having fun?' Emma asked.

'Yeah, thanks, Em. I'm so glad you're here.'

'Me too.' Emma hugged Alex.

'How's your skin?' Alex asked.

'Glowing.'

'Yeah, luminous green,' Alex laughed.

'Alex?'

'Yeah?'

'Why haven't you told Dan the wedding was off?'

'What? How did you know I haven't told him?' Alex asked.

'Something I said this afternoon and his response gave it away.'

'Well, I just didn't get round to it. I haven't told anyone at work yet. It just hasn't seemed appropriate.'

'He's got such a thing for you.'

'Maybe a bit.'

'More than that, Alex. Do you still like him?'

'Look, don't go there, Em. I'm not ready for anything. Anyway, I can't date people from work. It's the rule.'

'Yeah and like I said before, rules are meant to be broken,' Emma replied, steering Alex across the road. 'Come on, here we are.' They'd reached the club.

It was retro night and the music was cheesy eighties and nineties classics. As soon as they got past the entrance they had to shout to each other.

'I'll get the drinks,' screamed Emma.

The rest of the crowd gathered round the edge of the dance floor to watch the largely gay clientele strut their stuff. It was a postmodern ironic eighties dance floor, or perhaps just an eighties dance floor, and it was packed with guys in incredibly well-fitting trousers.

Alex watched and smiled at the sheer unadulterated fun of it all. There were no nervous men hanging round the dance floor plying themselves with Dutch courage here. The bar area was almost empty and it wasn't long before Emma returned with the drinks, an admirer in tow.

'Hi guys,' she shouted. 'This is Aaron.'

Aaron waved at them but couldn't keep his eyes off Emma. He was wearing tight-fitting pale denim jeans and a pristine white t-shirt revealing well-toned tanned arms. He was stroking Emma's sleeve.

'Isn't she amazing?' he said while looking up at her towering over him in her heels. 'You are stunning. I lurrrve the jacket.' He ran his thumb and index finger up and down the lapels of her sequinned tux jacket.

Emma smiled at the others and shrugged.

'What's he on?' Bex shouted to Alex.

'Dunno, but he looks happy on it,' she replied. 'Come on, let's dance.'

Alex pushed Bex towards the dance floor and they started to dance. Within moments a cute pocket-sized bald guy and his slightly punk sunken-cheeked friend were all over them; dancing round them, through them, behind them. Another astonishingly good-looking man appeared and started grinding up against Bex. All of them were laughing and smiling at them suggestively.

'Feeling threatened?' Bex shouted in Alex's ear.

'Nope. This is great!' she shouted back.

Alex watched as the guys around them flirted from group to group, dancing their socks off. It was great to watch and such a different vibe to a straight club. No one seemed remotely self-conscious and every time the girls tried a cheesy move or hammed it up the guys just lapped it up and begged for more.

She glanced over at Emma, who was now looking both flattered and irritated by Aaron's constant attention. He'd brought his friends over to worship his new find and his behaviour was becoming increasingly odd. When Alex saw him pretending to lick Emma's cheek she decided it was time to rescue her and she ran over and dragged her onto the dance floor. She looked back at Aaron, who had his hands on his hips and his bottom lip sticking out sulkily.

'Thanks, hun,' Emma said.

'Any time. Think you've got a new fan.'

'Yeah. Don't know why.'

They danced for hours to everything, stopping only to knock back ice cold beer and alcopops. By one in the morning they'd reached the stage where they were acting out every lyric to every song and were drawing a bit of a crowd including, of course, the omnipresent Aaron. When 'Jump' by the Pointer Sisters came on the whole hen party stepped onto the low stage round the DJ station and danced like podium dancers until the chorus, when they jumped in unison off the stage every time they heard the word 'jump'. The crowd were going crazy and the girls were falling everywhere in hysterics as they tried to scramble back onto stage for each chorus. By the end of the track they were all laughing so much they were crying.

Aaron sidled up to Emma again, 'Lady, you are crazy as well as gorgeous,' he said.

His friends were surrounding the rest of the group and begging them to dance to the next track. Alex and Bex didn't need asking twice and they were soon dancing with two very muscle-bound guys, one with bleached blonde hair and one with a shaven head.

The blonde man moved close up to Alex and then took her hand. He started throwing her round the dance floor in a series of increasingly ambitious moves. Alex's jiving repertoire was limited to two safe moves she'd perfected over the years with Elliott. This guy was taking her to a whole different level and one she wasn't entirely comfortable with. After one twist she found both his arms crossed in front of her while he ground up against her from behind. His friend was now on his knees in front of her, writhing around. Bex watched nervously, dancing on her own, as Alex felt increasingly uncomfortable. She tried to let go of Blondie's hands and escape but he was having none of it. He held her tighter and began swaying her from side to side. As he ground up against her again she tried again to get away. As she looked up she was amazed to see a familiar face heading towards her.

'Hey, that's enough now,' Dan shouted to Blondie.

'That's my wife. I want to dance with her.'

Blondie let go of Alex's hands and smiled suggestively at Dan. He was still dancing and was now moving towards Dan.

'Come on, Alex,' he said and steered her away.

They found a relatively quiet corner near the bar.

'What on earth are you doing here?' she asked him, realising that she quite enjoyed being the damsel in distress.

'It was Kim's idea. She loves clubbing and wanted to try out the London scene. Emma recommended this place to her this afternoon. I had no idea you'd be here.'

'Yeah but Emma did.'

'And maybe Kim did too. Do you think we've been set up?' he asked, a smile curving round his lips.

'Maybe,' she said, her mouth close to his ear as they struggled to be heard over the music. They were standing so close that her hair brushed against his cheek when they leant towards each other to speak. 'Thanks for saving me back there. I felt really uncomfortable even though those guys weren't remotely interested in me,' she said.

'My pleasure,' he replied, slowly placing his hand in the small of her back as he spoke.

His touch made her shiver as a feeling of longing pulsed through her. She turned her face towards his and returned his gaze. He drew her even closer towards him, both arms around her body now, and kissed her slowly and then more passionately. He held the back of her head in his hand now and Alex closed her eyes.

'Alex, is it true your wedding isn't going ahead?' he asked when they eventually separated.

'Mmm, yeah,' she replied, holding his hand now and staring at him dementedly.

'Why didn't you tell me?' he asked, moving her hair from her face.

'I don't know. I'm sorry. I guess I knew what might happen and I wasn't sure I was ready. I don't want to mess you about. I was trying to be professional, I suppose,' she said.

He pulled her closer and their lips met again.

After almost an hour holed up together kissing and talking, Emma confronted them.

'Ah, so you've met the stripper I booked for your hen night,' she said.

'Ha ha,' said Alex, holding onto Dan and smiling at Emma.

'Everyone's been staring at you two — you know, the weirdo straight couple snogging in the corner,' Emma joked.

'Well, I've never kissed a girl on her hen night before,' said Dan to Alex as he started to kiss her again.

'Don't let me stop you two lovebirds but I think everyone else is ready to go,' said Emma, nodding towards the rest of the hen party and Kim.

'It's not late, is it?' drawled Alex.

'It's four in the morning and we're off.'

'Alex, I need to take Kim home. She doesn't know her way about London,' Dan said apologetically.

'Okay,' said Alex, still holding onto him, disappointed that she wouldn't be taking another taxi ride with him.

Emma laughed. 'Come on, you two. You're like conjoined twins. Let's go.'

She bundled them out of the club in time for them all to witness Aaron being taken out on a stretcher.

'Time for a stomach pump, I think. Just say no, kids,' said the ambulance man to them as he went past.

'Bloody typical. The only man to fancy me in months was gay and off his head,' said Emma.

CHAPTER 23

Alex lay in bed hugging herself with excitement. She couldn't stop thinking about Dan. The best thing was, there was no guilt any more. She could actually dare to hope that something could work out between them. He'd kissed her one more time, as the hen party all whistled and cheered, before jumping in a cab to take his sister home, and he'd promised to call her.

Alex threw back the covers and danced to the shower, bringing her mobile with her just in case he called while she was in there.

Just as she started shampooing her hair the phone rang. She fumbled her hand round the shower curtain and grabbed the phone in her soapy hand. She stuck her head out of the curtain too and took the call, her eyes closed, as the shampoo dripped down her forehead onto her face.

'Hi. Dan?'

'Christ, Alex. Get a room, will you? It's me.' It was Emma.

'Oh, hi.'

'Just wanted to check you were okay and see if you wanted to grab some lunch. Our local does a great Sunday roast.'

'I'm fine, thanks. I had a great night.'

'Yeah, I noticed,' laughed Emma.

'Thanks so much for organising it.' She wiped the shampoo from her eyes with her free hand.

'No problem. I have to say, setting up the Dan thing was inspired. When I got chatting to his sister outside the spa I couldn't believe my luck.'

'Yeah well, thanks.'

'So, you and him. What's next?'

'Give me a break! He said he'd call today.'

'So let me guess, you're going to stay in all day and keep your options open in case he calls and wants to whisk you to Paris for lunch.'

'Something like that. Sorry, Emma. Do you mind?'

'Of course I mind. Go ahead – dump your mates as soon as a new guy comes on the scene.'

'Emma, please!' Alex was shocked by Emma's reaction.

'Only joking. Don't be silly. You sit around and moon over him all day for all I care. I'm just glad to see you happy again.'

'Thanks, Em. You're a top mate.'

'I know. Now get off the phone in case he calls.' Emma hung up.

Alex finished her shower and spent the rest of the day trying to work on the presentation for the final all-party meeting next week, but she kept finding her thoughts drifting back to Dan. She hadn't felt so excited for years. Her reaction to the realisation that there was nothing stopping them made her realise how strong her feelings for him were. The only nagging doubt in the back of her mind was the stupid firm rule about relationships, but damn it, she could do secrecy and subterfuge if that was what it took. Hadn't Lisa said that James had kept his relationship with his future wife a secret for years?

Her phone rang with the ringtone she'd already assigned to Dan's number, making her jump.

She took a deep breath and answered. 'Hi, Dan. How are you?' she said, trying to sound chilled.

'Hi, I'm great, thanks. Are you okay?' he answered.

'Yeah, I'm good.'

There was an awkward silence.

'Alex, about last night,' he began.

Alex could feel her heart pounding. Surely he wasn't going to say it was all a big mistake?

'Yes,' she said, almost defiantly.

'I can't stop thinking about it. Alex, you need to know I had an amazing time. I'm so glad you're not getting married. I mean, I'm really sorry it went wrong for you. Actually no, I'm not. Look, what I'm trying to say is that selfishly I can't believe my luck and if it's okay with you I'd like to take you out. Whenever suits you and whenever you're ready. I know it's going to be a crazy week at work with the presentation and tying up the deal.'

'Dan, it's okay. I feel the same way. Do you think we could wait 'til after the presentation? This week is going to be mental.'

'I suppose so, but I can't wait to actually finish a cab journey with you,' he replied.

They both knew what he meant.

'Look, Dan, about the firm rule. Do you think we could just play it careful? I know it's stupid and wrong but there's no need to jeopardise both our careers.'

'Okay. What about Lisa, though? She was there last night.'

Good point. Alex had forgotten about her.

'I'll talk to her. She's a friend; she'll be fine,' she said, suddenly remembering that Lisa had fancied Dan herself.

'So what happened with you and Elliott? That was his name, wasn't it? It must have been a difficult time for you. You covered it well at work. I had no idea. I kept hearing you on the phone talking to people about the wedding and the hen do, so I thought it was all still on,' he said.

They chatted away for almost an hour. It was easy, comfortable and tinged with the thrill of the connection between them. Alex explained that she and Elliott had grown apart. She didn't fill Dan in on all of Elliott's indiscretions. She was past the stage of character assassination.

'I guess I just wanted him to think of me occasionally and maybe suggest we do something I might enjoy. You know, maybe a meal out and tickets to the ballet rather than another gig with the boys.'

'So that's the secret, is it? Dinner and the ballet. I'll remember that,' he said, laughing.

Alex lay back on her bed as she spoke, unburdening

herself to him. She told him everything about when she and Elliott had met, how he'd moved into her house, how he'd proposed on one knee after coming off stage at a gig and how she'd buried herself in wedding planning while ignoring all the nagging doubts. He was a great listener.

'Are you sure you want to hear all this?' she said, conscious that she'd been monologuing for a while.

'Of course I do. I want to know everything about you. I know all about the professional side of you. I've been watching you in the office for almost two years in your sexy suits distracting me from my work. I want to know what else makes you tick,' he said.

'Well, to be honest, work and the wedding have been my main priorities. I guess my happiness has come somewhere down the list. Hopefully that will change.'

'I hope so too,' he replied.

On Monday morning Alex took more care than usual when choosing what to wear. Dressing for work was like dressing for a date now and she tried on several outfits before settling on a skirt, shirt and waistcoat combination that she hoped said both professional and sexy at the same time. She strode into reception and crossed the atrium to the lift. As she waited for it to arrive she went through the list of things she had to do that day as well as finalising the presentation for the big meeting tomorrow. As soon as she left the lift she was acutely aware she could bump into Dan at any moment. Emma was right. The sexual tension was more intense when she had to pretend her feelings towards him were purely professional.

She spent the morning at her desk drafting and redrafting the presentation. She had to highlight their positive findings while not skimming over the negative issues. She had a plan up her sleeve that she hoped would blow the whole Cassidy issue out of the water, but all the pieces of the jigsaw weren't quite in place. She'd wanted an excuse to see Dan all morning so she suggested a team meeting in her office.

She looked up as Dan entered the room and felt a frisson of excitement. His hair was dishevelled, his sleeves rolled up and his amazing smile beamed back at her.

'Hi, Alex, Ross. How are you?' he said, his eyes sparkling.

The three of them sat in the small office and discussed the presentation. They'd each been responsible for different sections and both Dan and Alex would be doing the talking on the day. Dan had some news on the US TV makeover show.

'It was a very similar format to the one your friend's involved in,' he said. 'But here's the interesting bit: it was based in LA about eight years ago and guess who the surgery provider was? A clinic owned by Equinox.'

'Really? That's fantastic! So they aren't averse to linking themselves to this kind of show. Very interesting,' said Alex.

'Oh and I was talking to Tom this morning and he's seen Albert,' Dan continued.

'And?' asked Ross.

'Well, Albert came to see him first thing. Tom thinks Audrey had tipped him off. He was contrite and begging not to be fired. He admitted that he'd been pumping Audrey for info, but only because he was nosey and fascinated by the celebrity clients. He said he knew about loads of names, not just the ones who've been leaked to the papers.'

'But did he 'fess up to leaking to the papers?' Alex asked.

'Not exactly, no. He says he's never sold a story and even showed Tom all his bank statements to prove he hadn't received payment.'

'That proves nothing. There could be bundles of cash under his mattress,' said Ross.

'Exactly. But what he did say was that he might have been less than discreet when he was out with his friends. It seems he likes to show off a bit when he's had a few drinks and one of his friend's boyfriends happens to be a freelance paparazzi. He thinks the pap might have sold some stories to the tabloids.'

'Does Tom believe him?' Alex asked.

'Not entirely, no. He's given Albert a written warning and told him that might not be the end of it. He said Albert was begging for his job and vowed never to say anything to anyone ever again.'

'Tom's well within his rights to fire him on the spot,' said Alex.

'Well, I don't think he wants to lose him. Apparently he's brilliant at his job,' Dan said.

Later that day Alex took a call from Rob Sweeney.

'Yo, Alex! How are you? I'm calling to thank you. I'm so grateful to you for recommending me to Tom. I had an interview with him and that Ben guy, the producer, and it seems they both want me on board. The job's mine if I want it.'

'And do you?' she asked.

'What do you think? My own TV show and working at one of the UK's best clinics?'

'Rob, it's not your show. You're just the surgeon,' she laughed.

'Yeah, whatever. But I'm the genius who'll transform the victims. I mean celebs. It's just what I've always wanted.'

'I thought you wanted to find a cure for AIDS,' she teased.

'Yeah well, that proved harder than I thought. Look, I owe you big time. Are you free tonight? Annabelle thought we could take you and your other half out for dinner.'

'That's really sweet of you but I'm already out tonight. There's a completion meal I'm supposed to be at.' Alex remembered that a group of them were going out for a curry tonight to celebrate the completion of the purchase of the condom business she'd been working on before the Beau Street deal.

'Okay. Let's do it next week. Monday okay?'

'Yeah, sure. That would be lovely.'

'By the way, what's your other half called again?' he asked.

She hesitated for a moment. Could she call Dan her 'other half', she wondered? Were they officially an item? What if Rob blabbed to the Beau Street guys and it got back to Truman?

'Dan. Look, I don't know if he'll able to make it but I'll check and let you know.'

At seven, after applying fresh make-up and brushing her hair, Alex walked down the corridor to Lisa's office. The trainee she shared her room with had gone home and she was alone at her desk. Alex closed the door behind her.

'You ready to go?' Lisa asked.

'Yep. Look, Lisa, about Saturday…'

'Alex, is this about Dan?'

'Yeah. I'm sorry, Lisa. But please don't tell anyone, will you?' Alex pleaded.

'Why are you sorry?'

'Well, I knew you fancied Dan.'

Lisa smiled at her. 'Alex, everyone fancies Dan. Even the men have secret crushes on him. It was obvious from the start he had no interest in me. He's besotted with you,' said Lisa.

'Really?'

'Er, yes. Wasn't it you he hunted down the moment he found out you were available and you he spent most of Saturday night wrapped around?'

Alex laughed. 'Yeah, I suppose so.'

'Don't be so coy. He fancies the arse off you. I'm so jealous. And Alex, there's no way I'm going tell anyone about you and him. I hate Margaret Kemp as much as the next woman. I'd hate to give her the satisfaction. Your secret's safe with me. Okay, let me get my lippy on and let's go and celebrate selling a small UK condom manufacturer to a bigger German condom manufacturer. How obscure a reason to do we need to go out for a curry?'

They'd reserved a table for ten in the small restaurant.

It was a traditional curry house with red carpet and large colonial-style ceiling fans over each table. James, who'd been the partner on the condom deal, was already there holding court and taking charge of the ordering. Lisa and Alex sat down on some banquette seating opposite a huge pile of poppadoms. James was regaling the more junior lawyers with tales of his days as a student on hockey tour in India and showing how hard he was by scooping up large mouthfuls of lime pickle with his poppadom. Predictably he ordered a vindaloo and some obscure vegetable side dishes while the rest of them opted for the traditional bhunas, kormas and the inevitable chicken tikka masalas.

'How's your plastic surgery deal going, Alex?' James asked.

'If one more person asks me that I'll explode. It's okay, I think. It's a big week this week. It's make or break time really. We'll know by Friday if it's happening.'

'It had better happen. I've promised the wife a new Rolex with my bonus,' he joked.

The orders started to arrive. James had ordered beers for everyone and once all the meals had been allocated to the right person he stood up, his napkin tucked in the waist of his trousers.

'Well, everyone, thanks for coming this evening and most of all thanks for all your hard work on the deal. I have to say Project Rubber was an eventful transaction but I was delighted with everyone's performance and effort. We can pat ourselves on the back and be proud that we've put the best of UK contraception onto the global stage.'

'I'll drink to that,' said Lisa to Alex, swigging at her bottle of beer.

The door suddenly swung open and a group of city traders barged in, clearly the wrong side of several hours of drinking.

'Table for six, mate?' asked one of the traders in a cockney accent.

The waiter seated them on the table next to the MacArthur Warren team.

'Six chicken phals, six bindi bhajis, six plain naans and six pilau rice,' the cockney barked at the waiter.

Alex was too busy watching the traders to notice Dan come in.

'Do you mind if I sit here?' he said, patting the space next to her.

'Of course,' she said when she saw him, blushing. 'Are you stalking me?' she whispered.

He leant forward and whispered back, 'Yes.'

'I wasn't expecting you here,' said Alex.

'Well, I did work on the deal for a couple of weeks when Lisa was on holiday. Didn't I, Lisa?' he said.

'You certainly did,' Lisa smiled. 'You're definitely technically allowed to be here.'

'Great, I'll get a beer then. James, can I get you a drink?' Dan asked.

'Furtado! Good to see you. Yah, I'll have a beer if you can attract the waiter's attention.'

It was quite cosy on the banquette now and Alex and Dan's bodies touched.

'When can we get out of here?' he whispered in her ear.

Alex suddenly went off her curry. 'Do you want some of this?' she asked Dan. As he finished her meal she was thankful that they'd both now smell of curry.

She watched him chatting with James and noticed several of the other female lawyers staring at him. He was hotter than James's vindaloo.

Suddenly there was a commotion on the next table. The city boys were standing on their chairs trying to balance their naan breads on the ceiling fan. Broken bits of naan were flying round the room and they cheered every time they successfully got another naan to balance on the fan before falling into its blades and disintegrating above the heads of the other diners. The waiters were ineffectually attempting to get the men down.

'Shall we go?' Dan whispered.

James was wading in with the traders, playing the diplomat and trying to calm everything down. A couple of the trainees were getting up to leave.

Alex whispered goodbye to Lisa and followed Dan out of the restaurant. They stood outside and smiled at each other nervously.

'Let's get a cab,' he said, taking her hand.

'Your place or mine?' Alex replied.

'Let's make it yours. We never seem to make it to mine,' he replied.

This time there was no U-turn in the cab. They arrived at Alex's house in silence. She fumbled with her key and then flung the front door open. Dan closed the door behind them and made the customary compliment about the house. He then gently put his hand under her chin and kissed her slowly as she dropped her keys and bag to the floor. Within seconds they were ripping at each other's clothes. In their frenzy they almost fell in a tangle to the floor but managed to steady themselves against the banisters in the hallway, laughing and kissing at the same time. They didn't make it to the bedroom. He lifted her onto the kitchen table, looking directly into her eyes as she wrapped her bare legs around his body and he thrust deep into her.

'Alex, you're amazing,' he panted.

She closed her eyes as her body moved against his, her heart racing and all inhibitions and awkwardness forgotten. She let her head fall back as she climaxed and he fell against her.

Then Alex took his hand and led him upstairs, where they made love again more slowly and with such gentleness and passion that she almost cried with the tenderness of it all.

'I can't believe this is happening,' she said, gazing at him dreamily.

He moved her hair from her eyes and kissed her again.

'I'm not going anywhere. I've never wanted anyone the way I want you,' he said.

CHAPTER 24

After a night of sporadic sleep, Alex woke first. She stared at Dan's naked chest next to her and admired his defined six-pack. She'd never shared a bed with a man who possessed one before. The flicker of desire crept over her again and she willed him to wake up.

He opened one eye. 'Good morning. What are you staring at?' He smiled sleepily.

'Breakfast,' she said and started to kiss him.

A couple of hours later, and at least an hour late, Alex almost ran into Fred as she flung herself through the revolving doors leading into the Beau Street offices.

'Morning, Fred,' she gasped, out of breath from running from the bus stop.

'Good morning, Ms Fisher. Another beautiful day but with a hint of cloud cover moving in from the west later,' he replied.

'Really? Must dash. Running late.'

'Quite typical, though, for the time of year,' he shouted after her.

Ross was already in the dungeon room. He looked relieved to see her.

'Thank goodness you've arrived. Tom has called twice to find out where you were. You're on in ten minutes. There's no sign of Dan either,' he gabbled.

'No panic,' she said, trying to convince him as much as herself. 'Dan called me. He's, er, on his way. Something about a cab breaking down,' she improvised, knowing full well that Dan was hiding behind a bus shelter a hundred metres from the Beau Street front door.

'Is all the IT stuff sorted?' she asked. She was doing a full presentation including some video footage.

'Yes. The IT guy has set it all up and I did a dummy run,' Ross replied.

Moments later Dan arrived as Alex and Ross were putting the final handout sheets into plastic wallets to distribute to the assembled professionals in the upstairs boardroom.

'Who's on at the moment?' Dan asked.

'The accountants. Tom said it was a full house up there. The top guys from Equinox are there, their CEO, Ryan, Brenda and Wickens and then there's King Alfred and that Meredith woman from the bank, oh and all the Beau Street management team.'

Alex was glad she'd been distracted from thinking about the presentation earlier in the morning. She was worried enough now to make up for it.

'Come on, Dan. We'd better go up. See you later, Ross, and thanks for doing all the prep,' she said, gathering up an armful of the plastic wallets.

Alex and Dan climbed the stairs together. They glanced at each other and Alex felt the electricity between them. She was beginning to understand the rationale for the firm's rule on employee relationships. How was she supposed to concentrate on her work when all she wanted to do was drag Dan into the nearest office and continue where they'd reluctantly left off earlier?

There were chairs lined up against the wall outside the boardroom. They sat down to wait until they were summoned. It reminded Alex of sitting outside numerous examination rooms as a child, when she took the piano exams which her parents had forced her to endure.

'Are you okay?' Dan asked.

She smiled back at him, grateful for the concern. 'I think so. This is going to be an interesting one.'

As she spoke they heard chairs being scraped back and muffled chatter from inside the boardroom. The door opened and a flushed Rachel from Payne Stewart and three of her colleagues filed out of the room.

'How did it go?' Alex asked.

'So so,' Rachel replied. 'Good luck in there. There's a cast of thousands.'

Tom Duffy appeared at the door.

'Okay, Alex. It's your turn,' he said, beckoning them to go in.

They entered the boardroom and registered the faces round the room. Alex nodded at Meredith and King Alfred as Ryan stood up to introduce his CEO to them.

'Alex, Dan, good morning. I think you know everyone here except Lawson Green, our CEO. Lawson, this is Alex Fisher and Dan Furtado from MacArthur Warren,' said Ryan.

A spherical man in his fifties, with remarkable jet black hair, struggled out of his seat and shook their hands.

Dan and Alex took their seats at the front of the room next to the laptop and screen that had been set up for them. The lights had been dimmed and they blinked back towards the expectant audience. Alex could see Wickens twiddling his ruler and Brenda Martinez leaning forward in anticipation as she took a deep breath and stood up.

'Good morning, ladies and gentlemen. As you know, I've been leading the team from MacArthur Warren over the past few weeks along with my colleague here, Dan Furtado. This morning we'll be presenting to you our key findings about the business at Beau Street,' she began.

She turned to the screen behind her and clicked to her first slide. She made a conscious effort to speak slowly, as she knew she had a tendency to rush when she was nervous, and tried to look at all the individuals in the audience and make eye contact. She spoke confidently for the first few slides about the property and employment law issues affecting the business. This was always going to be the easy bit as Beau Street had an experienced property manager and a competent HR director and the business was squeaky clean in those areas. Alex could see Lawson nodding sagely to Brenda, who was taking notes.

'The company's standard terms and conditions of employment comply in all respects with UK and European law and the procedures in place for dealing with grievances and employee welfare are satisfactory,' Alex finished.

'What about Cassidy? Has he got any grievances?' Wickens interrupted.

'We'll be coming to the Lloyd Cassidy issue in due course,' Alex countered, wishing she could shove his ruler down his throat. 'Dan, over to you,' she said as she sat down and Dan took over the laptop.

She watched as Dan seamlessly continued the presentation. He was talking about the regulatory issues that affected the business and the proposals that were being bandied about by politicians and in the press for greater regulation of cosmetic surgery businesses in the UK. He looked assured and professional in his dark single-breasted suit as he gestured towards the bullet points on the slide behind him.

'You're obviously familiar with the US regime for regulating the sector and if you look at the screen now you can see that I've highlighted the main differences in the current UK regime compared to the US. I've also included an additional column showing the differences should the proposals being suggested by UK consumer groups be adopted. As you can see, the impact isn't significant on a business that already conducts itself at a level that exceeds the current regulatory requirements.'

Warren was mumbling to himself about Cassidy

again and Alex saw Brenda frowning at him. Alex tried to ignore him as she stood up to continue.

'Quite the double act,' Wickens said under his breath.

Alex shot him a filthy look. 'Perhaps we could keep questions and comments to the end,' she said as she moved to the next slide, which dealt with the Beau Street reputation and brand. The time had come for her to bite the bullet and deal with the Cassidy issue.

'The legal documents that we've been negotiating with Brenda and Warren contemplate Equinox rebranding the business, and in the context of the unfortunate events surrounding Lloyd Cassidy and the recent leaks to the media we fully recognise this could be a sensible move if handled well. Moving on to the Cassidy issues, perhaps we could turn to the next slide.' Alex flicked to the next slide, which detailed the damage that had been inflicted upon the business. Along with the reputational issue, the fraud Lloyd had committed and the implications should any more Felicias come out of the woodwork, there was a considerable loss in revenue. Wickens sat up straight and seemed to be enjoying this part of the presentation.

'Dr Cassidy's secret practice and its impact on the business cannot be underplayed; however, we believe we may have come up with a way to attract celebrities back to the business, to generate new income and to launch the Equinox brand with a bang in the UK. Please would you turn your attention to the video we're about to show you,' Alex said as Dan switched the slides off and started the video running.

Cheesy music filled the room and then the screen was filled with the tanned, line-free face of a surgeon dressed in full scrubs with a scalpel in his hand.

'Hi, I'm Dr M.J. Daniels and today I'm gonna be changing this celebrity's life for ever,' he said as the screen panned to a blonde middle-aged lady.

'Hi, I'm Cindy Carson but you might remember me better as Tori Bellamy, the gun-toting cheerleader from the Emmy-winning primetime soap *Day by Day*,' said the blonde.

The video continued with the doctor counselling Cindy on how he could rejuvenate her.

Dan then paused the video.

'You may be asking yourselves how this is relevant to Beau Street?' Alex asked. 'Well, we've been in talks with a UK production company and a surgeon to recreate the format of this US TV show here in the UK. We already have a pilot show and a UK broadcaster has expressed interest in commissioning the show. On screen now is a letter from the broadcaster indicating their interest.'

Dan flashed up on screen the letter Ben and Bex had managed to procure from a major commercial broadcaster.

'Excuse me, Ms Fisher, but how is this going to fill the hole in the business's finances?' asked Lawson Green.

'Thank you, Mr Green. That's a very good question. Perhaps you could look at the next slide,' Alex replied.

Dan clicked up the next slide, which showed a graph that demonstrated a steady increase in income over a five-year period.

'This graph shows the increase in sales for the clinic where the US TV show was filmed after the shows were aired in the States. These figures compare exceedingly favourably to rival clinics in the States, as shown on the next slide. The other important factor for Beau Street is that Mr Duffy has secured the services of a successful UK surgeon who's been screen-tested by the production team and who's ready to join Beau Street and bring with him an already established practice, generating an annual income commensurate with Lloyd Cassidy's practice.'

A picture of Rob Sweeney grinning from ear to ear appeared on screen.

'What makes you think Equinox would want to be associated with such a low rent idea?' said Warren Wickens aggressively.

'Dan, perhaps you could move to the title credits of the US video?' said Alex.

They all stared at the screen as the title credits rolled and there in large white letters were the words 'Filmed at an Equinox US clinic and all surgery carried out by doctors employed by the Equinox Practise'.

'The US clinic was the Equinox's LA clinic. It was their sales that went through the roof after the show. We feel it would be a fantastic way to launch the Equinox brand in the UK market,' she said triumphantly.

Wickens looked crushed and Lawson seemed confused.

'Okay, let me get this straight. You guys are the lawyers, right?' said the CEO.

'That's correct, Mr Green,' Alex replied, suddenly nervous again.

'And you're telling me that you came up with this idea and found this Sweeney guy and the TV company,' he continued.

'Yes, that's also correct.'

'How did you know about the US show? That finished at least five years ago,' Lawson asked.

'Well, that was my colleague,' she said, gesturing to Dan.

'You're Mr Furtado, right? I've been hearing about you,' said Lawson.

'That's right,' said Dan, colouring slightly. 'I'm from Virginia, sir, and I had a vague recollection of the show, which actually finished eight years ago. I did some research and a friend of mine sent me the video clip,' said Dan.

Lawson turned to Tom. 'Did you know about this, Tom?'

'Well, Alex floated the idea with me a couple of weeks ago and I gave her the authority to work on it. But look, Lawson, if you don't like the idea we can dump it. We haven't committed to anything, have we, Alex?' Tom said.

'That's right, Tom. There are no legally binding commitments, but if you want us to press the button the show can go into production almost immediately. We have our first celebrity lined up.'

Alex searched Lawson Green's face for some evidence of a positive reaction. Warren was also staring at him, hoping for a very different pronouncement.

'Gee, I'm stunned by this. It's a bit of a curve ball but I love it. Why didn't our marketing guys come up with this, Brenda, instead of a Brit lawyer? No offence, Ms Fisher.'

'None taken,' said Alex, beaming back at Lawson.

'This is an idea we should run with. I'll speak to our marketing director and PR guys and then, Tom, you and I should meet with the TV people,' Lawson continued.

'Do you want me to go ahead and hire Rob Sweeney?' Tom asked.

'You should hire the guy anyway, with or without the show. Do his references check out?' said Ryan.

'I've known him for years. He's a bit flash but well qualified and has never had a claim against him,' Tom replied.

Lawson and Tom chatted together while Ryan was on his laptop trying to re-run the numbers, incorporating Rob's anticipated practice and then factoring in a similar uplift to the increase in sales generated by the US TV show. He started to get very excited.

'These numbers definitely plug the hole in the budget,' he said, sliding his laptop over to Lawson.

Alex and Dan smiled at each other with delight. This had gone so much better than expected. Alex signalled to Tom. 'Do you still need us?' she whispered. 'Our presentation is done.'

Tom got up from his chair and walked over to the two lawyers while the Americans were still pouring over the figures. He shook them both by the hand.

Alex watched Warren from over Tom's shoulder as he bent his ruler almost in two until it finally snapped and he jerked his right hand into Brenda's face. She berated him angrily.

As Dan and Alex quietly packed up their papers Ryan came over to them.

'Great job, guys. You're my kind of lawyers.' He gave each in turn a firm handshake.

Even Lawson heaved himself out of his seat again as they left. He took Alex's hand in both his and shook it firmly.

'Good work, Alex,' he said.

'Thank you, Mr Green.'

'Call me Lawson,' he smiled. 'And you too, Mr Furtado, great job.' He punched Dan on the shoulder.

As soon as Alex and Dan had run back downstairs she called Bex.

'Hi, Bex. Looks like the show is going to happen,' she blurted out.

'Really? How did the presentation go then?'

'As well as we could have hoped. Their CEO seemed to really get it and they've already committed to hiring Rob. They want to meet Ben and the whole team. Gosh, Bex, I really think we might have pulled it off. The best bit for me is that their lawyer is stuffed now and he knows it. His client is desperate to do the deal again, which means his bargaining position is pants.'

'That's fantastic, Alex. Wait 'til I tell Ben,' Bex replied.

'I was going to call him,' said Alex.

'No need. I'm seeing him later.'

'Oh yes? Anything I should know?' Alex asked.

'No. Well, yes. I don't know, maybe. We've been out a couple of times actually and I really like him.'

'Oh Bex, that's so great. He seems a really nice guy.'

'Well, we'll see, but so far so good. Oh and he's totally put me off the boob job idea. I think he likes me as I am and doing all the research for the show, well, let's just say I might wait 'til I've had my children and see how I feel when I'm the wrong side of forty.'

'Good for you, Bex. And you can use the money for something your granddad would have approved of.'

'I was thinking of a diving holiday in the Maldives. Don't know what Granddad would have thought of that. He couldn't even swim. Anyway, how are things with you and the delectable Dan?'

'Good, thanks,' Alex replied.

'Is that it? Come on, I want a blow by blow account,' Bex teased.

'Can't really.'

'Is he there?'

'Er, yes,' said Alex, placing the phone closer to her ear.

'Okay, message received and understood. You'll have to do yes or no answers then. Okay, so have you slept together yet?'

'Yes.'

Bex squealed down the phone, 'Ooh, good for you. And was it amazing?'

'Yes.'

She squealed again.

'Christ, Bex, are you trying to deafen me?' said Alex.

'Sorry. Just excited for you. Can we get together for a debrief?' Bex asked.

'I'm out with the team tonight at Bar Q.'

'So I'll come along with Ben.'

'I won't be able to talk really.'

'Oh of course, it's all a big secret at work, isn't it? What a nightmare. Okay, I'll come along anyway and we'll do sign language,' she said.

Later that afternoon Dan, Ross and Alex retired to Bar Q. They were in high spirits as Alex ordered a bottle of champagne and summoned Lisa and Emma to join them.

'Did you see Wickens' face when he realised he'd described the TV show that Equinox had backed as low rent?' said Ross, knocking back his second glass of bubbly.

'The best bit was when his ruler snapped,' laughed Alex as she watched Ben and Bex arrive hand in hand.

As Ben ordered a second bottle Bex sat down with them and bounced in her chair in excitement. 'So how is everyone?' she said, pointedly looking at Alex and Dan.

'Everyone's fine, Bex. Now have a glass of champagne,' said Alex, thrusting a glass into Bex's hand.

'Great,' said Bex, giggling and raising her eyebrows at Alex. 'Just great.'

CHAPTER **25**

'So Alex, do you think we'll be able to tell everyone about us when we're in our fifties and the kids have left home, or will we still be skulking around pretending we're just colleagues?' Dan asked the next morning as they took the lift from the atrium to the corporate floor.

'Kids, huh. That's a bit of a jump,' she said, pretending to look offended.

'At least three, I reckon. Seriously, if you had to choose would it be me or the job?' he asked, only half joking.

She stared back at him. The answer was much easier than she'd ever thought it would be. 'It's a no-brainer. If I can do the job here then I can do it at any City firm. I like MacArthur Warren but there are other firms.'

He looked at her with a serious expression, processing her answer. For a moment there was silence.

'Ever kissed anyone in an elevator?' he said, moving

towards her as the lift shuddered to a stop. The doors opened as he kissed her quickly on the lips. Thank God there was no one there. It was true there were other firms, but still she'd prefer not to be fired.

'See you later,' he whispered as she turned off the corridor first into her office.

'Hi, Ross. How's the head?' she asked as she saw Ross knocking back a glass of water and two paracetamols.

He'd still been at Bar Q when she'd left, exactly ten minutes after Dan. The whole subterfuge thing was already getting irritating. They'd spent the entire evening pretending to everyone that nothing was going on when the only people there who had no idea what was going on were Ross and Ben. Bex had been a disaster. She would have to keep her away from work dos in the future, Alex decided. Her 'nudge nudge wink wink' innuendo had been as subtle as Felicia's boob job.

'I've got a mouth like the bottom of a parrot's cage and a banging head,' Ross replied.

'Nice.'

'Oh and Wickens called,' he said.

'Did he now! How did he sound?'

'Less arsey than usual,' said Ross.

'That wouldn't be difficult.'

'He said he wanted to wrap up the agreement today. He has instructions to wire the money tomorrow so we can complete the deal.'

'That's great news!' said Alex.

'Not so loud, please,' moaned Ross, holding his

head in his hands. 'Oh and Tom called. Albert has confessed to everything.'

'No!'

'Yup. Tom had threatened to bring in the police about the leaks and Albert cracked. Apparently when he'd been getting all the documents together for us he'd had a good old rummage in Cassidy's office. Along with the information he'd pumped out of Audrey he had some serious material. He'd been leaking to a mate of his, Johnny someone, a freelance journalist.'

'What did Tom do?' Alex asked.

'Fired him but agreed not to go to the police. Albert is devastated but relieved apparently.'

'Well, that solves that mystery. At least the rest of Beau Street's clients can relax now. I suppose I should call Warren.' She picked up the phone and leant back in her chair.

'Good morning, Warren. How are you?' she asked chirpily.

'Just great, thanks. Look, let's get this thing wrapped up, shall we? After your show-stopping performance yesterday my client is keen to complete. But don't think I can't see beyond the smoke and mirrors, though. Oh and you can tell that Furtado guy that I know he's been sniffing around trying to get the lowdown on me,' he retorted.

'Okay, Warren. Look, why do you have to make it so personal? This is just another deal. Your client wants to do it and so does mine. Let's just facilitate it, shall we?' She couldn't believe his childishness.

'It was Furtado who made it personal. I'll tell Brenda all about him,' he replied.

What was he like? It was like negotiating a contract with a seven-year-old boy who'd taken his bat home. Warren sulked his way through the entire call but within a couple of hours they were there.

'Okay. I'll turn the agreement around and we can arrange signing tomorrow,' he said.

As she hung up her phone immediately rang. It was Truman's PA.

'Alex, hi. It's Pippa. Truman would like to see you in his office. He's been keen to speak to you all morning. Can you come down now?' she asked.

'Sure. I'm on my way.'

Alex brushed her hair and put on some more lipstick. When she arrived at Truman's office his door was open and he was smiling and beckoning her in.

'Alex, come in. Take a seat. Pippa, can you get us a couple of coffees, please?' he called out as Alex sat down. 'How are you, Alex?' he asked.

'Er, I'm fine, thanks,' she said. Where was this going?

'Good, good. And the wedding? It can't be long now.'

'Ah. Well, the wedding has been cancelled, I'm afraid, Truman. A few weeks ago actually now.'

Truman looked horrified and embarrassed. 'Alex, I'm so sorry. How dreadful for you.' His face was bright red. Alex thought he was going to ask her for Elliott's address so he could challenge him to a dual. He obviously thought she'd been dumped.

'All for the best, I think, Truman. It's a big

commitment. You need to be absolutely certain,' she said.

'Yes, of course. Well, I have to say that makes your performance on the Beau Street deal even more impressive. Yes, that's the kind of single-minded person we need here.' He nodded to himself and then looked up again. 'Look, I've had that scary woman from the bank on the phone. Melanie, is it?'

'Meredith.'

'Yes, that's the one. She's been singing your praises and from what I hear you've done an excellent job on the deal. She says it will complete in the next day or so and we'll get our completion uplift, which I'm sure I don't need to tell you is great news for the corporate team and great news for the firm. Between you and me, Alex, I've spoken to the senior partner and he's more or less told me that if you jump through the hoops your partnership's in the bag.' He lowered his voice as he said this as though his room might be bugged.

'Thank you, Truman. That's fantastic news. I should say, though, that it's been a team effort. Ross and Dan have both done a great job too.'

'Very generous of you to say so. Don't worry, I'll look after both of them when it comes to giving out bonuses.'

As he said this Pippa came in with the coffees. 'Excuse me,' she said, 'but I have Dan Furtado outside to see you.'

'Show him in. We were just talking about him,' said Truman, laughing as though it was the strangest coincidence.

Pippa showed Dan in and he smiled nervously at Alex when he saw her.

'Furtado, take a seat.'

Truman was hale and hearty now as though he was hosting a drinks party. Alex half expected him to ask Dan what he was drinking.

'What can we do for you?' Truman beamed.

'Should I go?' Alex asked.

'No, Alex, stay. This is something you should hear too,' Dan said.

Alex stared at him. What was he going to say to Truman? She'd just found out her partnership was safe. Was he going to spill the beans to Truman?

'Truman, there's no easy way to say this,' Dan said.

'Then maybe you shouldn't say it,' she blurted in.

'Alex, it's not that. Truman, I've been offered a job somewhere else. I'm afraid I'm resigning.'

Alex was gobsmacked.

'I couldn't tell anyone about it until today. I've only just had the formal offer letter. It's an in-house job at Beau Street, or rather Equinox UK, as it will be known.' Dan was looking at Alex as he said this, scanning her face for a reaction.

'Well, Dan,' said Truman recovering first, 'this is a bit of a shock and I have to say we'll be extremely sorry to see you go, won't we, Alex?'

'Yes,' she squeaked.

'Is there anything I can say to change your mind? You're in line for a good bonus this year, you know? Your prospects here are excellent.'

'Thank you, Truman, but no, I don't think there is.

I've been thinking about a move into business for some time now and the Beau Street deal presented me with the perfect opportunity.'

'Well, I suppose going to work for a client of the firm is different,' said Truman, perking up. 'That's an opportunity for us, not a threat. I do hope you're going to send all your work our way.' Truman smiled.

'Well, yes, I've already suggested that Alex be our first choice UK adviser,' Dan replied.

'Well, that's excellent news, although you'll be missed. Once you've accepted their offer let me know when they want you to start. I'd be delighted to give you an excellent reference, of course.' Truman's phone rang. 'Sorry, I need to get this. Well done, both of you.' He smiled at each of them before picking up the phone.

Alex and Dan left Truman's office in silence and found themselves facing each other in the corridor.

'Why didn't you tell me?' she asked.

'I wanted to but I was sworn to secrecy and I didn't know until this morning that I'd definitely got it. Warren Wickens was in the frame for the job as well.'

'No wonder he hates you then,' she said, the news sinking in.

'Well, he's not exactly my favourite person either. Now, talking about my favourite people.' Dan slid his arms around Alex's waist.

'Hey, Dan!' Alex panicked.

'What's the problem? I'm not going to be an employee here very soon. We can do what we like. In fact, I'm going to be your client, which means you have to do what I like. And at the moment I'd really like you to congratulate me on my new job.' He pulled her closer.

She smiled back at him as she realised he was right. The only remaining obstacle between them was gone. She put her arms around his neck and they kissed tenderly.

As Alex opened her eyes she saw, over Dan's shoulder, a matronly figure stomping towards them.

'Furtado! Ms Fisher! I knew it!' It was Margaret Kemp looking simultaneously furious and victorious. 'This is a matter for Mr Barry!' she shouted, marching straight to Truman's office.

Alex and Dan giggled and then walked down the corridor hand in hand.

'So, Alex, what shall we do tonight?' he asked. 'Dinner and ballet?'

She smiled. 'Maybe just dinner? I hate the ballet.'

ACKNOWLEDGEMENTS

From us both

We would like to say a massive thank you to everyone who has helped us on this wildly exciting journey from city slickers to authors.

To Midas PR - for believing in us right from the start and backing us all the way. Tony, Fiona and Tory, we couldn't have done this without you!

To Matador - for seeing the potential in the series, making the publishing process so user friendly and for putting up with our endless questions.

To afishinsea - for turning our outline ideas into genius, style icon covers and for the rest of our brand imagery. Your service is outstanding.

To Charlie Wilson - for your editorial support, patience and attention to detail. Our books were transformed from amateur scripts to real proper books under your watchful eye. Thank you!

To the Millennium Ten – for fun, friendship and providing us with endless material!

From Penny

I would like to thank all those that kept the world turning while I was locked away in my office for months on end. Lisa, Kate, Carolyn, Sofie and Graham – you are the best team anyone could hope for. I am so grateful to all of you and sorry if I forget to say so! These books are as much for you as anyone.

To my friends and family, for putting up with me droning on for hours about the books. At least now you can see them for yourselves, rather than just listen to me trying to describe them!

From Joanna

Thanks to Gemma, Faye and Kerry without whom the books would have taken twice as long. Thank you for everything you do and thanks for letting me bounce ideas off you!

To all my friends and family, especially the Wednesday morning coffee gang and the school run mums, who provide daily support and laughter. Also to Kath, Lucy and the Animals (you know who you are!) for keeping me in touch with the Legal world.